ROBERT B. PARKER'S
Angel Eyes

Gabby Leggett left her Boston family with big dreams of making it as a model/actress in Hollywood. Two years later, she disappears from her apartment. Her family, former boyfriend, friends—and the police—have no idea where she is and no leads. Leggett's mother hires Spenser to find her, with help of his former apprentice, Zebulon Sixkill, now an L.A. private eye.

Spenser barely has time to unpack before the trail leads to a powerful movie studio boss, the Armenian mob, and a shadowy empowerment group some say might be a dangerous cult.

It's soon clear that Spenser and Sixkill may be outgunned this time, and series favorites Chollo and Hawk ride to the rescue to provide backup. From the mansions of Beverly Hills to the lawless streets of a small California town, Spenser will need to watch his step. In Hollywood, all that glitters isn't gold. And not all those who wander are lost.

"Atkins gets the hardest parts right—his hero/narrator now sounds indistinguishable from Robert B. Parker's. . . . Readers who've always wanted to see Spenser in Tinseltown can cross that off their bucket lists."   —*Kirkus Reviews*

Robert B. Parker's Old Black Magic

"Atkins perfectly catches Spenser's breezy voice and Parker's knack for creating vivid characters."   —*Seattle Times*

"Atkins . . . again captures all the qualities Spenser fans love in the series: smart-ass humor, a touch of romance, plenty of violence, and, of course, Spenser's complex sense of honor."   —*Booklist*

Robert B. Parker's Little White Lies

"A taut, suspenseful story line drives Edgar-finalist Atkins's sixth Spenser novel, which deepens the relationship between the Boston PI and his significant other, therapist Susan Silverman."   —*Publisher's Weekly*

"*Little White Lies* will keep you eagerly turning the pages to follow his latest adventures in the mean streets. And boy, will it make you hungry."   —*Tampa Bay Times*

Robert B. Parker's Slow Burn

"A 5-alarm thriller . . . Atkins deftly recreates the Spenser character and his Boston milieu."   —Associated Press

"Sizzling . . . *Slow Burn* rises to a blazing finish and leaves Spenser with some major decisions to make. Can't wait to find out how it goes."   —*Tampa Bay Times*

"Scene-by-scene, line-by-line pleasures are authentic."
    —*Kirkus Reviews*

"Atkins tosses in a surprising change to his lead's status quo, and series fans will be eager to see what he does with it in Spenser's next outing." —*Publishers Weekly*

Robert B. Parker's Kickback

"Classic Spenser—the Spenser of wry wit, tasty food and drinks, hard workouts and lethal confrontations. It's a reader's guide to greater Boston and a nostalgic trip into the noir world of guys who privately investigate all manner of wrongdoing. . . . Once again, Atkins has delivered a thriller that evokes the best of Parker's Spenser series, not least the punchy back-and-forth of the dialogue." —Associated Press

"*Kickback* is the best one yet, with Spenser in fine wise-cracking fettle. . . . Fans of the series will be gratified that both Hawk and Susan Silverman, Spenser's brilliant and beloved squeeze, get plenty of presence, along with Pearl the Wonder Dog. There are just enough bursts of violent action as Spenser untangles the whole sordid mess and at least some justice is done. Good to have you in town, Spenser."
—*Tampa Bay Times*

"Another gritty and riveting Spenser novel in the best tradition of Robert B. Parker." —*The Huffington Post*

"You can always tell if you're reading a great Spenser novel because you start to read with a Boston accent. So it is with *Robert B. Parker's Kickback* written in impeccable style by Ace Atkins. . . . It's full of everything we've come to expect from the Boston Private Investigator—action, smart-mouthed sarcasm, the assistance of Hawk and most of all, justice."
—*Suspense Magazine*

THE SPENSER NOVELS

Robert B. Parker's
ANGEL EYES

ACE ATKINS

G. P. PUTNAM'S SONS
New York

PUTNAM
— EST. 1838 —

G. P. PUTNAM'S SONS
Publishers Since 1838
An imprint of Penguin Random House LLC
penguinrandomhouse.com

The Library of Congress has catalogued the G. P. Putnam's Sons
hardcover edition as follows:

Names: Atkins, Ace, author.
Title: Angel eyes / Ace Atkins.
Other titles: At head of title: Robert B. Parker's
Description: New York : G. P. Putnam's Sons, 2019. |
Series: A Spenser novel | Robert B. Parker's Spenser novel series.
Identifiers: LCCN 2019043685 (print) | LCCN 2019043686 (ebook) |
ISBN 9780525536826 (hardcover) | ISBN 9780525536840 (ebook)
Subjects: LCSH: Spenser (Fictitious character)—Fiction. |
Private investigators—Massachusetts—Boston—Fiction. |
GSAFD: Mystery fiction. | Suspense fiction.
Classification: LCC PS3551.T49 A85 2019 (print) |
LCC PS3551.T49 (ebook) | DDC 813/.54—dc23
LC record available at https://lccn.loc.gov/2019043685
LC ebook record available at https://lccn.loc.gov/2019043686
.   p.   cm.

First G. P. Putnam's Sons hardcover edition / November 2019
First G. P. Putnam's Sons premium edition / October 2020
G. P. Putnam's Sons premium edition ISBN: 9780525536833

Printed in the United States of America
1   3   5   7   9   10   8   6   4   2

For Maureen the Wonder Dog,

In life the firmest friend,

the first to welcome,

foremost to defend

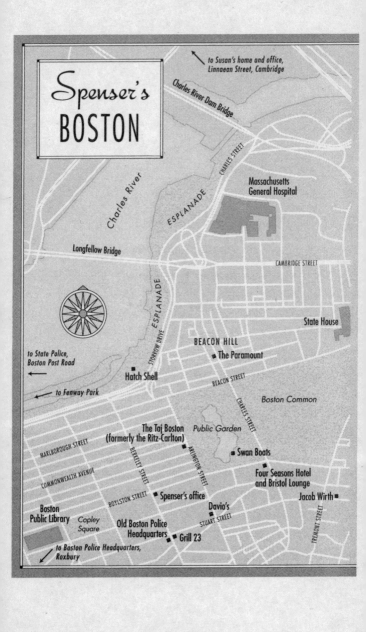

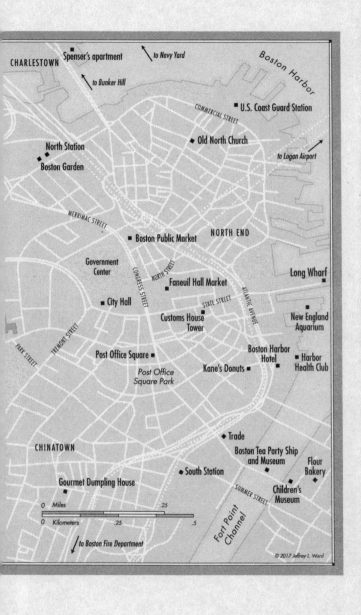

Robert B. Parker's
ANGEL EYES

1

"Whoever said it never rained in Southern California lied," I said.

"Albert Hammond," Zebulon Sixkill said.

"Albert Hammond wrote it?" I said.

"Albert Hammond and Mike Hazlewood," Z said. "Albert Hammond sang it. Nineteen seventy-two. I can't recall the label."

"I can recall record labels and ballplayers," I said. "It's one of my many gifts."

"What are your other gifts?"

I shrugged, trying to look modest. "I don't like to brag. But there's a reason Susan stays with me. Beyond my obvious good looks and stellar charm."

"Must be your fashion sense."

"I color-coordinated my ball cap with the T-shirt," I said. "Didn't you notice?"

"I did," he said. "You'll look right at home on Rodeo Drive. They'll think you're a wealthy eccentric."

"And they'd be half right."

We sat parked outside a midcentury-modern apartment building in West Hollywood, not far from the Runyon Canyon Park. I'd brought breakfast burritos and two hot coffees from my hotel and graciously shared with Z. Every few seconds, the windshield wipers on his highland-green Mustang would tick-tock across the glass. Downslope, the L.A. Basin spread far and wide from the hills. Tall palms moved as if blown by a gentle breath. "What do you know about 1972?" I said. "You weren't born yet."

"You live long enough in Los Angeles and you pick up things," Z said.

"Ray-Bans," I said. "Sports car. An office in Hollywood. You've become the cliché of a private eye."

"Might I remind you I am a full Cree Indian?" he said. "That gives me character."

"Character only gets you so far," I said. "Right now, I'd settle for a clue."

"Have you spoken with Samuelson yet?"

"I put in a call," I said. "He'll be thrilled to hear from me."

"You think the cops know more than us?"

"Wouldn't take much," I said, and opened the paper around the burrito and started to eat. I hadn't eaten since asking for an extra pack of pretzels on the flight from Boston. No one came from the building, which was guarded with a steel gate and punch-key entry. The rain continued to ping the car. It was overcast and cloudy at nine in the morning. But who was I to complain? It was like summertime compared to the Back Bay at the moment.

"Tell me again about Gabby," Z said. He was tall and thick-muscled, with a wide, flat face and long black hair. For three years he'd been my sleuthing apprentice, and now was on his own. His claim to fame was being the only mortal man who could out-bench-press me and Hawk. And he never let us forget.

"Gabrielle Leggett," I said. "Twenty-four. From Cambridge and played volleyball at BU. Her mother takes yoga with Susan. The girl came out here two years ago. She rented this apartment, joined an acting class, and got a job as a dog walker and personal assistant for a woman named Nancy Sharp. She did some modeling, shot a few commercials, and expanded her career as a social media influencer."

"Influencer," Z said. "Good work if you can find it. These people don't have to pay for a damn thing. They get comped clothes, meals, hotels."

"Maybe we should try it."

"What would you influence?"

"Beer and donut consumption," I said.

"And what does Gabby use to influence people?"

"Gabby," I said. "I scrolled through her Instagram before I flew out."

"Ugly?" he said.

"Hideous." I pulled out my phone and showed Z a picture. Blond, tan, long-limbed, and lithe, Gabby Leggett posed in a microscopic black bikini and a ridiculously large hat. Another photo had her in cutoff shorts and a crop top, a flower wreath in her hair, at some big music festival I'd never heard of. Z stared at the screen for a while and then let out a very long breath.

"Impressed?"

"Sure," he said. "My left leg won't stop shaking."

"Young enough to be my daughter," I said. "Or so Susan claims."

I handed him my phone and he scrolled through her account. He raised his eyebrows. "When did you get Instagram?"

"Yesterday."

"And your handle is Pearl the Wonder Dog?"

"She already has twenty followers," I said. "Don't tell her. She'll get cocky."

We both looked up as a white BMW wheeled into a space across the road and a thin young man crawled out and walked toward the apartment. He appeared to be the man we'd been waiting for all morning.

"What do you think?" I said.

"Could be," Z said. "Hard to tell. All you white people look the same."

I opened the passenger door and walked toward the young guy as he punched numbers on the keypad. He had a neatly trimmed beard and a Hitler Youth haircut and wore a three-piece navy suit with a skinny blood-red tie. He stood a little under six feet in tall lace-up boots favored by Victorian-era jockeys.

"Mr. Collinson?"

He nodded, a leather satchel hanging over his shoulder. The metal door sprung open.

"My name's Spenser," I said. "I work for the Leggett family."

"I know who you are," he said. "Sorry I didn't return your calls. To be honest, I don't feel comfortable with this."

"You agreed to let us into Gabby's apartment," I said.

"That was before I spoke to the police," he said, trying to let the door close. "I'd rather you handle your business with the family and leave me out of it."

I wedged my foot in the doorframe. I wore Red Wing boots with steel toes and didn't feel a thing. Z had gotten out of the Mustang and hung back, oblivious to the rain. Indians were like that. One with nature.

"Hey," Collinson said.

I gripped his upper arm and walked with him into the apartment building. "The Leggett family greatly appreciates your cooperation. I'm sure you realize they're quite concerned. They haven't heard from her in ten days."

The boy stopped, grunting, trying unsuccessfully to shake my grip. He had the general upper-body build of Mr. Salty. "Twelve."

"Excuse me?" I said.

"Twelve days," he said. "Gabby's been gone for twelve days. I've been looking for her since then. I've told the police all I know. I don't know what else to do."

"When did you see her last?"

"Would you please let go of my arm?"

"Sorry," I said. "I left my kid gloves at home. How about you let me into Gabby's apartment and we can talk?"

"Ouch," he said. "You're hurting me."

I let go and Collinson looked back through a large

plate-glass window. He seemed transfixed by the sight of the extra-large Native American standing next to the Mustang. Z leaned against the hood with his sizable arms folded over his chest. Collinson pointed his chin in Z's general direction. "Who the hell's that?"

"My associate," I said.

"What's he do?"

"Runs the West Coast office."

"And you?"

"Boston talent scout."

"You guys look like thugs," he said.

"Thanks," I said. "We do our very best."

"I told Gabby's mother I didn't feel comfortable with letting you in," he said. "I just need to pick up some scripts and contracts. Materials confidential to the agency."

"You used to date," I said. "And now you're her agent?"

"That's right," he said. "Is that a problem?"

"And you kept her key?"

"It's complicated," he said.

"Uh-huh," I said. "Any ideas of where she might have gone?"

"Why don't you ask her new boyfriend," he said. "Or her so-called friends."

"And who's her new boyfriend?"

"That's her business," he said. "And I have mine. Now, please."

"Did I mention I took the red-eye from Boston last night and had to sit next to a fat guy with halitosis and sleep apnea?" I said. "I'm tired, need a change of clothes, and wish to get into Gabby's building."

"You don't stop, do you?" he said.

"It's never suited me."

Collinson sighed and shook his head. "Maybe you should come work with me at the agency," he said. "You seem to have the temperament."

I looked over at Z and waved, following Collinson deeper into the apartment lobby. He punched up the elevator and waited with a cell phone in hand, staring down at the screen, scrolling with his thumb. There was a bulletin board by an empty reception desk with flyers for lost dogs, sofas for sale, roommates wanted, and a killer metal band seeking an intense drummer. Collinson hooked a thumb into the leather satchel's strap as we waited.

"You mind me asking what happened with you and Gabby?"

He looked up and said, "We weren't suited for each other."

"How's that?"

"She's six years younger," he said. "She said I was stifling her personal growth."

"I can see that," I said.

"Our relationship isn't any of your concern."

"That's where you're wrong, Eric," I said. "All this is my concern now."

The elevator opened and we zipped up to the third floor and exited, Collinson already ahead of me down an unremarkable hall and slipping the key into an unremarkable door. The carpet was an industrial gray, and black metal sconces dimly lit the walls about every eight feet. The air in the hallway was hot and stuffy, smelling as stale and musty as an old attic. As we walked inside, my eyes had to adjust to the darkness until Collinson found the switch.

The apartment was a wreck. Broken glass, stuffing from cushions, and upturned drawers. It didn't take a detective to see someone had been looking for something and wanted to find it very badly.

"Holy shit," he said. "What the hell?"

I walked over and picked up an overturned poster of Boston. A picture taken at twilight across the harbor with a wonderful view of the Custom House Tower and the city skyline. The kind of print you might find at the Quincy Market. I felt slightly homesick.

"God," he said. "What a fucking mess. These people."

"What people, Eric?"

"Whoever did this," he said. "I don't know who. I guess who took her."

I ran my hand over the back of my neck as I stretched my hands high overhead. My back and legs ached from the flight. I watched as he disappeared into a bedroom and returned a few moments later. I stooped down, looking through some scattered papers.

"I'd really rather you not do that."

"Do what?"

"Snoop."

"I'm a detective," I said. "Not a psychic. Snooping is my business."

"I don't know if the cops have been here yet."

"They have."

"Was the apartment like this?" he said.

"I don't know."

"Well, if it wasn't, they damn well need to know about it," he said. "I don't want to be responsible for anything you might mess up."

"I may look like a bull in a china shop," I said. "But I'm stealthier than a Sumatran tiger."

Eric Collinson rolled his eyes and shifted his weight in his stylish lace-up boots. He looked both bored and annoyed. I'd only just met him, but I wasn't a fan.

"If you know anything . . ."

"I don't," he said.

"But if you find out something."

"I will," he said. "Can I please go? I need to go."

"For her personal agent, you don't seem to be of much use."

He shook his head and tried to pass me through the narrow hallway. I took up a lot of space and kept my boots firmly planted.

"Why don't you just talk to KiKi?" he said. "She knows more than me. She knows all about Gabby's new beautiful life and new beautiful friends. I warned her. I warned her something like this would happen."

"And how do I find KiKi?"

"I don't know."

"Phone number or address works."

"All I know is she used to hostess at the Mirabeau," he said. "She provides bottle service for rich douchebags."

"Fantastic."

"Do you even know what the Mirabeau is?"

"I told you I'm a pro," I said. "I just mastered Google."

"They have a guest list," he said. "They have a huge wait to get in. It's pretty much the kind of place that you have to know someone."

"I know many people," I said. "And I just purchased a blazer that promises to be wrinkle-free."

Eric Collinson looked as if he doubted me. "It's a hangout for industry people. Beautiful people."

"I'm the definition of beautiful," I said. "Inside and out."

He handed me the key and said he was done with the whole thing.

"If you had to guess where Gabby went . . ."

"I can't."

"But if you did, where might she go?"

"It's Mr. Spenser?"

"Just Spenser," I said. "With an *S*, like the English poet."

"I know how to spell it," he said. "I went to Princeton."

"Of course you did."

He kept looking at me, as if appraising my trustworthiness, and then finally nodded. "If I had to guess what got her?"

I nodded.

"Ambition."

"Ambition?"

"Welcome to L.A., Mr. Spenser," he said, turning away. "What else is there? Gabby was a wonderful girl. I wish I knew what the hell changed her."

"Will you answer next time when I call?"

"Gabby's mother knows where to find me," Collinson said. "I hope you find her. But I'm done with all of this mess."

2

I spent the next hour going through Gabby Leggett's apartment with Z. It was hard, as most of her belongings had been tossed on the floor, but we made slow, deliberate work. She didn't have a lot of personal items other than clothes. And there were a lot of clothes, more than most boutiques on Newbury Street, and enough shoes to outfit an army of Kardashians. The interior seemed to have been recently renovated with a new manufactured bamboo floor and sleek gray cabinets in a Scandinavian style. Her furniture was basic and utilitarian, classic IKEA. In the drawers, there were no letters or personal photos. No suicide notices, hidden diaries, or maps to One-Eyed Willy's secret treasure. The only sense that Gabby Leggett had lived here was a MacBook computer slid halfway under her bed.

I pulled it out and showed it to Z. "Almost as if someone wanted us to find it."

"What did Collinson say?"

"Nothing," I said. "I think we made him feel a tad uncomfortable."

"Or inadequate," Z said as he upturned a massive framed black-and-white poster of Gabby Leggett from a modeling shoot. The glass had spiderwebbed across the image but the print was otherwise undamaged. "This girl would break that boy like a toothpick."

Gabby was posed in the corner of a shuttered business. The rolling metal grate covering the entrance had been painted with the faces of Tupac and Charlie Chaplin. She had on black jeans and a T-shirt generously cut out from the armholes. Her lean flank and the side of her breast were on prominent display. She looked right into the camera with her sleepy eyes, full lips parted as she touched the upper part of her chest as if holding back a terrific secret. *Shh.*

"I hate to say it," Z said. "But she's pretty average for this town."

"Tough critic."

"She could've gone anywhere," he said. "For all we know she could've skipped out on her rent and gone down to Baja for a few weeks."

"Then we go to Baja."

"I wish," Z said, hands on hips, looking over the mess. "We'll end up watching Motel 6 in Van Nuys."

On the way out, I tried to find the super, without any luck. I spotted two security cameras in the lobby and one out by the gated entry. I made a mental note of their placement as Z and I got back into his Mustang and drove back toward his office. I set her laptop in the backseat.

"Can you hack it?" I said.

"Hack it?" Z said. He zipped down Hollywood Boulevard, slowing at a red light. "You mean unlock the laptop without the password?"

"*Hacking* sounds more tricky and professional," I said. "Good for billing."

"I know just the girl," he said. "Works in K-town."

"Good to have friends."

"She knows a guy in Canada who can track Gabby's movements from her cell phone."

"I used to pull phone books at the Boston public library for addresses," I said. "That almost feels like cheating."

"Almost," Z said.

The office of Zebulon Sixkill, licensed California investigator, was at the corner of Highland and Franklin. Z had the corner space on the second floor of a double-decker strip mall. The other tenants included a Thai massage parlor, a vape shop, a movie-star tour bus service, a twenty-four-hour liquor store, and a nail salon. His office was twice as large as mine, with half the furniture and a secretary, a pleasant Latina named Delores. Delores was a little older than me but lacked my stellar charisma. She barely glanced up from her *National Enquirer* as we passed her desk. *Rob Lowe Reveals His Sex Tape Regrets!*

"I'd offer you coffee," Z said, "but I haven't bought a coffeemaker yet."

"I started out with just a jar of Sanka and a chipped coffee mug."

"Do you think someone tossed her apartment after the cops?"

"Probably."

"Why don't you think the cops took the laptop?"

"It wasn't there," I said. "Someone left it later."

"Collinson?"

I nodded. It felt odd sitting on the opposite side of the desk. I wasn't used to being the one in the client's chair and missed my accessibility to a bottle of Bushmills and a .357. Although I suspected Z's gun was handy. The Bushmills, not so much. Z had quit drinking almost five years ago.

"I have a list of friends from Gabby's mother," I said. "And the name and address of her current employer and acting school."

"What about her Instagram?" he said. "Friends in the photos?"

"I made a list," I said. "But most of her pics only feature herself. Gabby seemed mainly into promoting Gabby."

"You want me to hit up the friends and you stick with the acting coach and her boss?"

"Do I detect a hint of ageism?"

Z grinned. He stood up and hung his leather biker jacket on a hook on the back of a bathroom door and sat back down. Some pictures of him from his playing days at Cal Wesleyan lined the walls, along with a photo of him and Henry Cimoli when he worked at the Harbor Health Club. A few scars remained on Z's face from a nasty incident a while back at an old dog track in Revere.

"I am closer to their peer group."

"Maybe the woman she worked for is older than Maureen O'Hara and will take a shine to me."

The office had a lone window that looked into a narrow alley where some homeless people had made a small tarp city. An all-night diner pumped smoke and grease into the wide-open space over a dumpster. Rain tapped against the small window and pinged the puddles along the alley.

"Where's the glitz and glamour?" I said.

"Use your imagination," Z said. "It's all around us."

"I was thinking maybe I'd get a martini at the Cocoanut Grove," I said.

"I'd take you there," Z said. "But they razed it twenty years ago."

"Maybe have dinner at the Brown Derby?"

"Burned."

"Chasen's?"

"Gone."

"Clark Gable?"

"Dead."

"Damn," I said. I made a few notes on a pocket-sized spiral notebook I kept in my jacket.

"What's the girl's mother say?" Z said. He had on a gray T-shirt that said *Rocky Boy North Stars*. The short sleeves looked as if they might burst at any moment.

"I met her at Harvest with Susan the other night," I said. "She didn't know much about Gabby's life in L.A. Sounded like they were estranged. On the positive front, she hated Eric Collinson. Said he'd made a mess of her career."

"Maybe Collinson was jealous of Gabby's new friends?"

"Yep."

"Maybe we should've appealed to his better nature."

"You mean shaken the ever-living truth from him?" I said.

"Sure," Z said. "That."

"Sometimes I forget you've learned as much from Hawk as from me."

"What can I say?" Z said. "Boston was one hell of an education. Without you guys, I could never have come back to California as a professional."

"Professor Spenser?"

"Hawk called his class the school of hard knocks."

"At Harvard it would've been called 'A History of Violence Through the African American Prism.'"

Z laid his hand on the small silver MacBook. "I'll take this to K-town and see what I can find. Then I'll try and round up some of Gabby's friends, see what I can find out about where she's been and what she's been up to."

"Try and use some of that Native American charm."

"I'll do my best," he said. "Girls love stoicism."

"And I'll try that acting coach," I said. "Maybe he'll see some untapped potential in me. Maybe I could be the next Nat Pendleton or Ward Bond."

"Maybe," Z said. "And who the hell are they?"

"So young," I said. "So much to learn."

Gabby Leggett took acting classes twice a week at an old movie theater right across from a Ralphs in Studio City. I parked at a nearby Starbucks on Ventura for some much-needed caffeine, left a voicemail with Susan, and walked over to the studio. The rain had let up, but it was still dark and overcast, with a slight chill in the air. I hadn't expected Los Angeles to be chilly. The only clothing I'd packed with long sleeves was an authentic Pats sweatshirt I'd gotten as a gift from Kinjo Heywood.

I lifted the collar on my leather jacket, stepped under the aging marquee, and let myself into the lobby, searching for Jeffrey Bloom. Bloom was supposed to be an industry legend, according to his own website, featured in dozens of iconic film roles. After a quick viewing of IMDb, I found out he'd been in two space horror movies in the early eighties and had a reccuring role as a cop on *Matlock* in the early nineties. He offered something called the Bloom Method for several hundred dollars a month.

Testimonials on the site proclaimed the price a true bargain. His method nothing short of genius. I suspected Bloom wrote much of his own copy.

I found an empty office and wandered into the dimly lit theater. A man I assumed to be Bloom sat at the edge of the stage, leafing through a binder. He didn't look up as I entered and walked down the aisle, nor when I sat in the front row, perhaps three feet from him.

I hadn't been furtive in my movements. I crossed my legs and leaned back into the chair, curious as to how long it would take him to acknowledge my presence. He was a short, somewhat rotund man, somewhere in his mid-sixties, bearded and balding, with the rest of his curly salt-and-pepper hair pulled into a ponytail. His maroon guayabera shirt was unbuttoned to his chest and he wore tortoiseshell half-glasses down on his nose.

After a few minutes, he simply said, "I'm not payin'."

"Is that from *Twelfth Night* or *Merchant of Venice*?"

"Ha," he said. "You guys did shitty work. The lights still flicker on and off. Like I said, if your people in El Segundo have a problem, talk to my lawyer. I grew up in Brooklyn. I don't answer to shakedowns."

"Is it the size of my neck or my casual clothes?"

"Excuse me?"

"What made you think I'm an electrician?"

"Aren't you?"

"No," I said. "And I've never been to El Segundo. Not on purpose, anyway."

"What do you want, then?" he said. He had yet to look up, seemingly transfixed by what he saw in the binder. From where I sat, they appeared to be black-and-white head shots. "You're too old to be an actor."

"Be nice to people on the way up," I said. "You might meet them on the way down."

"I've been on both trips on that elevator, friend," Jeffrey Bloom said. He finally looked up and removed his glasses, letting them hang from a cord around his neck. "Would it be too much to inquire who you are and what it is exactly that you want?"

"I'm a blogger," I said. "I wanted to come to talk to you about *Horror of Party Beach Part Two*. How exactly did the Bloom Method serve you during the production?"

"Christ Almighty."

"Just Spenser," I said, offering my hand. "Nice to meet you."

"Nobody gives two shits about that rotten picture," he said, not accepting my hand nor moving from the stage. "It was a joke when it was being filmed and it was a joke in its minor release. How it's become a cult classic is beyond my understanding, but I'll take it. I took that part for the money. It allowed me to do summer stock for two years. I took an even worse picture that I won't name five years ago to do a one-man Faulkner play. Like I tell the kids, you do what you need to do to practice the craft."

"I can relate."

"And again, is it too much to ask what you do, Mr. Spenser, or are we playing some kind of game?"

"I'm a detective," I said. "I'm from Boston and have

just arrived in California to find a missing girl. In my craft, it's called a Wandering Daughter Job."

Bloom sat for a moment, face impassive, before he pushed away the binder and broke out into a loud, obnoxious laugh. I'd heard a better laugh from Francis the Talking Mule. "Oh, yeah?" he said. "And I'm Sam Spade. Or better yet, Philo Vance. Do you know Philo Vance, Mr. Spenser?"

"Sure," I said. "Years ago, I worked the *Canary Murder Case* with him."

He laughed again, but this time it sounded more genuine and real, coming from somewhere down in his protruding gut. He stood up on the stage, hands on his hips, and for a moment I wondered if I had time to get some popcorn and a Coke. I felt that a one-man play might be about to begin. But alas . . .

"Who's the girl?"

"Gabrielle Leggett."

He nodded. He looked down at me, solemn, and nodded some more. His beard had been trimmed into a somewhat devilish point, and as he talked he pulled at it, in what the acting folks called "giving their character some business."

"Gabby's missing?" he said. "I thought she'd just dropped out of the class. I'm sorry. I wish I could help you more, but I really don't know much about my students' personal lives."

"How long was she here?"

"Oh, I don't know," he said. "I'd have to check my records. Maybe a year or two? Too short of time to make any real progress. But she had a very interesting look about her, something feline in those eyes. When she didn't show up for the last few classes, I almost called her to say she had something really special to give the world."

"From my experience, that can be a curse."

Bloom found the stairs at the edge of the stage, walking down the first aisle toward me. The chairs were covered in thick red upholstery and had not aged well. Several had been sealed with duct tape, others showing exposed foam spilling from the seats. Ceiling tiles bulged and hung loose. Somewhere down there were vintage Jujubes stuck to the floor.

"Do you drink, Mr. Spenser?"

I showed him my Starbucks cup. "Pike Place Roast."

"Maybe some Irish coffee?"

"Why not," I said. "True to my heritage."

We moved out of the theater and into the bare-bones lobby, a wide, empty space of scuffed black-and-white linoleum tiles. The walls showed off dozens of posters of plays the Bloom troupe had put on. *Glengarry Glen Ross. True West. Deathtrap.*

"Eclectic," I said.

"I like to challenge the students," he said, reaching into a cluttered roll-top desk and extracting the largest bottle of Jack Daniel's I'd ever seen. He could have served half the state of Tennessee. I opened my cup's lid in an effort at solidarity and let him make a generous pour. Technically, the coffee was about as Irish as the Grand Ole Opry.

Bloom sat down at the edge of his desk. He offered me

a seat, but after being on a plane all night, I told him I preferred to stand. There were so many framed handbills and head shots on the wall that they formed a jigsaw puzzle of the man's life.

"So," he said, guzzling the whiskey from his mug. "What the hell happened to the poor girl?"

"I don't know," I said. "That's why I'm here."

"Any idea?"

"Nope," I said. "I was hoping you could tell me something."

"So very sad," he said. "So very L.A. I'd like to tell you this was the first time this has happened to a student. But it's not. Not by a long shot. It's drugs or boys. Or girls. Or both. Or money. Or power. Most often it's drugs. Did she have a habit?"

"Only one I know about is shopping," I said.

"You know, heroin is very chic again," he said. "Very cool. I thought all that went out of vogue when River Phoenix overdosed at the Viper Room. He was a brilliant kid. So much potential. One of my very closest friends produced *Mosquito Coast*. I knew Harrison long ago. When he worked as a carpenter."

He poured out some more whiskey. I thought about asking him if he needed help with the heavy bottle. It looked like I could do a set of one-armed curls with the jug.

"Was Gabby friends with other students?"

He shrugged. "Probably," he said. His cheeks brightening, eyes becoming a bit glassy. "Many of the kids go out for beers after class. I don't know which ones, but I'd be glad to ask. As far as my relationship, it was professional only. After five wives, I've learned to stay far and away from these hungry young creatures. Some of them are actually convinced I can help them with their careers."

"And you can't?"

"I tell them from day one," he said. "I can help you become a better actor. I can help you develop your craft. But I am not a businessman. You must separate the art from the business."

"Sounds like sleuthing."

"Are you not good with business, Mr. Spenser?"

"I'm a genius with money," I said. "But I spent it all on gambling and women. The rest I spent foolishly."

"George Raft."

"No one tossed a coin better," I said, toasting him with my Tennessee coffee.

"I have a class tonight," he said. "I'll ask about Gabby. How long has she been gone?"

"Twelve days."

"And nobody has seen or heard from her?"

"No one I've spoken to yet."

"That's disturbing," he said. "Highly disturbing."

"Yep," I said.

I shook hands with Bloom and let myself out.

Standing under the old marquee, I saw the rain had returned again, patting the little pools and turning the pavement slick. A lovely vision along Ventura Boulevard and out into the expanse of the Ralphs parking lot. I placed my hands in my pockets and waited for an opening in traffic. Back in Cambridge, it would be dinnertime. Susan would be done with her patients, probably opening up a nice bottle of Riesling and settling in with Pearl for the night.

I pulled the cap I was sporting that season, the Greenville Drive, down in my eyes. The coffee and whiskey sat heavy in my stomach.

I headed back to the hotel and waited for a call from Z.

4

Back at the Loews across from Z's office, I changed into gym clothes and did a series of push-ups and sit-ups. A hundred of each. Not my best effort, but better than nothing. After I got a little sweat going, I decided to journey out in the rain for a little jog. I often did my best thinking pounding the pavement or on a barstool. As it was not yet five o'clock, I laced up my running shoes.

I followed Highland a block over to Hollywood Boulevard and headed west for the red neon sign atop the Roosevelt Hotel, jogging away from the Egyptian Theater and the Pig 'N Whistle where Clark Gable and Cary Grant were known to knock back a few dry martinis. Made with gin, of course. Two men asked me for money. A woman tried to sell me a tour of the stars' homes. Another man tried to sell me either drugs or sex. He was so smashed, I couldn't understand him through his broken teeth. I was delighted to see Hollywood was as I'd left it.

I slowed as I ran past Madame Tussauds. A sign promised up-close-and-personal experiences of replicas of Michael Jackson, Madonna, and Shrek. The time-traveling DeLorean from *Back to the Future* was parked outside, surrounded by tourists taking selfies. Everyone had a camera. Everyone was smiling except for the homeless people sleeping in empty doorways.

Rain puddled all along the Walk of Fame. I ran over stars for James Garner. Steve McQueen. Kermit the Frog. I thought about something Gabby's mother had told me at Harvest. She said Gabby had always been a seeker. I wondered exactly what she'd meant. I should have asked more questions. But at the time all she knew was that her daughter was missing and she'd been unsatisfied by answers from LAPD. Sometimes you headed right into something and figured it out on the fly.

When I got back to my room, my clothes were soaked from sweat and the rain. I took a hot shower, shaved, and brushed my teeth. I pulled on a pair of 501s, a gray Henley shirt, and a lightweight navy blazer. It would do nicely to cover the shoulder holster and .38.

I picked up my phone and checked in with Z. He didn't answer but texted that he'd dropped off the MacBook in K-town. He could meet me later tonight at the Mirabeau on Sunset.

I sat in the chair by the window and dialed Susan. After several rings, she picked up.

"Let me guess, you've already found Gabby and are headed home," she said.

"How did you know?"

"No soap?"

"None whatsoever," I said. "But I did spend some quality time with her ex-boyfriend-turned-agent and her current acting coach."

"And?"

"They knew less than me."

"What about the woman she worked for?" she said. "Gabby was her dog walker."

"Next on the list," I said. "Maybe I'll interview the dogs, too. You know I'm good with animals."

"It's part of your innate mind."

"Thank you."

"Is there any chance this is a misunderstanding?" Susan said. "Maybe she just went off for a long vacation. Or in a new relationship? And maybe forget to tell anyone?"

"I went to her apartment this morning," I said. "Someone made a real mess of it. On the upside, Z knows someone in Canada who can pinpoint Gabby's cell within a city block."

"Is that even legal?"

"Probably not," I said. "I don't want to know."

"Have you had any luck with the police?"

"I have a call in to Samuelson," I said.

"This is so awful," she said. "No parent should ever go through this."

"This is Hollywood," I said. "I'll search for a happy ending."

"You do that."

"Love," I said.

"Love."

5

I wish I could help you more, but Gabby quit working for me six months ago," Nancy Sharp said. She was a trim, athletic-looking woman with premature silver hair, shoeless, in black yoga pants and a loose purple shirt that hit her right above the knees. Behind the door, dogs barked and made a lot of racket, Sharp having to shush them and push them back with her hands. Their names were Nanook and Willy.

"I'll take what I can get," I said. "Right now Nanook and Willy know more than me."

"And her mother?" she said.

"Worried sick," I said. "Can you help?"

"Of course."

She invited me into a classic 1930s Spanish bungalow with stucco walls and a barrel-tile roof. Outside, the landscaping was bougainvillea, lavender, oleander, and some interesting-looking big orange flowers. Some other stuff I could not identify, but knew would never make it through a Boston winter. West Hollywood seemed as exotic as a trip to Bora Bora.

As I entered, the dogs charged me and began to sniff my legs and hands. I got down on my knees and offered my hands, petting an old brown dachshund with a graying muzzle.

"That's Willy."

"Hello, Willy," I said.

Nanook was much more suspicious, a big Siberian husky with the trademark mismatched eyes, who stood on a couch, barking at me. It wasn't a mean bark, just a courteous warning. I let her sniff my hand, too. Whatever my smell, it seemed to satisfy her as I took a seat nearby, Sharp still standing.

It was a pleasant little house with what looked to be original hardwood floors and a small kitchen with an arched entrance framed in Spanish tile. A cup of hot tea sat on a coffee table in front of the leather couch and a television showing the local news was on mute. A small wooden bookshelf overflowed with meditations on Eastern philosophy and best-selling self-help authors. A medium-sized gong had been situated before a large brown sitting pillow.

The room smelled like the inside of a Cambridge tea shop.

"Her mother said Gabby mentioned you often."

"I liked Gabby a lot," Sharp said. "I'm sorry. Would you like anything to drink?"

"No, thank you."

"I have some good local beer."

"When in L.A. . . ."

She walked off into the kitchen and returned with an Angel City IPA. She popped the cap and handed it to me. I could see why Gabby Leggett liked Nancy Sharp. The woman liked dogs and had a fridge full of good beer. I decided she was a good and decent person.

"What can you tell me about Gabby?"

"What do you know?" she said.

"I know she worked as a model and wanted to be an actress," I said. "She was beautiful and some say talented. And I know she has many fans on Instagram wondering why she hasn't posted in a while."

"How many is she up to now?"

"Forty thousand and some change," I said.

"She only had about five or six thousand when she started working for me," Sharp said, taking a seat by Nanook and tucking her bare feet up under her. "She's moved up in the world."

Sharp reached for the hot tea while I sipped the beer. On the television, the news headlines scrolled *4.0 QUAKE STRIKES NEAR ALTA VISTA*.

"Did something change?"

"Gabby became a lot more aggressive with her social media," she said. "She cultivated famous people to follow her and repost. She did a lot of stuff in bathing suits. Some seminude. Not that I'm some kind of prude. Lots of nice trips down to Mexico with beautiful friends and a beautiful life. Parties on the beach. Cocktails at the best clubs."

"I often drink mimosas in a thong," I said.

"Ha," she said. "I bet. But for this generation, your life is not fully lived unless you're sharing it with the world."

"I prefer just to be."

"Exactly," she said. "I'd rather just experience what I'm seeing without a buffer, be in the moment rather than recording it for everyone else."

"I only take pictures when people are doing very bad things."

"Cheaters."

"Sometimes," I said. "But I prefer to eschew divorce cases. Unless money is really low. Or the money they offer is really good."

"And who hired you to search for Gabby?"

"Her mother, Amanda," I said. "Three days ago the police got involved, but her mother wasn't satisfied with what they knew or had learned. She asked me to come out here."

"And your services don't come cheap."

"Nope," I said. "They don't. Although I did fly coach."

"You look too big for coach."

"Premium economy," I said. "I need the legroom."

"Have you been to Los Angeles before?" she said. She held the tea in one hand and brushed back her straight silver hair with long fingers. Willy pawed at her legs to get up on the couch, his diminutive legs not quite able to make the leap from the floor. She pulled him up and he found a comfortable place in Nancy's lap. The two dogs continued to eye me with suspicion.

"A few times," I said.

"Know people?"

"A few," I said.

"And do you fear the worst?"

"I don't have much to go on," I said. "But I've come across a few details that cause me some concern. Did she ever mention a boy named Eric Collinson?"

"I know Eric," she said. "He was an agent of some kind at one of the big ones. ICM. Or maybe Endeavor. One of those Ivy League hipster types. Always backpacking in Argentina or heading up to wine country. He lives quite a curated, beautiful life, too."

I named the agency and she nodded.

"I know they had a rough breakup," she said. She had to lift her chin and hold her mug high as Willy tried to lick her face. "Eric was completely obsessed with her and wouldn't let her breathe. After they broke up, I told her to find a new agent."

"And why didn't she?"

"Apparently Eric is very good," she said. "And very connected."

"Was he abusive?"

"Not that I know of," he said. "But he called her all the time. She had to draw some boundaries between the personal and professional."

"Eric let me into her apartment today," I said. "I can't say we hit it off. He was reluctant to discuss Gabby."

"Eric was smitten," she said. "Gabby was beautiful and very popular. She went from a gee-whiz kid from the East Coast to a big-time player on the party scene."

"I doubt dog walking is that lucrative," I said. "Even in L.A."

"She made a decent amount making commercials," she said. "I seem to recall something for Carl's Jr. where she had to eat a cheeseburger in a string bikini."

"We've all been there," I said.

She laughed and reached over Willy to put down the tea. I smelled curry coming from the kitchen. Several brown bags of groceries waited on a table near the stove.

"Did you know any of her other friends?"

Sharp shook her head. "Other than Eric, I couldn't tell you," she said. "When she was here I was at work. We had some pleasant conversations, but often just in passing or when I was paying her for watching these guys."

"Where do you work?"

"I do on-set publicity for film and TV," she said. "I volunteer a little for a nonprofit."

"Eric mentioned she had a new boyfriend, but didn't give me a name."

"I wouldn't know," she said. "Have you talked to her friends?"

"My associate is on that," I said. I had drained the beer to the halfway point. "He has more cred with the young people."

"That happens fast," she said. "Doesn't it?"

"'Rage, rage against the dying of the light . . .'"

"There can't be that many literate detectives out there."

"Only one that I know," I said.

"I guess you want to find the new guy?"

"Yep," I said. "We're going to a place called the Mira-beau tonight. Eric mentioned a friend of Gabby's named KiKi worked there."

"Are you on the list?"

"Nope."

"I can help with that," she said. "One of the perks of being a publicist. I can open a few doors."

I finished the beer and stood. I thanked her for her time, left the empty bottle on her kitchen counter, and bent down to tell Willy good-bye. I scratched his long, soft ears. Willy licked my hand.

"They're good judges of character."

I smiled. "The best."

"Would you like to stay for dinner?"

"Thank you," I said. "But duty calls."

"Perhaps later, then?" she said. Sharp walked me to the door and leaned her bare shoulder against the frame. Like Gabby, she was quite lithe and had large green eyes.

"I would," I said. "But my girlfriend and dog back home might get jealous. Especially the dog."

"Sorry," she said. "I didn't see a wedding ring. And you sounded like fun."

"More than a barrel of monkeys," I said.

6

If Andy Warhol and Marie Antoinette had gone into the interior decorating business together, they might've come up with a place like Mirabeau on Sunset. Big crystal chandeliers, purple velvet sofas, oversized framed photos of famous people, many as naked as jaybirds, and random neon signs reading THE NIGHT IS YOURS and LET THEM EAT CAKE. No detail left unfettered, no extravagance too silly. The clientele was decidedly less beautiful than promised. Women in tiny dresses and six-inch heels and the men in slacker T-shirts and tight ripped jeans. I still remembered when a coat and tie were required at the best clubs. Now it seemed proper grooming would earn you a place at the back of the line.

"See what I mean," Z said. I ordered him a Coke while I worked on a Bulleit Rye on the rocks. "Your kind of club."

"My pants aren't torn."

"And we're both wearing jackets."

"For professional reasons," I said, patting over the .38.

A woman in a rhinestone bra and tight orange velvet pants leaned into the space between me and Z. She kissed the bartender on the cheek as he handed her a flute of champagne. Being trained detectives, we both watched her as she walked away. Her pants were so high and tight, I was surprised she wasn't yodeling.

"You're not in Cambridge anymore," Z said.

"Nope," I said. "Somewhere under the rainbow."

The music was pulsing, electronic nonsense, but no one seemed to mind. Four beefy-looking bald men in matching black T-shirts and with equally expanding guts gathered around a bucket of champagne. Several young women wore skirts the size of cocktail napkins and tops that looked as if they'd been knitted by mice. One of the older men clutched the champagne bucket, vape pen firmly in his teeth, as he poured another round. He caught my eye and blew steam from his nose like a bull.

I raised my whiskey in his direction. He glanced away.

Z finished the Coke and nodded to me. "What's the bartender say?"

"Never heard of KiKi."

"I'll ask the doorman," he said. He wandered off, leaving me alone with good whiskey and deep thoughts as the club started to rev up at midnight. A DJ worked the soundboard, a dance floor between him and the main bar and sectional sofas. One of those mirrored disco globes spun over the floor, the music reaching a vibrating crescendo as several servers appeared from a side door holding champagne bottles high. Sparklers had been lit against the bottles. The DJ played a song about partying like a rock star as corks were popped and the champagne flowed over glasses and onto the floor.

I pined for a slow night at the Ritz bar. A gentle fire, good conversation, with the Sox game on.

The bald fat guys near me were on their feet, gyrating their hips against the backsides of the much younger women. I wondered what Susan might make of all this. I wondered what Jane Goodall would think.

"Doorman didn't know her, either," Z said. "I gave him twenty bucks and he's going to ask around."

"So we wait?" I said.

"And enjoy the show," he said. "When's the last time you went clubbing?"

"'Ninety-nine," I said. "Right after Jerry Broz sent two of his worst guys for me. I kept a Louisville Slugger in my trunk."

I drank more whiskey and ordered another, this time with lots of ice and a generous splash of water. Always paid to be vigilant. When the bartender returned, I asked him if he'd see if the DJ might play some Johnny Hartman.

He looked confused and walked away.

"It's not as bad as you think," he said. "Some of these guys are really talented."

"Talent means playing instruments," I said. "Or at the least, carrying a tune."

"DJs have to know their audience," he said. "They have to feel the vibe of the place, know the flow of the night. Do you know this one? Tame Impala. The one before was Diplo."

"Sounds like someone making love to a synthesizer."

Z rested his elbows against the bar as an XXL bouncer walked up to us and whispered something in his ear. Z nodded at me and I left cash on the bar, following them through the crowd toward the front door. We walked outside, where a long line had formed against metal barriers. The bouncer looked me up and down and then back at Z.

"He's cool," Z said.

"It's true," I said.

"We don't need trouble," the bouncer said.

Z reached into his pocket and handed the man a little more cash. The man looked at me again and then back at Z. He reached for a walkie-talkie and turned his back.

"She goes by Caroline here," he said. "Her friends call her KiKi. She's one of the bottle-service girls."

I watched as two candy-colored sports cars pulled up in front of Mirabeau and opened their doors. One was a canary-yellow Ferrari and the other was a fire-engine-red Bugatti. The XXL bouncer lifted the rope for the drivers and more money was exchanged. The streets were shiny with the rain, the bright lights and neon along Sunset glowing in the asphalt. Lots of cash and bright lights, a warm wind coming down off the hills.

A few minutes later, a woman with a blunt-cut bob and the standard outfit of black bra and black hot pants came outside. She sucked on a vape pen and said something to the bouncer. He nodded toward us and she walked our way, head down and shoulders slumped. She had on thick eye makeup and looked a little like Louise Brooks.

"KiKi?" I said

She nodded. I introduced Z and told her that we were hired to find Gabby. She listened as she sucked on the device, squinting her eyes into the haze, not sure what to make of us. An electric-blue Lamborghini wheeled up as I told her what we'd seen with Eric Collinson.

"Eric is such a fucking prick."

"Most likely," I said. "He said you and Gabby were friends."

"Best friends," she said. "We were the very best of friends."

"'Were'?"

"Gabby got judgmental," she said. "She didn't like me working here. She didn't like what I did or my lifestyle."

"Why not?"

"I've already talked to the police," she said. "I don't really know anything more."

"What did you tell the police?" Z said.

"I told them I hadn't seen Gabby in months," she said. "We had a nice pasta dinner at Republique and she kept on bashing this club and what I did with my life. And the men I dated. I told her I didn't need another mother. Not to mention, I wasn't into half the shit that Gabby was into. I mean, this is just a fucking job. What Gabby did, the men she dated, that was really messed up."

"Like Eric."

"Like I said, Eric was a prick," she said. "But he wasn't the worst."

"Who was the worst?" I said.

KiKi looked back to the door and then back to us. She sucked hard on the pen and then shook her head. "I got to go," she said. "I don't know where she went or what she got into. But I wasn't about to sit there and have her run down me and my friends. All I know is that she was acting strange. Like maybe she was high or something. She was just so calm, talking in this really irritating, level voice, telling me that I had options. That there was a bigger world out there I needed to experience. That I didn't have to be the person I was."

"Maybe she was channeling Carl Sagan."

KiKi looked confused and shook her head. "I didn't stick around. Once she started getting totally judgy, I paid my share and left."

"Did you talk to her later?"

"She called," she said. "But I didn't answer. I don't know who she's met or what she's done. But that wasn't Gabby that night. Gabby used to be the most wild, fun girl I ever knew. You ever been to Joshua Tree at three a.m., out of your mind on mushrooms?"

I shook my head. "Not since Gram Parsons died."

"I really have to go," she said. "I have three tables tonight."

"Do you know anything about a new boyfriend?"

She looked at me and Z and shook her head. "Just one?"

"Eric was convinced she'd been seeing someone new," Z said. "Someone special."

"Eric's mad he got dumped," she said. "He was so controlling. Had to have her check in with him all the time.

Kept on pestering her to move in with him. I mean, really. What a total dick."

"Someone broke into Gabby's apartment," Z said. "And made a real mess."

"I wouldn't know anything about that."

Z named several women he'd spoken to earlier in the day. He was very exact and precise about each one mentioned. He asked KiKi if there was anyone else we should find.

"Not really," she said. "They haven't seen her in a while, either. She left us for whatever she'd found."

"Did Eric ever threaten her?" I said.

KiKi shook her head, pointing the vape pen at my chest. "You want to know what I really think? I think Gabby got herself into her own mess. I think she pissed off the wrong people and something really, really bad happened. There, I said it. I'm sorry. I loved her like a sister. But she brought up some really painful stuff to me. Things that I told her in confidence. It was almost like she wanted to blackmail me or something."

"Blackmail you into what?" Z said.

"That's the thing," KiKi said. "I never gave her a chance to go ahead with her threats. I left. I turned her away. I don't have time for that shit."

I watched the bouncer ushering in more beautiful people and some who slipped him a little cash. It was midnight in Los Angeles and way past bedtime in Boston. I looked at my watch and nodded to Z.

KiKi turned to leave. We watched her walk away in wobbly tall boots.

"Gabby Leggett is a woman of many secrets."

"Even among her closest friends," Z said.

"You remember Spenser's number-one Crime Stopper tip?"

"Keep bugging the shit out of people until the bad guys get nervous."

I grinned. "You were listening."

7

Samuelson graciously agreed to meet for breakfast at the Original Pantry downtown on Figueroa. Samuelson, being Samuelson, had gotten there early and was already studying the menu when I walked in. He was still bald but had grown his mustache back, long and droopy, like a member of the Earp family. He wore a navy suit and white dress shirt with a flowered red tie, and had on gold aviator glasses with tinted lenses.

"Nice tie," I said. "No wonder you made captain."

"I made captain because I closed a shit-ton of cases," he said, shaking my hand and passing me a menu. "Sit down, gumshoe. The French toast will break your goddamn heart."

I sat, put the menu down, and leaned back. Outside, the sun had finally decided to make an appearance, and light streamed through the blinds onto the old tables.

Samuelson didn't ask what I wanted, but I gave a two-minute rundown of Gabby Leggett and what I knew so far. He listened intently and nodded, taking a break only when the waiter appeared. I got the French toast. He had country-fried steak with eggs sunny-side-up. The restaurant was a long shot from the front door, with a big sizzling grill against the far wall. Cream-colored globes glowed overhead, and there were slatted blinds over the windows. A sign read: SINCE 1924. NEVER CLOSED WITHOUT A CUSTOMER.

"You told me the woman's name in your message," he said. "As you've done such a stellar job keeping in touch over the years, I made a few calls."

"You didn't get my Christmas cards?"

"Must've gone to the wrong address," he said.

"And the fruit baskets?" I said.

"Please."

The waiter brought ice water and coffees. I added one pack of sugar to a thick mug and stirred.

"Girl was reported missing about a week ago."

I nodded. "By her mother."

"You know how many girls go missing in Los Angeles County and then are found a few days later?"

I nodded. "How many go missing and are never found?"

"You really want to know the answer to that question?"

"Not really."

There was the dull murmur of conversation all around us. Men and women in business attire and laborers in heavy overalls and paint-splattered shoes. Historic photos of L.A. hung on the wood-paneled walls. The air smelled of crisp bacon and black coffee. All the things that made diners wondrous places.

"The detective who caught the case did his job," he said. "He talked to some of the girl's hippie friends and the girl's ex-boyfriend. Guy named Collinson."

"I'm on the same track," I said. "Although Collinson hasn't been her boyfriend for some time. Now he's just her agent."

"Good for him."

"And I don't know if I'd call these kids hippies," I said. "Or hipsters. To be honest, I don't know what to call them."

"Call 'em fucking dumb kids," he said. "They're all the same. Same as you and me when we were that age. Looking to screw over the old guys."

I toasted him with the mug and took a sip.

"As an ex-cop, you know we're looking at the boyfriend," he said. "Most of the time that's our answer. It's not exactly Agatha Christie out in the real world. Unless it's Colonel Mustard lurking around the corner with his dick in his hand."

"Never did trust Colonel Mustard," I said. "Or Collinson. He seemed reticent to assist me. And for the record, I wasn't fond of his haircut."

"*Reticent?*" he said. "Jesus. You need to get out of Boston more often. And yeah, the detective had the same impression of Collinson. But here's the thing. That's not the boyfriend I mean. I mean the most current boyfriend, that I never for one single goddamn moment mentioned to you."

"I have the feeling I'm springing for breakfast."

"What did you expect?" he said. "I didn't come for the stimulating conversation."

The waiter brought breakfast. Samuelson had told the truth. The French toast was truly heartbreaking. Out of respect, I lightly applied the maple syrup and took a third and fourth bite.

"You sure you want into this?" he said. "I don't know if you really want to go there."

"Where's that?"

"Shit City," Samuelson said.

I shrugged. "Oh, I've been there once or twice," I said. "Always glad to get my passport stamped."

"And that doesn't always work for you."

"I've made a few mistakes over the years," I said. "A big one out here that both of us will never forget."

Samuelson nodded and cut into the country-fried steak and eggs. He worked around the eggs, slicing and slicing until finally breaking the yolk. The yellow spread out across his plate. "See, the boyfriend isn't just a boyfriend," he said. "He's not some twiggy, jittery little hipster. Looks like your girl Leggett's last boyfriend was a goddamn nine-hundred-pound gorilla in his town."

I held up my hand. "Gabby was dating Mighty Joe Young?"

"Pretty much," he said. "Ever heard the name Jimmy Yamashiro?"

"Sounds like a Japanese steak sauce."

"Even better," Samuelson said, pointing the end of his fork at my chest. He explained Yamashiro was the president and CEO of a major studio that now had offices on the old MGM lot in Culver City.

"Ah," I said. "That's entertainment."

"This was told to me with the utmost confidence."

"You know me," I said. "Ol' trustworthy Spenser."

"I never said that," Samuelson said, taking another stab at the eggs. "I just thought the family should know. Yamashiro is a big fucking deal. The chief has taken a personal interest in keeping this quiet."

"Why tell me?"

"Off the record?" Samuelson said. "Maybe I think the current chief is an asshole. If this gets out, it'll be a three-ring media circus. Fucking *Entertainment Tonight* and those smug a-holes at *TMZ*."

"Yeah," I said. "They won't leave me alone since I broke up Brangelina."

Samuelson shrugged and continued to eat. "This won't end pretty," he said. "Things like this never do."

"Don't I always come out smelling like a rose?"

"Don't get cocky," he said. "Even if Yamashiro is clean, these people have too damn much to lose and won't go easy."

"Did the detective mention anything about Gabby's apartment being torn apart?"

"Nope," he said. "They said the apartment was empty and clean."

"Hmm."

"And now?"

"Might want to have them check on it again."

"Find anything?"

I set down my fork and leaned back into my chair. The front door opened and gust of cool air blew through the diner.

"Wait," Samuelson said, holding up the flat of his hand. "I know you too well, Spenser. Please don't answer that question."

8

I called Z twice without luck. I left a message on his cell and with his secretary, Delores.

"Does your heart go pitter-patter when you hear my voice?" I said.

"No, sir," she said. "It does not."

"Even just a bit?"

"Nope," she said. And hung up.

"She'll come around," I said, setting the phone in the rental's console.

I was on my own the second morning in L.A., dipping in and out of traffic on the 10 West toward Culver City. In my experience, there were several different ways to get to the center of a Tootsie Pop. But the most expedient was always crushing it in your back teeth. I had several other friends and acquaintances to find. But when you get a big lead from a cop you trust, you don't waste your time.

After breakfast with Samuelson, I dug deep into my Rolodex and called a producer I'd worked for in Boston many moons ago. Sandy Salzman had assigned me to track down a guy in Boston stalking a big-time actress named Jill Joyce. While the outcome wasn't what we'd expected, we remained friendly.

"You want to get in with who?" Salzman said.

"Jimmy Yamashiro."

"You're kidding me," he said. "I can't even get in with Jimmy Yamashiro. He runs the whole fucking studio in Culver City."

"I know," I said. "I'm headed that way now."

"What, did you write some cockamamie pilot about a Boston tough guy?" he said. "You trying to sell your life story?"

"How'd you know, Sandy?"

"I expected it," he said. "I'd change a few details, though."

"Like what?"

"You're too much of an old-fashioned good guy," he said. "White knight and all that crap. I'd make the hero fresh out of prison."

"Really?"

"Sure," he said. "Gives him some mystery and edge."

"Ah."

"And I'd tone down that friend of yours, Hawk," he said. "He makes me nervous as hell. The black hat and cowboy boots. Jesus Christ. He'd make viewers really nervous, too. I get the chills just thinking about him."

"Can't have a show without me and Hawk," I said.

"Maybe make him a young kid from the streets," he said. "Shows some promise but real green. Can't shoot. Can't throw a damn punch. You could take him under your wing. A real *Boys Town* kinda thing."

"Like a big brother?"

"Exactly."

"Hawk would love that," I said. "He's always admired me. But, Sandy?"

"Yeah?"

"I'm not pitching a show," I said. "I'm out here working a case. I'm looking for a missing girl and Jimmy Yamashiro might know a thing or two. It needs to be handled delicately. And I figured there are many layers to get to a guy like Yamashiro."

"More than a fucking rotten onion," Salzman said. "Let me make some calls. I know he started out over at CBS. A guy who used to work for me, fetching coffee, later became Yamashiro's mentor. Blase McCarthy. Great guy. Blase has a direct line to Yamashiro. He can relay a message."

"Perfect."

"Spenser?"

I waited. Since we'd been talking, the interstate traffic had moved all of four feet. Over the rails and down the slopes, the jacaranda trees bloomed bright purple as the sun shone weakly through the city haze. "I wouldn't do this for just anybody," he said. "Don't make me look bad."

"Discreet is my middle name."

"You weren't so discreet back when you worked with Jilly," he said. "Christ. You put that poor woman through the fucking ringer."

"And she was better for it."

"Have you spoken to her lately?"

"Nope."

"She's a damn mess," Sandy said. "What's Yamashiro's connection to the girl?"

"I can't tell you."

"Christ," he said. "What'll I say, then?"

"What did I say?" I said. "Discreet."

"But he'll want to see you?"

"Mention I work for Gabrielle Leggett's mother," I said.

"How do you spell that?"

I told him and he repeated it as he wrote it down. Traffic moved another two inches.

"And that'll get his attention?"

"Like a ten-thousand-watt cattle prod."

"Yikes."

9

I rolled through a gigantic Art Deco arch at what used to be the old MGM Studios and stopped behind two cars at the guard shack. The other cars drove in and I slid up to a wiry old man in a blue uniform. He looked to have gotten to Hollywood slightly before Thelma Todd.

"Hello, Jonesy," I said. "I'm here to see Mr. DeMille. Where's he shooting today?"

The old guard looked at me with a proper amount of annoyance. He tapped at his clipboard with a pen, wishing for me to get on with it. Behind us, a humorless person honked their horn.

"Spenser," I said. "I have an appointment with Mr. Ya-mashiro."

He walked into the shack and after a few moments returned with a parking pass. He asked me for my ID, which I showed him, and the gate lifted. I followed signs

to guest parking. Billboards of many famous films covered the walls of soundstages and Art Deco buildings.
The Wizard of Oz. Ben-Hur. Singin' in the Rain.

I left my rental and walked past the old studio commis-
sary and then a large building named after Jimmy Stew-
art. *Spenser, private eye to the stars.* I was told Yamashiro
had his office in the main building on the studio campus.
The structure was newer, constructed in a mod style, with
mirrored windows and an austere lobby. A security guard
checked my ID against his list and followed me to an elevator, punching up the fifth floor and holding the door
wide. Upstairs on the fifth floor, I met Yamashiro's secretary, a bubbly young black woman in a bright yellow dress
overlain with a navy cardigan.

She offered me coffee, tea, or bottled water.

I accepted the coffee.

She offered me a blueberry muffin.

I accepted the muffin. Who was I to try and buck the
Hollywood system?

"I don't suppose you have a Bloody Mary cart?"

"I can check."

I held up the flat of my hand in surrender.

The waiting room was austere to a point that followed
form over function. The walls were black marble and the
floor four-foot-by-four-foot sleek white tile. Most of the
trim done in weathered beach wood. A glass-topped table
the length of half a football field prostrated along a long
black leather couch. A grouping of industry magazines
had been neatly aligned. *Variety. The Hollywood Reporter.*

On the walls, several posters of recent hits had been framed. None of them I wanted to see.

I checked the messages on my phone. I used the bathroom. I drank coffee. And I waited. Twenty minutes turned into nearly an hour.

"Mr. Yamashiro must be a very busy man."

"Mmhmm," the secretary said from behind her over-sized desk.

"Very nice for him to fit me in so quickly."

She nodded and tilted her head, without a smile. "It was unusual," she said. "You must be very special."

"I am," I said. I gave her the full smile that was known to melt steel beams and make women lose all self-control. "I helped solve the Fatty Arbuckle case."

"Really?" she said.

I nodded.

"Won't be much longer."

A half-hour later, she appeared again and ushered me down the hall into a glass-walled conference room. A long oval table filled the center of the room, with several comfy rolling leather chairs. Orchids flowering in white lined the center of the spotless table. Our movements echoed in the room, as the secretary disappeared and two men entered. One was about my age, or a bit older, with weathered skin and whitish hair fashioned into a severe crew cut. The other man was younger but twice as large, with a bald head shaved close. They wore dark suits and waited by the door until a short, chunky Asian man walked through the door and came over toward me.

He offered his hand. "James Yamashiro."

"Spenser," I said, shaking it.

"Can we get you anything?" he said. "Coffee, tea?"

"Already had coffee," I said. "Tasted as if the beans were picked by Juan Valdez himself."

"Fine, fine," he said, beaming. He wore a tightly tailored gray suit, a pressed white shirt, and a long black tie. He had dark skin and black eyes, hair so silver it seemed metallic. His haircut was precise and exact. His fingernails buffed and manicured. His smile so white and blinding, I nearly reached for my sunglasses.

As he moved toward the opposite end of the long table, Yamashiro nodded to the two men and they walked out the door. They followed orders like two dopey yet faithful golden retrievers.

"So you know some people," he said. "Sandy Salzman is a name I haven't heard in some time. He was doing some producing work over at CBS when I first got started in the business. I believe he's been retired for some time. How do you know him?"

"He hired me years ago to help track down a stalker."

"Fascinating," he said, still-beaming eyes taking me in, his palms spread out flat on the slate table. "Absolutely fascinating."

"When people aren't shooting at you."

I crossed my legs and looked back at Yamashiro. He'd chosen a seat eight places away from me at the head of the table. He looked like the kind of guy who refused to sit anywhere but the head of the table. I rocked a little in my chair and smiled back. *Spenser, O, Friend of the World.*

"I heard you are also friends with Miss Leggett."

"Never met her," I said. "I work for her family."

"The family," he said. "Of course."

He nodded, smile dropping, hands disappearing from the table. He took in a long breath and leveled his black eyes at me. I assumed this was the kind of look that struck fear in producers with hopes and dreams armed with dynamite pitches. I wondered if I needed to sit on my hands to make them quit shaking.

We didn't speak for a while. The silence was so long and protracted, I wondered if we were playing some sort of game.

"I know why you're here," he said. "Do you people have no shame?"

I shrugged. "Did you see me pocket an extra muffin?" I said. "But you tell me. Why am I really here?"

"You've come to embarrass and humiliate me if I don't play along," Yamashiro said. "But my answer is no different than it was two weeks ago. I don't answer to bribes and threats. If you want to go and whisper in the ear of some dip at *The Hollywood Reporter*, be my guest. What Gabby and I had was nice, pleasant, and consensual. I didn't know who she was and the kind of people she consorted with."

"Okay," I said. "What kind of people did she consort with?"

"The only reason I let you get one toe past that front gate is to stop this nonsense once and for all," he said, ignoring my question. "I'm not afraid of you or what Gabby has to say. My wife and I have a strong and very modern relationship. She knows I am a grown man with lots of pressure and many needs. My arrangement with Gabby was nothing unusual. And nothing to be embarrassed about."

I held up my hand like a confused kid at school. I swiveled a bit in the nifty chair, leaning forward. "I am employed by Gabby's mother in Boston," I said. "Gabby went missing nearly two weeks ago and no one has seen nor heard from her. I have been out here less than twenty-four hours and have spoken to several people who knew her. But you seem to be the only person I've met who has a semblance of an idea who she really is. Or has been in touch with her recently. So may we press rewind and start again?"

He leveled a hard look at me. I tried not to quiver. His nostrils flared and he swallowed. I smiled back at him. The lid of his right eye twitched ever so slightly.

"Who is trying to shake you down?"

He didn't answer.

"How is Gabby connected to them?"

He still didn't answer. I started to worry he'd spit in my coffee and poisoned that muffin. I knew those blueberries had a little something extra.

"I will tell you what I told the police, Mr. Spenser," he said. "Gabby isn't missing. She may not be at her old apartment, but she's never been gone. I'm sorry she's put her family through worry and trauma. She's not really the kind of girl that you see. She's someone very, very brilliant. And someone who is very, very devious."

"And someone who is blackmailing you?"

Yamashiro stood up. The two men in dark suits entered the room. The older one with the throwback crew cut held the glass door wide. "I am done here," Yamashiro said.

I pulled out my card, the one featuring my image clutching a bowie knife in my teeth, and tossed it on the table. "A little cooperation never hurt anyone."

He walked toward the open door and briefly turned back to me. "Do I look like a man who needs help?"

"Those two look like they just escaped from the circus," I said. "I, on the other hand, am bonded and insured and the best in the business."

Yamashiro disappeared. The two men stood there, arms folded over their chests, and stared at me. I waited a moment to see if they would growl or bark at me.

"This is the scene when you offer the easy way or the hard way," I said. "And I run away with my tail tucked between my legs."

"Yeah." The older man with the crew cut was leather-skinned and flinty-eyed. "You got that right, bub."

"'Bub'?" I said. "Boy, that is a hit from the past. How long have you been doing this?"

"Too damn long."

"I know the feeling." I walked myself back to my rental with dashed dreams and waved to Jonesy on the way out the gate.

I met Z at Chunju Han-il Kwan, a tiny restaurant in a K-town strip mall wedged between a dry cleaner and a nail salon. I slid into a hard wooden booth across from him and told him about my power meeting with Jimmy Yamashiro.

"If Yamashiro saw you," Z said, "he must be scared shitless."

"Maybe," I said. "But he still seemed pretty full of shit."

"Having a mistress is hardly a scandal in L.A.," he said. "It's more of a job requirement."

"He feels the same way," I said. "He called his wife a thoroughly modern woman who understood his pressures and needs."

"Just like Susan?" Z said.

"The complete opposite of Susan."

Z looked around the restaurant at the small gathering

of mainly Asian customers huddling over steaming bowls of soup.

"The tech is meeting us here," he said. "I figured you might be hungry by now."

"You know me," I said. "I'm always hungry."

Z had on a sleeveless black Mickey Mouse T-shirt with faded jeans and well-broken-in brown cowboy boots. He looked like an extra from *The Outsiders*.

"There's no shame in eating while you work," I said. "It's what efficiency experts called multitasking."

"I also figured you'd dig their *budae jjigae*," he said. "It's a spicy kitchen-sink stew. Has about everything in it you can imagine."

"I can imagine quite a lot." The restaurant was paneled in dark wood and lit by bronze lanterns, looking almost like a Korean Cracker Barrel. The air smelled of onions, garlic, and spice.

"What else did Yamashiro say?" Z said.

"He admitted to the affair and said before she disappeared Gabby had tried to blackmail him."

"Wait," Z said. "Repeat that again."

I repeated it for him. He listened and nodded along with the details. "And he thought you'd been sent to shake him down?"

"Correct."

"But he knew Gabby was missing?"

"Also correct," I said. "But somehow didn't believe it. He said she was both highly intelligent and devious. He said she may not be in her apartment but definitely hadn't been abducted."

"Did he elaborate?"

"Right up until the time he had his people toss me out."

"That didn't go well."

"Believe it or not," I said. "I went quietly."

The waitress arrived and Z ordered for both of us without a glance at the menu. Besides the *budae jjigae* and a side of *kimchi*, I had no idea what was for lunch. The waitress stared at each of us as she jotted down the order, looking dubious that we could put away such a Korean feast.

"Don't worry, ma'am," I said. "We're professionals."

Z leaned back into his chair and rubbed at his chin. "So we have a jealous ex-boyfriend and a powerful married man with something to hide."

"Both men would have reasons to make Gabby disappear," I said. "One for love. One for money."

"Any more from the cops?"

"Not yet," I said. "The Yamashiro angle has been buttoned up by the LAPD. I was lucky to have gotten what I did from Samuelson."

"I know he's a big fan."

"Besides Quirk?" I said. "The biggest."

When the feast arrived, it covered every inch of the table. The *budae jjigae* came out bubbly over a butane burner and smelling of rich garlic and otherworldly spices. The waitress needed help arranging all our side items around the burner. I ate a little *kimchi* as we waited for the stew to cool.

"My friend is very good," Z said.

"How good?"

"She handles a computer the way Vinnie handles a pistol."

I nodded in appreciation.

I was on to my second helping of stew when an attractive young woman walked in the door. She turned the heads of most of the men in the restaurant, wearing a black biker jacket over a cropped white hoodie and tattered blue jeans. Her hair was pink, the color of cotton candy, and she was clutching the small silver MacBook we'd taken from Gabby's apartment. I could tell it was Gabby's by the stickers.

Z watched my gaze and looked over his shoulder. He smiled and waved her over. I stood and she took a seat across from me and next to Z. The table was so crowded, she seemed confused where to put the laptop. The woman's name was Jem Yoon. It appeared she and Z had been friendly for some time.

"Are you in?" Z said, not looking at her as he dipped an oversized spoon into the large bowl.

"Scoot over," Jem Yoon said, pushing at Z's shoulder for more space. "Am I in? Of course I'm in."

Jem Yoon had large brown eyes and very delicate features. Her ears were almost elflike and peeked out from her short pink hair. She slid out of her biker jacket, showing off a sleeveless hoodie and several leather bracelets on her slim wrists. "Doesn't look like this machine had been used in a while," she said.

"How long?" I said.

"A few weeks."

I nodded.

"I was able to access her iCloud," she said. "That would include documents and photos taken on any other devices. I would think that'd be pretty helpful to your purposes."

"That would be most helpful."

Jem Yoon rested her hands on top of the table and stared directly into my eyes. If I hadn't been so tough, I might have blushed.

"So this is him?" she said. "The one who trained you? The master?"

"Yep," Z said.

"He looks just like you described him," Jem Yoon said, as if I weren't actually present. "He looks like a tough guy. With the busted nose and scarring around the eyes. Very authentic, Zebulon. Very authentic."

"I have a certain image to uphold," I said. "And, of course, the Spenser brand."

"You shoot many people?" she said.

"One or two."

"Did they all deserve it?" she said.

"Of course," I said. "Once I shot a man just for snoring."

"When I first met Z, I thought he was joking about being a private eye," she said. "I'd never met a real private eye before. And then he told me about being from here but then meeting you in Boston. He said you took him in and trained him."

"Yes," I said. "But I had help."

"And that you and your friends all have some kind of code," she said. "Some kind of honor system?"

I nodded. The waitress brought us over cans of Coke

and clean plastic glasses. I sprung for an extra can for Jem Yoon.

"You passed on that code to Z," she said. "He has rules about what he will and won't do. I understand. But it can get a little tiresome. Especially when you are trying to get shit done in this town."

"I also taught him advanced surveillance techniques and firearms safety," I said. "Not to mention ballroom dancing. He was a quick study."

"I bet," she said. "How about this girl you're looking for? That's this Gabby Leggett woman?"

I nodded.

"She has thousands and thousands of pictures in her cloud," she said. "I looked through as many as I could stomach. Some of them she should have protected more. They were definitely not safe for work. I don't like to judge. But she's pretty wild."

"Any with a rotund Japanese man with a bad disposition?"

"Not that I recall," she said. "Most were just showing off her tan lines. That girl took a lot of pictures in the bathroom mirror. Some in the shower. She really seemed to be only in love with herself."

"What about with a skinny hipster-looking dude?" Z said.

"Nope," she said. "But I did find a massive amount of deleted emails to a man named Yamashiro. The messages had been taken off an email account and placed in a special folder. Looks like that folder was trashed only three days ago. Does that make sense?"

"Absolutely," I said.

Z looked over at me, beaming. "Thanks, Jem," Z said. "You're the best."

"No shit." Jem smiled, reached into her coat, and pulled out an envelope. "Of course I am. But I come through for a price. Your invoice, Zebulon. This time, don't be late. Or I'll sic my uncle on you. He doesn't like accounts that go past thirty days."

"Is that your natural hair color?" I said, intercepting the envelope and sticking it inside my jacket.

"Don't you like it?"

"I love it," I said. "How do you think it would look on me?"

"Like a pit bull in a tutu," Jem Yoon said.

I looked at Z and grinned. "I like her."

"He'd be nothing without me," Jem Yoon said, punching Z in the biceps. "I'm the real brains of the team."

"You have a team?" I said.

"Sure," Z said. "Just what do you think I've been doing out here?"

11

'm sorry, but I'm going to have to ask you to quit following me," Eric Collinson said.

"No harm in asking," I said.

"My agency is full of the best lawyers," he said. "We have top-notch security."

"You should've had them wipe the laptop," I said. "You did a terrible job. Everything you deleted is still there."

Collinson's cocky expression deflated like an old birthday balloon, shoulders slumping, in line at Starbucks. We stood there waiting for his caramel macchiato while I, on the other hand, already had my black coffee and had helped myself to a pack of sugar. Simplicity has its rewards. Overhead, Ella sang, *"It don't mean a thing, if it ain't got that swing."*

"I didn't touch any of it."

"You deleted a batch of emails dealing with Gabby's relationship with Jimmy Yamashiro."

"I did no such thing."

"That was awfully nice of you," I said. "But I thought you were on Team Gabby. Why are you protecting him while she's the one missing?"

This was pretty weighty conversation to be having in line at Starbucks. But I was sick of chasing Collinson and having to wait for him to leave the agency. He looked down, hands in his blue plaid suit pockets, the barista calling his name twice before he responded.

"Why do you think I took her laptop?" he said. "You're the one who found it."

"You had it in your satchel when I made you let me in," I said. "And we saw video footage of you coming to her apartment a few days ago. You came empty-handed. You left with a laptop."

The second part was a lie, but a decent one. Collinson started to sweat and walked over to a plate-glass window facing Fairfax and the old Farmers Market. He wiped his face with a napkin and left his macchiato untouched. He looked up, beard looking as if it had been cut by laser, and stared hard at me. His cream tie had been knotted very tightly at the throat. He blew out a long breath and simply said, "Shit."

"Most eloquent for a Princeton man."

"I didn't make that mess, if that's what you were thinking," he said. "I took the laptop and then returned it. You and I saw that mess at the same time."

"Why'd you take her computer?"

"Like I said, I didn't want any part of this," he said. "But Mr. Yamashiro is a very important man who works with many of our top-tier clients. He has nothing to do with this. It would've only embarrassed him and his family. You ever heard, 'You'll never work in this town again'?"

"Similar threats have been leveled at me," I said. "I never paid much attention."

I drank some coffee and watched the afternoon rush hour along Fairfax. A winding path of red taillights snaking their way into eternity. Traffic bottled up for a half-mile down the road. I was happy to stay here and discuss Eric's dishonesty for as long as it took.

"Something happened between them and Yamashiro had it covered up."

"Why protect him, then?"

"I wasn't just protecting him," Collinson said. "I was protecting me, too. Gabby and I were done, but I didn't want to destroy my goddamn career. I said some awfully nasty things in those emails, Mr. Spenser, about Gabby and Yamashiro."

"That laptop would've been a big help to the cops," I said. "Finding Gabby is a little more important than moving up the agency ladder."

"Gabby was a mess," he said. "Her first boyfriend out here was unemployed. Then she met a guy in a band. And then she met me. And then there were two actors after. And then she shuffled far ahead and hooked up with Yamashiro. I think it was one of the actors who actually made it happen. Like a goddamn pimp. The whole thing is so sick and twisted, it literally turns my stomach."

"The actor introduced her to Jimmy Yamashiro?" I said.

"Yeah," Collinson said. "And it got him a damn good part in a feature."

"Who was the actor?"

"I can't say," he said. "He was one of ours."

"Ah," I said. "Loyalty."

I watched Collinson's face soften. He bowed his head and began to cry. Not so much sobbing, but tears did fall at the Starbucks. I reached over and grabbed a handful of napkins. Eric Collinson hadn't moved on from Gabby Leggett.

"You loved her?" I said.

"Yeah," he said. "Of course I fucking loved her."

"Did you and Gabby discuss Yamashiro?"

He nodded.

"And how'd that go?"

"Awful," Collinson said, wiping his face. He blew his nose into the napkins. "I warned her about getting involved with him. I don't know how much research you've done, but Yamashiro is a collector of beautiful young women. As you can imagine, he brokers favors for jobs."

"In Hollywood?" I said. "I'm shocked."

Collinson pursed his lips and nodded. He reached forward and touched the coffee, finally taking a sip. "In today's culture, that's not entirely accepted," he said. "Yamashiro's image is based on that of a stalwart family man. He's built his brand on being a real and decent man."

"He told me his wife was complicit in his extracurricular activities."

"She probably is."

"But that doesn't matter?"

"This doesn't have a damn thing to do with his wife," he said. "Yamashiro can't have his image tarnished. If Gabby spoke publicly about their arrangement, it might end his career."

"And yours if he knows what you said about him."

Collinson nodded. He again wiped his face and nose.

"What has Yamashiro actually done for Gabby?"

"She played a murder victim on *SVU* and a dominatrix on this new Netflix show," he said. "Jimmy's not exactly beating down doors for her. Come on. I really can't say any more. I do not and will not be a part of this. Gabby was my client. End of story. Yamashiro scares me. He knows people. Really bad and scary people."

"Badder than me and Sixkill?"

"Who the hell is Sixkill?"

"The big, mean Indian you met at Gabby's place," I said. "The one who never smiles."

"I want Gabby home safe and I want these people held accountable."

"Jimmy Yamashiro?"

"This doesn't have anything to do with him."

"How can you be so sure?" I said. "He's top of the list for me."

Collinson swallowed, his Adam's apple nervously jumping up and down like a banjo string. He sipped on his macchiato and wiped the foam off his lip, looking to me and then across the street again. And then around the Starbucks and deep into the packed parking lot.

"You're going to fucking get me killed."

"That's a little dramatic, Eric," I said. "Even for Hollywood."

"Have you ever been with a woman that you loved so deeply that she could crush your heart with a snap of her fingers?"

"Absolutely."

"Did she destroy you?"

"No," I said. "We worked out a long-time exclusive arrangement. Not to mention share a wonderful dog."

"That didn't happen to me," he said. "You flew out here to find a sweet, innocent girl that left Massachusetts a few years ago. You believe some bad guys had her killed for what she knew. Or maybe it was even me who killed her in a jealous rage. *I know. I know.* I see it in your eyes. But that's too easy. Way too fucking easy."

"Then tell me what I need to know."

"Talk to Mr. Yamashiro."

"I have."

Collinson widened his eyes, taking another sip. He looked suitably impressed.

"Did he tell you how he and Gabby met?"

"Nope," I said. "Yamashiro was less forthcoming than I had hoped."

"It wasn't by accident," Eric Collinson said. "And he wasn't the one preying on her. Yamashiro was the target."

"A studio head was being played by a twenty-four-year-old Instagram model?"

"Do your job, Spense," Collinson said. "I can't do that for you. What the hell do you guys do in the movies? Follow the fucking money."

I nodded. "I appreciate the advice," I said. "But if you call me Spense again, kid, I might have to knock you onto your bony ass."

"Gabby always wanted to find a deeper meaning," he said. "She really believed she was on to something. A bigger take on the world. She's what you call a searcher."

"Yamashiro claims she's not missing," I said.

Collinson snorted. "Then where the fuck is she?"

I tilted my head and eyed him. I took a sip of coffee. "Quit trying to be Deep Throat and talk sensibly and straightforward and maybe I'll find out."

"To hell with you," he said. "To hell with all of you. Her mother should've hired better."

I shrugged. "There is no better."

"Not from where I'm standing." Collinson's face turned red and he trashed his macchiato in the bin, storming out of the Starbucks.

Ella kept on singing. *"Used to ramble through the park, shadow boxing in the dark."* I found a table by the window and finished the rest of my coffee. As I watched the sluggish traffic going nowhere fast, I texted Z to meet me back in Hollywood.

12

High on the Loews fifth-floor pool deck, I stood with Z, looking down into the open shopping complex at Hollywood and Highland. Huge pillars and an elephant reproduced from a D. W. Griffith Babylonian epic accented Forever 21, American Eagle, and Sephora. Eagle gods adorning mammoth arches peered down upon Dave & Buster's and the Cabo Wabo Cantina. Z and I took it all in as we rested our forearms on a metal railing like rustlers peering down into a canyon.

"Eric Collinson can't keep his stories straight."

"He's an agent in L.A.," Z said. "He lies for a living."

"He first said he was protecting Yamashiro out of professional courtesy."

"Do you believe it?"

"Nope," I said. "But then he said he tried to purge

inflammatory emails he sent. Not-so-nice words about Gabby and Yamashiro that could hurt his career."

"Also would make him look bad to the cops."

I nodded. "How did it go with Gabby's young pals?"

"It was hard to keep them straight," he said. "They were all so young and perky. Bleached blond and very positive. Two of them were named Kaitlyn."

"Spelled the same way?"

Z shook his head. "One with a *K* and with a *C*. One had a *Y*. One didn't."

"Vive la différence."

"I heard pretty much the same thing about Gabby," he said. "She was beautiful and full of life. Wonderful style. Everyone seemed to be in shock that she'd disappeared. Every one of them offering to go on social media for her. They all promised to do all they could to help."

"Who saw her last?"

"A girl named Jade Phillips," Z said. "She said she'd seen Gabby two weeks ago, a couple days before she disappeared. She said they'd had brunch together at a place in Santa Monica. I went through every bit of the conversation and didn't get anything. She said Gabby seemed happy and positive. Was very excited about getting some callbacks on some gigs. Jade said she'd never seen Gabby more present and alive."

"I heard she'd been recently cast as a dominatrix," I said. "How is she with a whip?"

"Didn't ask," I said. "And didn't see it listed on her IMDb profile."

"Did Jade mention anything about Jimmy Yamashiro?"

"Nope," he said. "But that was before you found out about him. She said Gabby had been dating around and had been better off after ditching Eric."

"Does anyone like Eric?"

"Nope."

"Can you really blame 'em?"

Z shook his head. "I spent the afternoon going through her laptop and Instagram," he said. "She last posted the day before she disappeared. She was playing pool at some dive bar in Studio City. I couldn't ID the people but thought I might head that way next."

"Eat and investigate," I said. "Drink and investigate. Just like Boston."

"I thought we should start putting together a timeline," he said. "Jade Phillips would start that forty-eight-hour period. Didn't you get into her credit card account from her mother?"

"Gabby hasn't made a purchase in twelve days," I said. "At least with the accounts I know about."

"No witnesses," Z said. "No other credit cards we know about. No one has found her car. Her apartment was tossed. And all I've found on her laptop so far is bikinis, boobs, and avocado toast."

"And emails from Yamashiro."

"Yep," he said. "Some sexy stuff. But nothing that implies blackmail or threats."

We left our lofty perch and wandered past the hotel pool, the deck crowded with women at a bachelorette party passing around bottles of white wine and champagne. Some of the women were floating along in big white inflatable swans, holding plastic stemware and pointing to the Hollywood hills, almost close enough to touch in the golden light. Everything as ethereal and golden as a Cialis commercial.

"Or we could stick around here," Z said.

"Wouldn't get much done here."

"Speak for yourself."

We took the elevator down to the third floor and cut through the banquet rooms and into the shopping complex. We rode a second elevator from there into the parking garage, where Z had left his Mustang.

"Nothing on the security cameras?"

"Samuelson hasn't said," I said. "But they'll see Eric Collinson coming and going twice in the last few days. I heard back from her acting coach. He gave me some more names. Friends from class that'll speak to us."

"Jem Yoon said she can dive deeper on the hard drive," he said. "But she'd need a few days."

"Seems like a good woman to know," I said. "Just how'd you meet her?"

"Would you believe Comic Con?"

"Yes," I said. "I would."

Z paid at a kiosk and we walked into the garage, following a long row of cars and turning down deeper below the shopping center. As we got within twenty feet of Z's car, I noticed a light go on in a black Mercedes SUV. We kept walking, Z's cowboy boots making dull thuds in the cavernous space.

Two men emerged from the vehicle and watched us as we got closer to the Mustang. The men didn't look like tourists.

They moved with authority and knowledge, standing on each side of the car, eyeing us as we passed. One of the men had a mustache and slick black hair. He had on a bright blue tracksuit and appeared to have a tattoo on one side of his face.

The other one was young, sallow-faced, with a shaved head. He had serious black eyes and took great interest as Z mashed the unlock button on his keychain. The Mustang's taillights flashed on and off.

"Hey," the tracksuit guy said. "Hey, you."

Being the curious type, I turned around.

"You the one they call Spenser?" he said.

I didn't answer, as I felt it was a rhetorical question. Z walked up next to me, both of us a few feet from the trunk of his car. Z and I were both armed. But in the trunk was a twelve-gauge Mossberg that Hawk had given Z as a going-away present from Boston. In close spaces it gained respect and immediate attention.

"Stop looking for this girl," he said. "This is none of your business. Go back to where you come from."

His accent was thick and Slavic, sounding almost Russian to my untuned ear.

"And who might you be?" I said.

"Mr. Nobody," he said. He looked to his younger friend, the driver, and the man snickered. He had horrible-looking teeth.

"Did you get a deal on that tracksuit?" I said. "Or did you lose a bet?"

"My friend," he said. "You listen. You listen to me? Where I'm from, we have this saying. There are no second warnings."

"Oh, yeah," I said. "Where I'm from, we have a saying, too."

The dark-haired man waited, hands loose at the sides of his sweatpants. In my best Dorchester accent, I told the guy to go have intercourse with himself.

"Looks like me and you," he said. "We have problem."

I shrugged, hand resting on my belt, a quick move up to my holster. Neither man showed a gun. I watched their hands as they walked forward and then noticed a light go on in another car, five spaces down from where Z had parked. Three men, looking just as rough and ugly, emerged from a blue sedan. Perhaps some kind of self-help group.

"How many clowns have you packed in there?" I said.

"Throw down your guns," he said. "You come ride with us. Okay? We not bite. We talk. Like men."

I didn't answer. Z didn't say a word. We all stood there as the three men walked up the ramp, the other two standing still. Z watching the three, my eyes still on the other two.

Just then a car wheeled around the lower ramp, heading up toward us, sending the three men off to one side and cutting us off from the two by the Mercedes. The headlights roved across us and over the men's faces. Z mashed another button on his keychain and the trunk popped open. As he reached for the shotgun, I watched as Mr. Nobody pulled a pistol from his tracksuit pants. I pulled my gun as Z warned the three to stay back. I kept my eyes on the two men. I had my back to Z now. The concrete walls seemed to grow closer in to us.

Mr. Nobody yelled something in a language I didn't understand and I heard the *blam* of Z's shotgun and several pistol shots. Z pushed me hard out of the way as if stiff-arming a linebacker. I stumbled and we found cover behind the Mustang. More shots and the back window shattered into tiny pieces. Z shot again. *Blam*. I fired my .38 three times, squeezing off the rounds at Mr. Nobody as he climbed back into the black SUV, the taillights clicking on and the car reversing.

I turned back to see the three men had retreated. Z kept his shotgun trained in their direction as he stood and walked down the ramp. They'd left their car empty, doors open, and had run into a stairwell up to ground level. Above, I could hear the Mercedes's squealing tires as they headed up and out of the garage.

I walked up on Z, sliding my gun back in the holster. Z set the Mossberg back in the trunk and we followed where the stairwell door had just slammed shut.

We made our way to the third level and heard the door. Both of us arrived at the landing at the same time and pushed through the doors into a wide-open space by a store that sold Dodgers gear and a designer sunglasses shop. The Hollywood and Highland Center was open-air and four stories tall, lined with railings down into a common area filled with kiosks and small cafés. We looked for the men in both directions without luck. The shots had been fired deep underground, the shoppers blissfully unaware.

"Glad you left the shotgun," I said.

"People may have started to stare."

Blood began to drip onto the concrete. I looked up at Z. His face was ashen and his left arm hung loose at his side.

"How bad?" I said.

"Only hurts when I laugh."

"I'll try to keep jokes to a minimum," I said. As we started to move back to the elevators, it seemed like everyone we passed was watching us. Z had a great deal of blood splattered on his jacket and across his jeans. He held his arm tightly with his right hand.

We heard the sirens and saw two prowlies cut off the exit to the shopping center.

"Can you make it out?" I said. "We'll find a doctor."

"I'm fine," he said. "We can cross the street to my office."

I didn't like the look on his face or the way his arm hung ragged in his hand. It looked as if some bones had been shattered in the scuffle. The elevator seemed to take forever, blood pooling at Z's feet. He clenched his jaw and set his gaze at the doors, waiting for them to open.

When they did, two LAPD officers had their guns raised and asked to see our hands.

It wasn't a request.

13

I don't see you for years and now I see you twice in two days," Samuelson said. "Wow. Just wow."

"Some people are just born lucky."

"Not you, Spenser," he said. "According to the patrol guys, you and Sonny Sixkiller turned a Hollywood parking garage into the O.K. Corral."

Samuelson sat down in the interview room at LAPD headquarters and shook his head. The officers had taken me to the county lockup for processing and Z to the hospital to look at his arm. It took three hours before I could convince them to call Samuelson and check my story.

"We were just getting into Mr. Sixkill's vehicle when they ambushed us," I said. "They'd been waiting. Probably followed Z to the hotel and then waited for us to come back."

He nodded without an iota of empathy.

"We impounded the car they left," Samuelson said. "A

2012 Chevy Malibu. Stolen, of course. It was boosted in
Marina Del Rey two days ago."

"No style with hoods these days," I said. "Think they
could've stolen a Corvette."

"When we catch 'em, I'll let you tell them that."

I leaned forward in a very uncomfortable metal chair.
My wrists were sore from being cuffed and my fingers
were stained from being printed.

"Did you recognize 'em?"

"Nope," I said. "But one recognized me. He knew my
name and kept calling me his friend. Thought maybe it
was from my bubble-gum cards."

"Your what?"

"You know, trading cards of famous private eyes," I
said. "Sam Spade. Philip Marlowe."

Samuelson leveled his eyes at me, fingering at his droopy
mustache. "Not in the mood," he said. "How about you
just tell me what these assholes looked like?"

I described the man from mustache to blue tracksuit to
the rubber soles of his Nikes.

"And they had accents?"

I nodded.

"Eastern European?"

"I once had a run-in with Ukrainians," I said. "They
sounded very similar."

"Ah," Samuelson said. "A guy sporting a funny tracksuit and speaking in a funny accent. I'll put out an APB.
Can't be too many of those in the city."

"Maybe I should have asked them for their passports,"
I said. "And birth certificates."

Samuelson tilted his head and looked at his phone and then back at me. He wore an expression less telling than that of a sphinx. "Your friend is stable at Cedars," he said. "After we're done, I'll take you over to see him. He lost a decent amount of blood and the bullet broke a few bones. I guess it's good news he got shot in the left arm."

"Sure," I said. "If only he wasn't left-handed."

"Damn," he said. "Your southpaw gunslinger is benched."

I nodded.

"Guess you better leave this to us now," Samuelson said. "If I remember my Saturday-morning serials correctly, the Lone Ranger wasn't jack shit without Tonto."

"Or his horse," I said. "Silver was a pretty big part of the deal, too."

"Do you own a fucking horse?"

"Not yet," I said. "My landlord can be particular about farm animals."

Samuelson leaned his head back and stared at the ceiling, letting out a long breath. For some reason he'd never quite taken to my charm the way Quirk and Belson had. I knew I only needed to give him more quality time. He kept staring up at the sagging tiles.

"Looking for divine intervention?"

"Something like that," he said. "You're a fucking classic. You know that?"

"Thank you."

"A fucking classic pain in my ass."

I shrugged as someone knocked on the door. Samuelson excused himself and left for several minutes. I spent my time trying to wipe the ink from my fingers and studying the collection of anti-drug and anti-gang posters, many of them in Spanish. One particularly harsh poster showed a coffin being loaded into a hearse with the tagline *You Can't Pimp This Ride*.

I'd nearly cleaned the ink off my thumb with a Kleenex when Samuelson opened the door and walked back into the room. This time he didn't sit. I was still sitting and I continued to sit. I was tired.

"You were close," he said. "Not Russian. Your guys are Armenian Power."

"Is that a cover band?"

"Nope," Samuelson said. "A well-known and nasty group of killers and crooks. Some of our gang people took a look at the garage video and IDed two of them. They work for fucking Vartan Sarkisov."

"Should that concern me?"

"Yeah," Samuelson said, nodding. "Probably should. How the hell did you manage to piss off this crew in less than forty-eight hours? Really, Spenser. That's goddamn amazing. Some kind of fucking record."

"The only person I've intentionally pissed off is Jimmy Yamashiro."

"Yamashiro has been very cooperative in the girl's disappearance," he said. "He's been completely open and honest about having the affair and given us access to his whereabouts."

"Maybe they're hired muscle?"

"Maybe," he said. "But guys like Yamashiro tend to send out an army of attorneys. Not some Armenian gangbangers."

"You say that with the utmost certainty."

"I'm not certain about shit," he said. "But Yamashiro did send word he wants to see you. He wants to make contact with Gabrielle Leggett's family and even put up a reward."

"That's very big of him," I said. "And he's not a very big man."

"Would you quit being a hard-on for maybe two seconds and pay attention to what's going on?"

"Sure," I said. I did my best to look serious and solemn. I waited for the answer as I drummed my fingers on the table. "You want to tell me what's going on?"

"I would if I could," he said. "But *Vartan Sarkisov.* Holy mother of Christ. You better watch your ass. Don't expect anyone to do it for you."

"Can you call around for my horse?" I said. "I'd like to ride over to the hospital to see my friend."

"How about a slightly used Crown Vic," he said. "And as a bonus, I'll let you sit up front like a big boy."

"Will you flash the lights?"

"Yes," he said.

"You're too good to me, Captain."

14

Early the next morning, I drove back to downtown and Olvera Street to find Chollo.

In the past, Chollo preferred more opulent surroundings in Bel-Air, working for a heavy hitter named Victor del Rio. But after a few well-placed phone calls, I was told Chollo had some of his own interests in the oldest section of the city.

I parked near Union Station and walked across to the mouth of the old Mexican market. Many of the shops and kiosks hadn't opened yet, and workers were spraying down the pebbled streets. The ones that were open offered piñatas and wrestling masks, T-shirts, and leather goods. Many professed pride for both Mexican heritage and being an Angeleno.

I found Chollo sitting in the shade of a twisted fig tree,

so old it had to be propped up with metal beams. He was speaking in Spanish with two old men tuning their guitars. Behind them was a small arcade with its doors propped open. I could feel the blast of air-conditioning and smell the tortillas.

"Chollo," I said, nodding.

Chollo nodded back. He wore dark jeans and a denim shirt overlaid with a long tan suede coat. All of it slim-fitting and seemingly molded to his body. He looked up at me and shook his head. *"Hombre."*

The two older men stopped tuning their guitars, as if they expected trouble. Chollo stood and stretched to his full lean, medium height. The suede coat hung low over his belt and the gun he always wore. I started to whistle the theme to *The Good, the Bad, and the Ugly*.

"How did you find me?"

"Haven't you finally realized I'm the best there is?"

"No," Chollo said. "Not yet."

He put out a hand, but in a single quick movement feigned a move to the left and then the right, wrapping me in a big hug. As he patted my back, I noticed the posture of the two old men ease. They went back to tuning their guitars as the T-shirts and linen dresses fluttered along the kiosks.

"I heard you have interests here."

"Sí."

"Not the same interests of Mr. del Rio?"

He shook his head, pointing down into the arcade, toward a number of Mexican fast-food offerings. "My accountant told me I needed to diversify," he said. "Invest."

"Chollo's Churros?" I said.

"*Sí,*" he said. "Has a certain ring to it. Don't you think?"

"Service with a smile."

Chollo nodded down the street, away from the men and away from the little restaurant down Olvera Street. We walked in the brisk morning, the old street smelling of flowers and wet stones. He kept his hands in his jacket pockets, the street hustlers averting their gaze as he passed.

"You didn't come for the churros, my friend."

"But should I?"

"*Sí,*" he said. "They are quite delicious."

"Perhaps later," I said. "I understand Mr. del Rio employed Sixkill last year."

"*Sí,*" he said. "He was concerned about the welfare of his daughter."

"And did he fix the issue?"

Chollo shrugged, moving toward the end of the street, a large wooden cross at the other entrance of Olvera Street. "Sixkill relayed useful information," he said.

"And then?"

"Bobby Horse and I acted upon it."

I nodded. The less I knew about Victor del Rio's business, the better. A large woman who looked a lot like Katy Jurado, dressed in a purple peasant top and long, flowing dress, hung handmade wooden puppets on a sidewalk display. She smiled as we passed, commenting to Chollo about it being a beautiful morning. Chollo agreed, calling her by name.

"Last night, five men ambushed me and Z at the parking garage at Hollywood and Highland."

"Terrible place for an ambush," Chollo said. "Hard to escape."

"Sixkill was wounded," I said. "He's fine. But had to have surgery last night to fix his arm."

"And now you want to take me and Bobby Horse away from Mr. del Rio?" he said. "Like the other times."

"No. Not right now," I said. "Right now, I only need information."

"Bueno," Chollo said. "Mr. del Rio doesn't go anywhere without Bobby Horse. These are strange times, my friend. The lines are not so clearly drawn. Honor, respect. Men don't understand these words."

"These men had little honor and no respect," I said. "They tried to scare us. And when that didn't work, they tried to blast us into kingdom come."

"Who were they?"

"Armenians," I said. "They work for a guy named Vartan Sarkisov."

Chollo stopped cold by the wooden cross. He reached into his pocket and dropped several bills into a wooden box for a local church. He looked at me, the sun growing high over our heads. He squinted and nodded with understanding.

"You know him?"

"Sí."

"You like him?"

"The man is a snake," Chollo said. "The worst kind of scum in this city. Why are you here, Spenser?"

I told him a condensed version of Gabby Leggett's disappearance and crossing paths with Jimmy Yamashiro. And the possible plan to blackmail him.

"Blackmail, intimidation," Chollo said. "Yes. That's Sarkisov."

"If that's true," I said, "then Sarkisov might know what happened to Gabby Leggett."

"*Sí*," Chollo said. "His people, the Armenian Power, used to do business at a mini-mall in East Hollywood."

"And now?"

"They have expanded."

"Diversified?" I said.

"More than churros, my friend," Chollo said. "They sell big truckloads of stolen goods from a small town south of here called Furlong."

"L.A. County?"

"*Sí*," he said. "But there's no law there. Sheriff won't go there. Only law is from the AP."

"Good to know."

"If they had this girl, she'd be dead by now."

"We've faced worse odds."

"Proctor," Chollo said.

I nodded.

"Furlong makes Proctor seem like Disneyland."

"It's a Small World After All."

We walked back the way we'd come. "Is Susan with you?"

"No."

"Hawk?"

"No."

"So now you are here, alone?"

"*Sí,*" I said.

Chollo stopped and gave me a hard look. "No," he said. "Not anymore."

"What about the churros?"

"Churros can wait, my friend."

15

I called Susan from the waiting room at Cedars.

"Oh my God," she said. "How is he?"

"Z ate two In-N-Out burgers with fries," I said. "And now he's resting."

"But his arm?"

"Shattered," I said. "The doctors put in some pins. He's going to be out of commission for some time."

"Getting shot isn't like twisting your ankle," Susan said.

"He said it only hurts when he laughs."

"Good thing you're not funny," Susan said.

"I know you don't mean that," I said. "My humor isn't an easy thing to contain."

I'd found a grouping of empty sofas and chairs in the emergency room lobby. It was a grand, tall-ceilinged space with serpentine leather sofas and a glass wall that looked out to the entrance. The front doors were pneumatic and opened and closed frequently. Chollo sat in a tall, upright chair, leafing through a medical journal.

"Should I let Hawk know?" she said.

"No," I said, looking to Chollo. "Not now."

"Are these men in custody?"

"No," I said. "Not yet."

"Have you been able to link them with Gabby?"

"I have solid suspicion."

"And are you sure these men won't continue to attempt to do you harm?"

"Nope," I said. "I can pretty much guarantee it. At least I know where to find them. A lawless little town within L.A. County called Furlong."

Susan didn't say anything. She let the silence fall and hold for several seconds between Los Angeles and Boston. The stillness was prolonged and electric, as Susan Silverman wasn't a woman who was ever at a loss for words. Chollo crossed his boots at his ankles in repose.

"Do you think that's where Gabby might be?"

"Perhaps," I said. "Or maybe she's at a Holiday Inn in Reseda. Or Knott's Berry Farm."

"How will you find out?"

"It's complicated," I said.

I told her more about my meeting with Jimmy Yamashiro. And that Yamashiro had accused Gabby of trying to blackmail him.

"Gabby?" she said. "That doesn't sound like the young woman her mother described. The headstrong student athlete from BU."

"California changes people," I said. "Don't you East Coast shrinks know that?"

"Or maybe Gabby is just being used."

"That scenario has crossed my mind once or twice," I said. "Samuelson said Yamashiro wants to talk with me. Apparently he withheld some key information."

"So you will make some discretionary planning before you barge into Far Far Away with both guns blazing?"

"Furlong," I said. "It's supposed to be a lovely little town."

Chollo lifted his eyes from the magazine and then glanced back down, licking a finger, and flipping a page. He shook his head.

"To get killed," she said.

"Would you rather me get killed in Plymouth?"

"Plymouth is too far," she said. "How about Chelsea?"

"Perfect," I said. "I'll save my demise for my own turf."

16

Jimmy Yamashiro lived in Beverly Hills, right along Sunset Boulevard, in a mod-looking mansion only slightly smaller than the Quincy Market. The house was mainly concrete, built in a harsh, angular style, with gigantic picture windows making the house almost seem naked as we drove through the gates. Along the roadside, a sprawling orange grove stood with trees planted in a neat, orderly symmetry.

I parked my rental in a circular drive and Chollo and I got out and walked toward the front door. Before we had a chance to climb the steps, the older bodyguard with the crew cut opened the door. He was wearing the same dark nondescript suit from when we'd met in the studio. His face was as weathered and worn as a secondhand pair of boots.

"You said you were coming alone," Crew Cut said.

I looked to Chollo and shrugged. "I changed my mind."

"Who's he?" the man said, jacking his thumb at Chollo.

"My life coach," I said. "He's helping me sleuth to my maximum potential."

He looked over to Chollo with clear blue eyes and then back to me. He didn't answer, walked back inside, and shut the door behind him.

"Is that it?" Chollo said.

"Maybe we could steal a few oranges," I said. "The vitamin C wards off seasonal colds."

"Sure," Chollo said. "I could sell them at the freeway exits."

"Is that a local ethnic joke?" I said.

"*Sí,*" Chollo said.

A minute later, the door opened again and Crew Cut ushered us inside. The house was big and airy, with gray slate floors and some kind of trickling waterfall along a rock wall decorated with live orchids. The back of the home was wide open, looking out onto a courtyard and then a large swimming pool. Everything smelled bright and clean of citrus and chlorine.

"Pays to be the boss," I said.

"Mr. del Rio's house is much nicer," Chollo said. "He would never live in Beverly Hills. Too common."

"Have you forgotten your roots?" I said.

Chollo didn't answer, only grinned.

Jimmy Yamashiro was seated at a wrought-iron table in the middle of a courtyard. He looked up from his morning *Los Angeles Times* and lifted his chin to the open chairs. He wore a white terry-cloth robe, tight and snug against his rotund frame. "Mr. Spenser," he said. "You didn't say you were bringing a guest. I thought this was a private conversation."

"This is Chollo," I said. "Whatever you say to me can be said in front of him."

"So you say."

"Yep," I said. "I do."

"Chollo?" he said. "No last name?"

"Cher, Madonna, Prince," I said. "Chollo and Spenser."

"Really?" Yamashiro said.

Chollo hung back by the hedgerow as I took a seat. Crew Cut lingered on the pathway, trying, but not succeeding, in looking inconspicuous. I watched as he took in Chollo, spotting a slight bulge on Chollo's right hip under the suede coat. It was ever so slight but comforting to know.

"Would you like anything to eat?" Yamashiro said.

"Sure," I said.

Chollo shook his head.

"He doesn't talk much," Yamashiro said. "Is he your sidekick or something?"

"I'm his," I said. "I do the talking. He does the shooting."

Yamashiro laughed, believing I'd made a joke. I looked to Crew Cut, who had his eyes on Chollo now, hands on his waist, as if trying to look tough and in charge. Chollo lifted a hand to his mouth and stifled a yawn.

"My apologies on our first meeting," Yamashiro said. "I thought you were trying to extort me."

"That's okay," I said. "I thought you might have kidnapped my client's daughter."

Yamashiro's friendly smile dropped and he leveled his

black eyes at me. I tilted my head, staring back at him, and waited. A Hispanic woman dressed in a gray-and-white servant's getup appeared with a carafe of orange juice. She poured me a sizable serving.

"Fresh squeezed," he said.

"Living amid a citrus grove?" I said. "What are the chances?"

There was black coffee and then a basket filled with assorted pastries. I grabbed a croissant and reached for the butter. "How is L.A. suiting you?" he said.

"Like a sharkskin suit."

"I heard there was some trouble last night?"

I shrugged while I buttered the warm croissant. The butter spread nice and smooth off the knife. He asked if I would like anything else and I told him I was dandy.

"Captain Samuelson said a friend of yours had been shot," he said. "By some hoods."

"A crew of Armenian gangsters," I said. "They wouldn't happen to be friends of yours?"

"I can see how you might think that," Yamashiro said. "But if I wanted to get rid of you, I could use more threatening means through legal channels."

"The calls of high-paid attorneys weaken my knees."

Behind Chollo's back, two women in bikinis appeared, holding straw bags. They set up shop in a couple of lounge chairs before one mounted the diving board. The whole time I watched them, Chollo never took his eyes off Yamashiro or Crew Cut. I figured I had the better view. The women giggled and frolicked. Their bikinis seemed to have been made of dental floss.

"Tell me about the blackmail attempt," I said.

Yamashiro didn't say a word as the server appeared again with a plate of lox over a bagel, slathered in cream cheese and sprinkled with capers. He seemed not to even notice it as the woman reached gently around him and ground pepper for what seemed like half an hour. When she disappeared back into the kitchen, Yamashiro said, "I don't see why not," he said. "Captain Samuelson said you could be trusted."

"Shucks."

"And always deliver on what you set out to do."

"True."

"Two weeks ago, the threat came to my personal email account and contained a four-minute video," he said. "The video contained an old encounter between me and Miss Leggett."

"I take it that you two weren't playing rock, paper, scissors," I said.

"No," he said. "We were not. The images were of an intimate nature."

"Ah," I said. I reached for the coffee. Before I could even touch the pot, the stealthy Hispanic woman had it and performed the task for me. I thanked her before she again disappeared. She exchanged some quick words with Chollo in Spanish and she walked away, smiling at something he'd said.

"You have described the relationship between you and Gabby as consensual," I said. "And that you and your wife had what you called a modern agreement."

"That's correct."

"Do you think Gabby sent the email?"

Yamashiro nodded. He defied convention and dropped the knife-and-fork act and went right for the second half of the bagel. "I had some very good tech people on this," he said. "It was a junk email account sent from a coffee shop in Burbank."

"Why would she blackmail you if she was complicit in the relationship?"

"As I'm sure you've read, Hollywood is going through tremendous changes," Yamashiro said. "What might have seemed commonplace in the old days is frowned upon now. Just the idea that I had had this relationship with Miss Leggett might be construed as harassment by the twenty-four-hour outrage machine. The truth wouldn't matter. This whole so-called Me Too movement has taken down powerful men."

"Many have done some very bad things," I said. "To both women and to potted plants."

"And some have been vilified for just being men," he said. "What are we supposed to do? Subvert our masculinity? Surely, as a man, you understand that."

"I don't think being a man gives you a freebie for acting like a creep."

"Are you saying I'm a creep, Mr. Spenser?"

"I'm not sure," I said. "I'm still gathering information."

Yamashiro didn't seem pleased with the answer and went back to eating his bagel and lox. As he chewed, I noted a slight tic in his right eye.

"Did you abuse your position at the studio to cultivate this relationship?"

"Of course not."

"Then what did this email exactly say?" I said.

"They wanted ten million," he said. "If not, they'd send the email out to all the gossip sites."

"May I see this threat?"

"No, you may not," he said. "It's not something I'm proud of."

"Are you sure the message was sent by Gabby?"

"Yes," he said. "It said I was a lecherous old fuck that was about to get a taste of his own medicine."

"Ouch," I said. "And then?"

"And then nothing," he said.

"No follow-up?" I said.

"No," he said. "When you appeared, apparently representing Gabrielle's interests, I assumed the extortion had ratcheted up. And that her so-called disappearance was timed to make me look more sinister."

I finished the last of my croissant and brushed the crumbs from my lap. Despite my best efforts, I remained a messy eater. Where was Pearl when you needed her? "Besides you, can you think of anyone who might like to see Gabby disappear?"

"I wouldn't know," he said. "Our relationship was purely physical."

"Like them," I said, nodding to the frolicking girls.

"Yes." Yamashiro nodded. "Exactly like them."

"Ah," I said. "The stars of tomorrow."

As he smiled, his robe opened up at the top, exposing his saggy and hairless chest.

"I guess I don't really know if Gabby actually sent it. Or if someone put her up to it."

"The timing looks bad for you," I said. "Before I even have a chance to unpack my underwear, some local toughs try to intimidate me and my associate into leaving this alone."

"Not my doing," he said.

"So you say."

"That is correct," he said. "Don't you know who I am?"

"I know you're a top-notch movie fireplug who follows his privates like a divining rod."

"Excuse me?

"None of this looks good, Jimmy."

"If I'd kidnapped or killed Gabby and then sent some Hungarians to threaten you, why would I now be meeting you?"

"Not sure," I said. "And they were Armenian. Not Hungarian. Different as baklava to goulash."

The server swept away his plate and refilled both of our coffees. Yamashiro took a long sip, watching the frolicking mermaids by the pool. They both had long legs and curvy hips, wet hair plastered down their bare backs as they dried in the sun like contented seals. I was pretty sure the Smith & Wesson I wore under my coat was older than both of them.

"I want this stopped," he said.

"Okay," I said.

"I'm willing to pay for this to stop."

"And what does that have to do with me?"

"Find Gabby," he said. "However this started and whoever is involved, she's the start of it. Without her, there wouldn't have been a tape."

"Did you consent to a video of your activities?"

"Of course not," he said. "I'm not a goddamn idiot. But how would I know? These days, they can put a camera in a ballpoint pen or the eye of a needle. You find Gabby and stop this and I'll pay for your services. The longer she's missing, the worse things look for me."

I shook my head and stood up. I took one last sip of coffee and nodded over at Chollo. Chollo nodded back, his eyes still on Crew Cut. They didn't seem to like each other very much.

"You don't want my money?" he said.

"Nope," I said. "I have one client. Gabby's mother. I'm being paid to find her and return her safely. Your blackmail issue is not my problem."

"Even if she's involved?"

"Even then."

Yamashiro shook his head and gave a little chuckle. He looked over at Chollo, who leaned against a low brick wall, arms crossed over his chest.

"Your friend," Yamashiro said. "Is he always this stubborn?"

Chollo nodded. *"Sí."*

"Okay, good," Yamashiro said. "I think this was a productive meeting. Are we at least clear with the situation?"

"Nope," I said. "Not in the least."

Chollo and I walked back out through the house and the front door. Before I got into the rental, Chollo snagged a fresh orange from a nearby tree.

17

That afternoon, Chollo and I parted ways.

I returned to the Loews, worked out in the hotel gym, ate a club sandwich with fries, and followed up with some phone calls. A few hours later, I found myself drinking beer with five of Jeffrey Bloom's acting students in North Hollywood. Besides the hazards of the industry and their latest auditions, they talked a little about Gabby Leggett. To hear them tell it, Gabby ranked somewhere between Sister Aimee and Mother Teresa.

"She was lovely," said a young woman, fittingly named Bridget. She was very tan and very blond, looking like she'd just stepped off the set of *Bikini Beach* in a cropped red gingham top, high-waisted jeans, and tall clogs. "Inside and out. She was so giving. Like when you were in a scene, she was totally present with you."

"Being present is good," I said. "I like being present."

"Actually," Bridget said, fingering a large gold hoop earring, "it's everything."

A few of her classmates nodded along. There was Bridget, Olga, and Claudia.

The boys were Austin and Dani. "Dani with an *i*," he said.

We all sat in a beer garden in back of a Depression-era building shaped like an enormous whiskey barrel. In the garden was another vintage roadside attraction, a small café shaped like a bulldog smoking a pipe. The whole bar exuded a vibe of the Hollywood of yesterday. It was cool and pleasant in the little garden. An attentive waitress continued to refresh my Lagunitas IPA on draft. I could think of no finer place to conduct interviews while I watched the bubbles rise in my pint glass.

"Do you think she's, you know, dead?" said Austin, a serious, dark-eyed guy. He had shaggy, greasy hair and a sallow face. His T-shirt advertised a band called Perfume Genius.

"I don't have a reason to think she is or isn't."

"But it's possible?" said Dani with an *i*. He was a tallish young man with sunken cheeks and slick brown hair. He wore a pink tank top and skinny black jeans and had the deliberate, fluid movements of a dancer. He reminded me physically of Paul Giacomin but was decidedly more pretentious.

"Sure," I said. "Anything is possible. Your class seems to be the only constant in her life. Maybe you might have noticed or heard something."

"What the hell would we know?" said Bridget, playing

with the ends of her bleached hair and biting her lower lip. "Let's all be honest, after Gabby got that Carl's Jr. commercial, she didn't hang out with us anymore. She became a real asshole. Once she flashed her perky little boobs all over TV while eating that sloppy burger, she was ready to move to the next level."

"That was late last year?" I said.

The young thespians nodded in unison. Olga and Claudia were huddled off at the far end of the corner and talked in whispers. I wanted to ask if they had something to share with the class.

"I heard she was going to get a recurring role on *The Good Doctor*. Some kind of chick with mental problems," Austin said. "Like a real head case."

Dani shook his head and snickered a bit.

"Gabby was a very spiritual person," Olga said. "She was very open to many ideas. Many religions. She and I would sometimes get coffee after class and speak spiritually."

Olga was a tiny woman with enormous breasts, speaking in a slight Eastern European accent. Her hair was brown with blondish highlights and her makeup was airbrushed to perfection. Some of the other students seemed surprised by what she said. I drank some more beer and listened.

"She said she had quit drinking alcohol," Olga said.

"Ha," Dani said, with a flick of his wrist. "She drank like a fish."

Bridget nodded in agreement.

"Drugs?" I said. I still wasn't able to connect Gabrielle

Leggett of Cambridge, Mass, with a crew of Armenian gangsters. There were few ways to bring up organized crime with the troupe.

"Oh, no," Olga said. "Not now. Not in a long time. She had such a hard time after her breakdown."

No one seemed to make much of this detail. But Dani sat upright and cocked his head to listen more. He, like me, apparently hadn't been aware of a breakdown, either.

"Were you not listening?" Olga said. "When she performed the monologue on the breakup? How she found herself groveling on the floor, picking cigarette ash from her hair, not knowing where she'd been. Or how she'd gotten home."

"Come on," Bridget said. "You actually believed that? That was all some bullshit she made up for Jeffrey."

Dani snickered some more. And so did everyone else, but Olga. Olga shook her head, gathering some silver bracelets on her delicate wrist. "It was true," she said. "Had you not been so self-absorbed and listened, you would have all seen it. She cut her hair, quit wearing makeup. Her backpack so full of self-help and discovery books. She let me borrow many of them. Gabby said she was into finding true meaning in life."

Bridget seemed to bristle a bit at "self-absorbed," toying with the hoop earring and rolling her eyes. Dani bit his lip, tightly crossed his legs, and tilted up his red wine.

"What the hell does that have to do with her being gone?" Austin said. "This guy isn't trying to do a character study. He's trying to find out what happened to her."

"Maybe a little bit of both," I said. "One often facilitates the other."

"And what do you know?" Bridget said.

"That maybe Gabby kept a very private and compartmentalized life," I said. "What about a boyfriend? Did she mention one?"

"The agent?" Bridget said.

"No," Olga said. "No. She left him long ago. Eric Something-rather. The one who broke her, broke her heart, was much older."

I nodded. *Warm.*

"And married."

I nodded again. *Getting hot.*

Claudia sat at the end of the table, shook her head, and stared at me. She was a tall black woman, the height of a runway model, with an additional few inches on top consisting of a bouncy, curly Afro. She tapped at the table with long red nails and stared at me intently, as if waiting for her turn to talk.

"You mean The Creep," Claudia said.

"You know him?" I said.

"Don't know his name," she said. "But she called him The Creep in class. He promised her all kinds of parts and big trips that never came about. They were first going to Hawaii and then maybe Paris or some shit. None of it ever happened. At one point, she told me he was leaving his wife. How's that story always work out?"

"They lived happily ever after?"

"Bullshit," she said.

I signaled to the waitress for another round. In my vast experience, I knew sources were more apt to speak up after a few drinks. And I was glad to supply beer and a few glasses of wine for the cause. Claudia touched the edges of her bouncy locks, seeming a bit uncomfortable with the discussion. She met my eyes for a moment, shifted her gaze over my head, and then looked down at her iPhone, tapping at the screen.

"Did she ever mention the married man's name?" I said. "To any of you?"

No one said anything. A few shook their heads.

"But there was a breakdown?" I said.

"Probably," Dani said. "We're actors. Not fucking accountants. I had two breakdowns last week."

Everyone laughed. More drinks came and they were loosening up. Claudia excused herself. As the talk shifted from Gabby to Jeffrey Bloom and his many eccentricities and shortcomings, I watched Claudia on her cell phone, talking and pacing inside the big whiskey-barrel bar.

When Claudia walked back, she said she needed to be going.

"Nice meeting you," Claudia said.

"May I walk you out?" I said.

She nodded and I walked with her out through the bar and out onto Vineland. She slung a sleek little leather purse over her shoulder, moving fast in very tall heels. With the heels and the hair, she stood nearly an inch taller than me. She had on a man's plain tank top with a silver necklace around her neck. A long silk skirt shifted in the soft, cold wind.

"You wanted to say something away from the group?" I said.

"What makes you say that?"

I cocked my head. "Detective's intuition."

"It's probably nothing," she said. "Jeffrey says we all come to acting with our set of hang-ups."

"In my business, nothing often turns to something."

"I didn't want to piss off Olga about Gabby's spiritual growth," she said. "If Gabby's dead, that'll make them all feel better."

I nodded. The sun was going down, casting Vineland in a wonderful golden glow. I reached for the black Way-farers in my pocket and put them on.

I was going native already.

"I grew up outside New Orleans," Claudia said. "In the church. And I guess I'm still not really open to the way some people talk out here. Everyone telling me that they know more than I do. That they have the answers."

"Gabby thinks she found the answers?"

She nodded.

"To what?" I said.

"Life," she said. "Being a woman. Breaking through what we grew up with. Male dominance. At first, I figured it was something that would pass. But then she put pres-sure on me to attend one of her classes. Thought I could maybe benefit from the strength and power she was offer-ing on a silver platter. Gabby said she looked up to me."

"You are quite tall," I said.

"Thank you," she said.

"Where did Gabby take you?"

"I promised her I wouldn't say anything," she said. "I even had to sign some kind of bullshit legal form. They said if I ever talked about what they talked about, they could sue me. I can't afford to get into all that mess."

"Gabby invited you to *Fight Club*?"

She laughed and gave me a side eye. "HELIOS," she said. "Group called HELIOS."

"And what, may I ask, exactly is HELIOS?"

"Gabby swore it helped her get straight after her breakdown," she said. "We mainly sat around and listened to all the folks talk about what HELIOS did for them. There was some little video presentation and they gave us crackers and fruit juice. Kind of like church. Only without Jesus."

"And what did they offer?"

"That's the thing," Claudia said. "Beyond making a stronger and more resilient woman, you don't know what they do or how they do it until you sign up for more. And you can't sign up for more unless you put up some money."

"How much?"

"Five thousand."

I gave a low whistle. "And do you have that much?"

"I had an uncle that died," she said. "Back in Louisiana. Left me some money."

"And Gabby knew about this?"

"Yeah," she said. "Sure did. I talked about him in class. I talked about what he meant to me and how I was going to put that money to work to make it out here."

"Ah."

"You think Gabby invited me because of the money?"

"Yep."

"Damn," Claudia said. "This the first you're hearing about HELIOS?"

"Yes, ma'am," I said. "When did all this start for her?"

"A few months ago," she said. "After I told her I didn't want no part of it, it never came up again."

"Never?"

"Not a word," she said, biting her bottom lip. Her skirt ruffled around her long legs. "Almost like she dared me to say it had ever even happened. You think that's important?"

18

The HELIOS outreach center was in a small bungalow on La Brea across from an old studio Charlie Chaplin had built. There was no signage to show this was the outreach center, only an address I'd found online. The bungalow had gray stucco walls with wooden accents, and cacti and jade plants for landscaping. As I walked up a short concrete staircase with a broken metal railing, the sun had nearly set, leaving the house in shadow. Cars raced up and down the street, unbridled by rush hour.

It was cool and pleasant up on the porch. I knocked.

No one answered. I knocked again.

Being the pushy East Coast type, I opened the door and walked inside. It reminded me of a waiting area at a dentist's office. There was a well-worn sofa and a few folding chairs. A glass-topped coffee table in the center piled with self-help pamphlets about alcohol and drug abuse, dealing with the death of a loved one. The room smelled musty and worn, everything dingy and shopworn. Along a far wall was a partition with a sliding glass window. A shade covered the window from the inside and beyond the wall I could hear the murmuring of voices.

I selected a slick flyer with the word *HELIOS* spread across the top in a fancy font. I sat down and flipped through it, looking at pictures of attractive men and women playing games along a beach, at peace at some kind of yoga retreat, and zip-lining somewhere in wilds of the Pacific Northwest. The opening statement was *UNLOCK YOUR HIDDEN POTENTIAL.*

I was intrigued. I knew I had tons of hidden potential. But the more I read about HELIOS in the four-page spread, the less I knew. They held the answers that no one knew. There were more pictures of women rafting and hiking. One of a giant sunset and a woman in a lotus pose. *A Sisterhood of Power*, announced one of the cutlines. *BREAK THROUGH EXPECTATIONS!*

"Wow," I said to myself.

A side door opened and a woman walked out, looking very surprised to see a guest this late. She looked harmless enough, small and bony, with her brown hair in a pixie cut. Her clothes were just a longish navy T-shirt, bell-bottom jeans, and Birkenstocks. She had enormous blue eyes, freckles across her cheeks and the bridge of her nose, and a slight gap in her front teeth. She looked as wholesome as a slice of apple pie.

"How the hell did you get in here?" she said, sounding less wholesome than she looked.

"Let me see. I knocked several times. Then I opened the door and walked inside. It was really pretty simple."

"Do you have an appointment?"

"No," I said. "But I have lots of untapped potential."

"Who sent you?"

I shrugged. "L. Ron Hubbard?"

"Very funny," she said. "Are you a reporter?"

"No."

"A lawyer?"

"Never."

"Then who sent you?"

"HELIOS came highly recommended by one of your members."

"Oh, yeah," she said. "And who might that be?"

"Gabby Leggett," I said.

She looked at me as if the name meant nothing to her. She stared for a moment, biting hard on her lower lip. Her teeth and the ends of her ears appeared sharp and pointy. "I don't care who you know," she said. "We're closed."

"I'll come back tomorrow," I said.

"You'd still have to have an appointment," she said. "You can't just walk in here off the street. That's not what we do."

"And what do you do?"

"We are a private organization," she said. "We respect the privacy of our members."

"And according to this pamphlet, you are outdoorsy as hell," I said. "Hiking, rafting, swimming. The only thing I didn't see was hang gliding. That might be a deal-maker for me. If I'm going to join, I really need some time in the air."

"Would you like me to call the police?"

"Sure," I said, still sitting. "Why not?"

"I will, you know."

"I kind of doubt it."

"What exactly is it that you want?"

"I want to know more about HELIOS," I said. "I'd like to frolic with attractive women. I'd like to reach deep in myself and maximize my fullest potential. Did you know that the average human only uses ten percent of their brains?"

"You're mocking us," she said. "You're mocking our materials."

"Why have materials if you don't want anyone to join?" I said, looking down at the pamphlet.

"You have to be selected," she said. "You must have an invitation."

"I have an invitation," I said. "From Miss Leggett."

"I don't know that name."

"Sure you do," I said. I pulled out my phone and showed her a photo taken from Gabby's Instagram account. She looked very happy, smiling in a short blue dress while holding a sunflower. "Check your team roster."

"We have many members," she said.

"So glad to hear it."

"Thousands across many continents," she said. "Most of us are women."

"There's a man in several of these photos," I said. "The guy with the beard and the wild blue eyes. Who is he?"

"Again, this is a private organization," she said. "Right now, you are trespassing. I don't have time for questions."

"I'm wearing shoes and a clean shirt," I said. "All that I request is some service."

The woman brushed past me toward the front door and held it open wide. She continued to give me a dirty look until I finally stood and stretched. I tried to muster a look of disappointment, calling on the shoptalk I'd heard from Bloom's students. As I moved, the old floor creaked under my feet.

"Your loss," I said. I moved toward the door and handed her my business card. "I'd be a true and great asset to the HELIOS organization."

The young woman glanced down at the card and then at me. She didn't seem to be the least bit impressed.

"Tell Gabby to call me."

"I don't know anyone named Gabby," she said.

I glanced around the shabby room, seeing nothing but dull paneled walls and outdated furniture. No signage on the outside and nothing but a splay of pamphlets on the table. I'd seen lemonade stands with more investment in infrastructure.

"Ask around," I said. "Or I can ask the police to make inquiries."

As I stepped onto the landing, the door shut hard behind me. A sharp click sounded from the deadbolt being turned.

Hooray for Hollywood. I was making friends everywhere.

19

Early the next morning, the hospital released Z and he immediately returned to work. He typed with his right hand, his left arm in a sling, while I sat across from him at his strip-mall office at Highland and Franklin. It was raining again, as it had been the day I'd arrived, and we didn't seem any closer to finding Gabby Leggett.

"I don't know what to say," Z said. "These HELIOS people are everywhere and nowhere at the same time. They call themselves an executive success program that seeks to free their participants from the shackles of self-doubt and confusion."

"We did the same thing with Henry Cimoli."

"But unlike Henry Cimoli, HELIOS also seeks to end world hunger and looks to promote a lasting peace for all of humanity."

"At least they have realistic goals."

I'd brought more burgers and fries from In-N-Out that morning in my effort to support the local economy. Z had two burgers. I wanted three burgers but had only one. Z's secretary had finally come around to my lingering presence and dropped off a tall coffee before leaving the room without a word. I thanked her. But Delores didn't answer.

"I think deep down she really likes me," I said.

"She said you remind her of her ex-husband."

"That can't be all bad."

"Yes, it can," Z said, still pecking away with one hand. "She ended up shooting him. Judge ruled it was self-defense."

"Wonderful."

"Don't worry," Z said. "It was years ago. She's changed. Completely reformed."

"Who's worried?" I said. I lifted my hand and made it shake.

Z nodded, pushing a button on his computer, a printer on top of a file cabinet humming to life. "I've found a few profiles on the HELIOS founder," he said. "A man named Joseph Haldorn."

"The man from the pamphlets with the piercing blue eyes," I said. "What do we know about Joe?"

"Not much," Z said. "He's cryptic when it comes to his programs. Haldorn says you can't really understand his methods without attending a HELIOS class. He was some kind of CEO of a Silicon Valley start-up and then transitioned into helping others with their success goals."

"Was he successful?"

"According to Haldorn," Z said, "he's known nothing but success. He claims to be some kind of child prodigy who grew up outside St. Louis with an IQ off the charts. He says he was playing piano concertos by the time he was five. And mastered college-level algebra in elementary school. He also says he was a record-setting sprinter that could've been an Olympian, had he not had a higher calling."

"Sounds reasonable," I said. "I'm sure all these details have been verified."

"A reporter with the *Los Angeles Times* made the point that Haldorn offered no proof for his claims," Z said. "Also the reporter had tried to find school records back in Missouri and found nothing."

"So cynical," I said. "Can't you trust a man at his word?"

"Nope," Z said. He slid a manila file over to me. "According to his personal narrative, Haldorn says he had some kind of epiphany while on a trip in the Far East."

"Poughkeepsie?"

"Farther," Z said. "Somewhere in Thailand. He'd dropped out of high school for a while and decided to travel the world. It was there that he'd had the idea for HELIOS while watching the sun rise on a beach with a group of monks. He said it took him more than twenty years to develop what he'd experienced into a successful program. He credits what he calls the science of HELIOS to a woman named Riese, who does appear to actually have a Ph.D. At least according to the *Times* piece. This Riese woman developed the HELIOS method based on clinical trials and thousands of successful students."

"But yet, no one knows what they do."

"Correct."

"You must pay to play."

Z nodded and handed me a stack of printouts on Haldorn, understanding I still preferred a physical file to a computer screen. Before I read, I pulled a pair of cheaters from my jacket pocket.

"How's the arm?" I said.

"What arm?" he said. "I'm on so many painkillers I barely feel it."

"Could have been much worse," I said.

"Could've shot me in the groin," Z said.

"Or it could've been me if you hadn't body-checked me out of the way."

"You'd do the same for me," he said. "I got hurt worse in high school. Broke my leg in two places in the state playoffs."

I looked down at a picture of Haldorn from the *Los Angeles Times* piece. He didn't look like a guru. He looked like a guy rattling change in a bucket along Newbury Street. He had long brown hair and a long gray beard, a tattered corduroy jacket over a Western shirt. Lots of silver jewelry around his neck and on his fingers. His eyes appeared clear, nearly translucent, his face showing a sly, knowing smile to the camera.

"Any connection to Jimmy Yamashiro?"

"I knew you'd ask that," Z said. "But no. I couldn't find a thing. I did a deep search for anything HELIOS-related for Yamashiro and anyone in his orbit at the studio. I also looked for anything with Gabby Leggett, but those came up empty, too."

"Terrific," I said. "Where can we find him?"

"Nothing in the DMV or property records," Z said. "I read one account that says he doesn't drive. He's reputed not to own any worldly goods. No cars. No homes. I'll keep trying."

"Can't you type any faster with one hand?"

"Glad you got Chollo to watch your back," he said. "He helped me out on something last year. He and Bobby Horse are even better than you told me."

"Bobby Horse can't leave security on del Rio," I said. "There are some threats."

"Mr. del Rio has a target on his back," Z said. "Don't know how he's lived this long. I understand he's given up half his territory in the last ten years."

I watched the rain fall in the alley between the strip mall and the row of old storefronts along Highland. A man in a tattered raincoat peed against a brick wall. I drank some coffee and wondered how the weather was in Boston. No matter the rain, it had to be at least forty degrees warmer. I'd worn only a black T-shirt with Levi's and a pair of Nikes that morning.

"How did everything go with Jem Yoon and Gabby's laptop?"

"She's looking for any mention of HELIOS in Gabby's emails and files," he said. "And she's trying to find that sex video with Yamashiro, since Yamashiro has cold feet about sharing."

"If it exists, let's pray it's as short as Yamashiro," I said. "I don't know if I can stand a double feature."

"There are thousands and thousands of emails and pictures to go through," Z said. "But nothing has really stood out. I've been slow and methodical. But what struck me is that nothing Gabby posted online was distinctly personal. Very few photos with friends or details beyond good food and good California vibes."

I drank coffee and watched the rain, leaning back in the old wooden chair. When Delores turned to ask Z a question about billing, I craned my head over my shoulder and gave her my million-watt smile. She acted as if she didn't see me.

As I contemplated where we should go next, my phone buzzed on my leg. Someone named M. Riese had texted me. M. Riese said they were with HELIOS and would be glad to meet me at any time about their organization. I texted back: How about now?

M. Riese agreed and sent me directions to a restaurant not far away.

"Hot date?" Z said.

"That woman at the center must have been more concerned than she let on," I said. "Message from someone named Riese, like the psychologist."

"Could be a setup," Z said.

"I certainly hope so," I said.

"Maybe bring Chollo with you."

"If I can pry him away from selling churros."

"I'll stay on what we know about the Armenians," he said. "I have a buddy who works with the Feds. He's pulling Vartan Sarkisov's file. Should give us a good place to start. Maybe some kind of connection to Yamashiro or his security people."

"You might be more useful with one hand than with two."

"Online detecting, yes," he said. "Not with Jem Yoon. She's made several highly offensive jokes regarding my delicate condition."

"Maybe she's worried certain acts might be harmful," I said. "And best tackled alone."

"I'm wounded," he said. "Not dead."

"Excellent point."

"Would Susan ever suggest such a thing?" Z said.

I picked up the file and tucked it under my arm. I reached for my coffee. "Only when she's angry."

I met a woman named Mallory Riese at The Henry in West Hollywood. The restaurant was decorated like a mod Parisian bar, with soft leather furniture, softer glowing lamps, and dozens of small oil paintings. There was a full coffee bar and patisserie and an entire wall filled with newspapers and magazines. The outdoor patio faced a concrete plaza and sat empty in the rain.

Riese waited by the windows, a cup of coffee before her. She stood and offered a smooth, delicate hand with very long fingers. She had large black eyes and slick black hair. Her eyebrows had been professionally arched and she had a pair of winsome dimples in her cheeks. Her clothes were black, neat, and professional. A simple pantsuit and a white silk top open wide with lapels spilling on her coat. A golden sun pendant hung from her neck.

"Thank you for meeting me," she said. I figured her to be somewhere in her mid-twenties, too young to be Haldorn's HELIOS partner.

"Thank you for texting," I said.

I set my damp ball cap on an empty chair beside me and looked up as a waiter filled my water glass.

"You gave one of our night attendants quite a scare," she said. "You can only imagine the kinds of people who walk into our offices."

"Aren't outreach centers for outreach?"

Riese smiled at me, touching the edge of her coffee, steam swirling from the top. "During normal business hours," she said. "Yes. But I heard you stopped by after we were closed?"

I smiled. "The door was open."

She smiled back. "We have so many satellite centers," she said. "Perhaps you should have tried our main office."

"Which is where?"

Riese didn't answer as a waiter appeared and I ordered a coffee. "I'm sure you understand this is a very private group with many high-profile members," she said. "We are very selective about our time and only answer serious inquiries."

"So you checked me out?"

"We wanted to clear up any questions or misconceptions you might have."

"Why would you think I have any misconceptions?"

"I heard you were looking for one of our members," she said. "You said that she'd gone missing?"

"Gabby Leggett," I said. "She's originally from Boston and has been in California for the last two years."

"I don't know Miss Leggett," Riese said. "And I definitely wasn't aware we had any missing members."

"Her mother hasn't heard from her in two weeks," I said. "There's an active police investigation that I've been hired to supplement."

"Sometimes our members go off the grid for a while," she said. "They eschew the use of modern devices and go on extended retreats. We promote the idea of retreating from modern life and getting back to our primitive selves. People have become entirely corrupted and enslaved by technology."

"Not me," I said. "I just got an iPhone a few years ago."

She smiled at me, showing off her dimples, as if I were joking. "How do you spell her name again?"

I told her. I was about to tell her how to spell Spenser, too, but recalled I'd left a card at the HELIOS center. I didn't want to be patronizing.

"We don't monitor activities of all our members," she said. "But I'd be happy to check with our people. Perhaps there's been some miscommunication."

"No miscommunication," I said. "Her mother paid for me to come all this way. I've been looking for her for three days straight. And my associate was shot in the arm while we searched."

"Shot?"

"Although he was grateful for not being shot much lower," I said. The waitress appeared, heard the word *shot*, and turned on a dime, not wanting to interrupt us.

"And you think this has something to do with the disappearance of Miss Leggett?"

I nodded. My coffee arrived and I added a single sugar. I stirred slow and neat and tapped the spoon at the edge of the cup.

"How can you be so sure?"

"My detective senses were heightened when one of the shooters told me to quit looking for Miss Leggett or he'd kill us."

"Oh my God," Riese said, putting her hand over her mouth. If she was acting, it was impressive. "We will do whatever we can to assist anyone in the HELIOS family."

"Is that what it is?" I said. "A family?"

"In a manner of speaking," she said. "Simply put, our goal is to assist our members in becoming more successful human beings."

"And how exactly does that work?"

Riese looked bemused, tilting her head. "I wish it was simple enough to explain over coffee," she said. "But our teachers and our leaders have spent decades of their lives training to perfect what we do. Even those at the highest level are still learning. We're not just a couple of seminars you attend. HELIOS is a lifestyle."

"Ah," I said.

"I've been studying with HELIOS since I was fourteen," she said. "My mother is a trained psychologist. She and Joe Haldorn originated the method nearly a decade ago, based on some of her research at Stanford."

"I've read about your mother," I said. "I don't want to brag, but my girlfriend has a Ph.D. from Harvard."

"Really," she said. "I'm sure my mother would love to meet her. She might be able to understand all the hard work that goes into our seminars."

I smiled. I drank some coffee. All was right with the world. "I've read more about your leader, Mr. Haldorn. He seems almost too good to be true."

"Joseph Haldorn has accomplished about everything in life he's set out to do," Riese said. "From athletics to music to academics, he has done so much that at one point he got bored. He wanted to share his talents with the world."

"Wow," I said. "That's truly amazing."

She folded her long, delicate hands over each other and gazed right at me. Her eyes seemed even darker and bottomless up close. Behind her, beyond the glass, I watched as two men in black raincoats passed by the window at separate intervals.

They both tried to glance furtively from the small plaza into the restaurant, without much luck. I could tell one of the men had a shaved head. The other, at a distance and in the rain, might have been one of the shooters from the garage.

I kept listening to Mallory Riese, touching the edge of my coffee mug. "I heard you've really done some amazing things for Jimmy Yamashiro," I said, throwing a curveball into the dark.

She continued to smile, keep eye contact. She gave a little shrug. "Should I know that name?"

"Jimmy?" I said. "He runs one of the biggest studios in L.A."

"Mr. Spenser," she said. "Again. I can't talk about our

members or our methods. You've come to us concerned for the safety of one of our people. And we will do our best to assist you and her family."

"So you can confirm Miss Leggett is a member of HE-LIOS?"

"Again, I don't know that name," she said. "We have thousands and thousands of members in four continents. But if she's part of our organization, I promise to do everything humanly possible to reach her. And if she's missing, as you believe, we will assist the authorities."

"How can you assist if you can't even tell me the first thing about what it is you do?" I said.

One of the men in the raincoats had doubled back along the plaza. He stopped to look at his watch, head hidden deep under a hood, and then kept walking toward the sidewalk along Robertson.

"Is something the matter?"

"You didn't happen to ask some friends to accompany you?"

"No," she said. "Why would I do that?"

I didn't answer. I was pretty sure I'd been followed from Z's office. But I couldn't rule out the possibility of these men being close-and-personal friends of Mallory Riese's. Despite her dazzling style and nice dimples, she might be content as hell to have me shot in the back.

"May I reach you at the same number?" she said.

"You may."

"I'll make some calls," she said. "We prefer to head off any issues with our members before information has gone out to the press."

"Are you asking me if we've spoken to the press about Gabby?"

She didn't answer. She sat up straighter and pulled her shoulders behind her, lifting her chin up. She had a very neat and precise way of talking.

"My mother has devoted her life and her work to forming HELIOS," she said. "You must understand that I'm very protective of her legacy."

"And you should understand, the more I know," I said, "the less I have to reach out to outside sources."

I thanked her for her time, picked up my Greenville Drive cap, and stepped back out into the rain. I walked the opposite direction from where I'd parked my rental, glancing in storefront windows, waiting to see if the gentlemen in black raincoats followed.

21

Robertson Boulevard was close enough to Beverly Hills to feel its silly effects. There was Chanel, The Ivy, with its celebrity clientele barely hidden by a white picket fence, a designer boutique selling matching clothes for couples, a medicinal marijuana distributor that resembled an Apple Store, and a luxury pet store called Max Bone. I darted into the pet store to see if the two men might pass rather than wait for me. And perhaps find a gift for Pearl while I was at it. Leather collars, even the smallest, started at more than a hundred bucks. Dog shampoo cost nearly fifty.

As I reached for a knitted sweater made for either a Chihuahua or a well-groomed rat, I saw one of the men. He walked under the canopy of the shop, hood down around his shoulders, exposing his bald head. When he turned, I knew it was one of the men from the garage.

I set down the pink sweater and felt under my jacket

for the leather strap over my gun. I unbuttoned the strap and turned back toward the door.

"Isn't that so cute?" said the young man behind the register. He was blond and lean, wearing the logo of the store on a black T-shirt. He reached down to pat the head of a Great Dane that lay on an oversized pillow.

"Too cute," I said, my right hand moving away from the gun.

The front door was propped open and I could smell the rain. The big dog was sound asleep, snoring deep.

"Want me to ring that up?"

"Too small for my dog."

"What kind of dog do you have?"

"A brown German shorthaired pointer," I said. "Her name is Pearl."

"Perhaps a raincoat, then?" he said. "I bet Pearl would love a slicker. We have some new ones in stock on the rack over there."

"She likes to get wet," I said. "She also likes mud."

"We have booties," he said. "That way your dog doesn't track mud in the house. My dog just loves 'em."

"I can hardly imagine," I said, acting as if I were interested, checking out the canine footwear and glancing out onto the sidewalk and across the street. I saw two women pass, one old and one in her twenties. The younger woman was pushing a stroller. I didn't see the other man in the raincoat.

I didn't see Chollo, though I knew both to be out there.

A woman in tall heels, wearing a Western fringe jacket, walked in with two leashed Siberian huskies. She began to talk to the guy at the register about how to stop constant shedding.

The trick was to follow one of the men, or both, without them knowing they'd been spotted. Or at least that was the plan. If I could separate one from the other, so much the better. I might be able to appeal to his better nature and find out exactly why they wanted me to stop looking for Gabby Leggett. And perhaps who had sent them.

I headed back in the rain. The clerk thanked me for dropping by. I continued to walk south on Robertson. As I turned, I looked in the opposite direction but didn't see anyone. I put my hands in my jacket pockets and continued to move. I had on an Under Armour zip-up workout shirt that hung a few inches below my belt line. I could reach for my revolver faster than Killer Miller. Although shooting someone so close to Beverly Hills might be viewed as tacky.

While I walked along the tree-lined street, I spotted Chollo a block over, heading in the opposite direction. The rain had picked up and he darted into a large glass-front specialty store called Kitson. I ran across the street and joined him inside the shop, which sold novelty items for L.A., including hundred-dollar T-shirts that proclaimed Bloody Marys to be the Breakfast of Champions.

"I followed him up to Third Street," Chollo said. "There was a car waiting for him. Silver Mercedes SUV. He got in and headed West. I would have followed, but I parked near you."

"The other one?"

"I only saw one," Chollo said. "Maybe the other was the driver?"

"Perhaps," I said. "Or maybe the other one is still out here."

Chollo nodded.

I picked up a terry-cloth robe with I'M KIND OF A BIG DEAL embroidered on the back. "For Hawk?"

"Hawk doesn't need to be reminded."

I looked at the price tag and set it back on the table. Chollo headed out the front door. I waited a beat and then followed, walking in the direction of my rental. I got in and started the engine, the windshield wipers going back and forth. A block over, I watched as Chollo walked into the plaza between the office building and The Henry.

Five minutes later, he reappeared, trailing the bald man. I drove out into traffic and U-turned toward the sidewalk. Chollo opened the door and pushed the man inside. He had an aggressive face with beady eyes and a hooked nose, and the stubble on his face was slightly longer than the hair on his head. Under the raincoat, he had on a denim shirt unbuttoned low, showing off the edge of a colorful tattoo. Everyone out here seemed to have tattoos. I was starting to feel left out.

"This him?"

"Yep," I said.

"You always shop with a Glock?" Chollo said. "You afraid one of these rich old ladies going to take you down, *ese*?"

The bald man didn't answer as I pulled into traffic.

"This one stinks," Chollo said. "Too much cologne, my friend. Just a touch. A touch."

I headed back toward Z's office and my hotel. I wasn't sure if the men knew where Z worked or if we'd just been tailed from earlier that day. When I'd brought up the issue with Z the day before, he'd outlined the many security measures in place to stop someone from getting inside his office. The front door was locked at all times and a multitude of video cameras kept watch on his floor and down in the alley beside him. He promised he had more ammo than the Bolivian Army when they cornered Butch and Sundance.

"Where to?" I said.

"Somewhere quiet," Chollo said. "Where we might have a pleasant chat."

A few miles down Sunset, I pulled in behind an empty strip mall. I killed the engine. Rain tapped at the windshield. Chollo was right, the bald man had been generous with the cologne. I started the car again and cracked a window. I breathed in the sweet smell of the back alley.

I glanced into my rearview. No one said a word. Then the man jumped for the door handle and Chollo coldcocked him with his gun. The man held his head, a respectable goose egg beginning to form, a trickle of blood zigzagging down his face.

"Although it would give me great pleasure," Chollo said, "I don't want to shoot you."

The windshield wipers cut on, slapping once to clear the glass. The back of the strip mall was crowded with overflowing dumpsters and busted delivery crates. Nearby stood what looked like some kind of lean-to fashioned with trash bags and old grocery carts. When I flicked on my high beams, it looked to be abandoned.

"Why do you want to harm this man?" Chollo said, nodding toward me.

The Armenian didn't answer.

"Why does Sarkisov care about a missing girl?" I said.

Again no answer. The bald man shuffled in his seat. He glanced up to the rearview with his black eyes.

"We didn't want to shoot your friend," he said. "That was your problem."

"Why don't you want us to find Gabby Leggett?" I said.

"I don't know."

"Does Sarkisov know her?" I said.

"It's just a job," he said. "Just a job. They say nothing to me."

"Do you know a man named Jimmy Yamashiro?" I said.

He didn't answer. Harpo Marx, Marcel Marceau. He was up there with the great ones.

"You know that woman I met today? Were you there to watch out for her?"

He looked over to Chollo and then again at me in the rearview. He finally gave a quick and easy nod and smiled. He had very bad teeth. Small, sharp, and yellow. "You don't know who you fucking with, man. Sarkisov will eat up your assholes."

I looked to Chollo. "Yikes."

"Not so appetizing," Chollo said, speaking with a lot of force. "But I'm not so afraid."

"Me either," I said. "Although it did make me tighten up a little."

"What do we do with him?"

"Take his gun," I said. "Leave his *cojones*."

"Get out," Chollo said, pocketing the man's pistol. "And don't look back. Unless you want to get shot."

The man walked away briskly. He did not look back.

22

I met Z at the Frolic Room later that afternoon. I drank a Dos Equis as he sipped on a Coke, waiting for Jem Yoon. Z had sent her over to a HELIOS outreach center in Echo Park, hoping she'd gather some useful information.

We sat along the long vintage bar, staring at the multi-colored liquor bottles and framed black-and-white photographs. Behind my back, Hollywood legends scowled at me from a Hirschfeld mural.

"I heard this is where the Black Dahlia had her last drink," Z said.

"That's not a good omen."

"Or maybe she wasn't here at all," Z said. "Never know what's real in Los Angeles."

"Those Armenians were real."

"Don't I know it," Z said, lifting his Coke with his

right hand. He wore his black leather jacket over his shoulders and arm sling like a bullfighter's cape. "Glad you brought Chollo today."

"Now we know HELIOS sent them to watch us."

"Are we sure?"

"Pretty sure," I said. "Although that guy we picked up may have just wanted out of the car."

"With Chollo holding a gun on him?" Z said. "A more-than-distinct possibility."

I ordered another Dos Equis with lime. I figured after a hard day's work I deserved it. The old jukebox played Louis Armstrong singing a duet with Louis Jordan. "Life Is So Peculiar." One of my all-time favorites.

"Is this what you'd call real music?" Z said.

"Louis and Louis?" I said. "Would you like me to sing along?"

"Would you be offended if I said no?"

"Not at all."

"Should we talk with LAPD?" Z said, absently stirring his Coke with the straw. "About what you suspect with the Armenians and HELIOS?"

"Not yet," I said. "We only have a possible connection to HELIOS through a very disreputable thug with a horrible dental plan."

"And what are we?"

"Reputable thugs with good teeth," I said. "Trying to stay one step ahead of the bad guys and the cops."

I drank more of the beer, trying to prolong the second cold bottle.

A half-hour later, Jem Yoon walked in through the front door. Her hair was blue today, pulled back in a ponytail, and she wore big black sunglasses along with her black biker jacket. Her T-shirt read THE RUNAWAYS. Without a word, she tossed down a handful of pamphlets and a few DVDs onto the bar. "They fucking loved me," Jem Yoon said. "Wanted me to sign up for an executive leadership course right away."

"That hair screams success," I said.

"Was it okay to put the five grand on your credit card?" she said. "I lifted your numbers online last night."

"She's kidding," I said, looking to Z. "Right?"

Z shrugged, hunkered over his Coke, glancing down the bar toward a flat-screen television playing highlights from last year's Super Bowl. Sony Michel scoring the only touchdown in the entire game. The whole thing what they called a defensive battle, no one scoring a touchdown until the fourth quarter. I'd watched the entire game with Hawk at Vinnie Morris's bowling alley.

"These people are very intense," she said. "They asked me a lot of personal questions. They wanted to know where I'd heard of them. I said I'd read some good things online."

"Jem is the best at bullshit," Z said.

"Excuse me?" she said. "I was prepared and ready. I made up a brand-new life. I have several online identities I use from time to time. One is a rich L.A. socialite with more money than brains. I acted that one up. I played very ditzy. Very curious about personal growth and all that. I told them that I yearned for a deeper philosophical meaning to life. I did that whole bullshit vocal-fry thing. You know what that is? Right?"

"Can I buy you a drink for your efforts?" I said.

"Jack Daniel's, double," she said. "Water back."

"Wow," I said. "My admiration for you only grows."

"Even at the height of my boozing," Z said, "this woman could've drunk me under the table."

I flipped through the reading material, much more detailed than the pamphlets I'd found at the center on La Brea. They were slick and bold and offered dates and times of courses being taught in Los Angeles and New York. Many of the pages highlighted big pictures of Joseph Haldorn with words like *visionary* and *genius* in the cutlines. Women encircled him as he raised his hands and offered what I assumed were nuggets of wisdom. In most shots, he intently looked at the camera with his pale blue eyes.

The bartender laid down Jem Yoon's whiskey on a cocktail napkin.

"Did they talk much about Haldorn?" I said.

"They pretty much only talked about Haldorn," she said. "According to the two women I met, his success programs can change my meaningless life. They said he's figured out a system to hack into the human brain."

"And then?" Z said.

"And then we don't know," Jem Yoon said. The jukebox now playing some Lee Hazlewood with Nancy Sinatra singing "Some Velvet Morning." I figured Hazlewood and Sinatra were an acquired taste, too. I needed to stick with them longer.

"When can you start?" I said.

Jem Yoon smiled. "First, we must discuss my hourly rate."

I turned to Z. "Is she worth it?"

"Every nickel," he said.

"You boys don't have a choice," Jem Yoon said, draining her glass and motioning to the bartender for another. "I got the impression that it's women only. Unless you and Z want to go deep undercover. Wigs, makeup, the whole nine yards."

"I'm confident in most things," I said. "One being that I would make a very ugly woman."

Z nodded in agreement. I flipped through the guidebooks and worked the second half of the beer. I continued to read and scan through the pictures. I looked at picture of Haldorn on a horse. Haldorn playing volleyball. Haldorn being adored by a huge audience. Haldorn shaking hands with the Dalai Lama at a private reception. I kept on reading until I spotted a familiar face in a crowded photograph.

I lifted my chin at Z and pointed to a group photograph of the HELIOS executive board. I tapped at one face at the far end. An attractive middle-aged woman with a silver bob. I tapped at the photo with my index finger.

Z looked down at the page, reading the names. "Nancy Sharp."

"Gabby's old boss," I said. "The one who knew so little about her life. I'd never even given her a second thought."

"I know I'm still new at this," Z said. "But I take it we've found a clue."

Z and Jem Yoon looked over at me from down the bar. I took a dramatic pause to lift my beer and drain the rest of the bottle.

"Good work?" Jem Yoon said.

I nodded. And ordered her another drink.

23

I waited with Z outside Nancy Sharp's bungalow for nearly three hours until she finally showed up. We were parked across the street and watched as she let herself in a side door and began to turn on the lights. The front door soon opened and she had both dogs on leashes and looked to have changed from heels into running shoes.

The moon was high over Hollywood, coating the perfect square lots and sprawling hills with a bright silver glow.

I got out and met her on the sidewalk. Z remained in the passenger seat and watched me through the open window. Sharp still had on her dress clothes, wide-legged black slacks with a gray sleeveless velvet top. When I walked up, she seemed genuinely glad to see me.

"Hello, stranger," she said, brushing away her silvery bangs. "A little late for dinner."

"I was in the neighborhood," I said, squatting down to pat her old dachshund on his head. He licked my hand as the husky eyed me with great suspicion. Willy and Nanook. Nice animals. But then again, Hitler loved dogs.

"Of course," she said. "Anything on your mind?"

"How about HELIOS?"

Her face changed very little, a little softening around the mouth, as if I'd just hurt her feelings. "Of course," she said. "Why do you ask?"

"Gabby was a member."

"Where exactly did you hear that?"

"A woman she tried to recruit," I said. "Were you the one who brought her in? Or is that how you met?"

She stared at me, gathering the leashes into one hand. "I really must walk these dogs," she said. "They haven't been out all day. And it's very late."

"I understand," I said. "I'll walk with you. I'm good with animals."

We walked for a bit along Orange Grove Avenue, block after block of small mod houses and classic California bungalows. Her dogs seemed to accept me tagging along for their nightly routine as they sniffed at hidden messages along walls and mailboxes.

"I hope you understand why I didn't mention Gabby's involvement in the group."

"Not really."

Nancy Sharp cut her eyes over at me briefly as we walked. Nanook strained at his leash, choking and panting, while Willy seemed content hobbling along.

"I don't know why you'd waste your time wanting to

know about an executive training course while Gabby is out there still missing."

"The devil resides in the details."

"What is it you wish to know?"

"Quite a bit," I said. "How long has Gabby been a part of your group?"

"I'm not sure," she said. "Again, what does it matter?"

I didn't answer as we waited for Nanook to take care of some very important business. The suspense of will he or won't he was killing us both. She reached for a large plastic bag in her pocket. Speaking with Nancy Sharp, I felt I needed to prepare the same way.

"The whole time she's been in L.A.?"

"Oh, God, no," she said. "She was really new at this. She'd just gotten started. A real newbie in the program. Gabby had a lot of issues that she wanted to work through. Very deep and very emotional issues. I believe she was making a lot of progress when she disappeared."

"Did you mention your group to the police?"

"They didn't ask," she said. "HELIOS is an executive training program with branches all across the country. I know hundreds of women in L.A. who've benefited from the seminars and online classes. Actresses, executives, multimillionaires. They say it saved their lives. This dealt with her professional life. Her career. And had nothing to do with whatever happened to her."

"Is that why you kept bringing up Eric Collinson?"

"Exactly," she said. "I really am very worried about her. I told you they had a very unpleasant breakup. Have you made any progress?"

"You bet," I said.

Nanook wasn't able to complete the task at hand, and we kept on walking down the street, searching for his perfect target. We followed. Just a nice couple out for an evening stroll talking missing girls, little white lies, and secret empowerment clubs. I thought about offering my arm and serenading her with "Buffalo Gals."

"Why all the secrecy about HELIOS?"

"The program isn't a one-and-done seminar," she said. "It's a lifestyle."

"And to my understanding, the more recruits you bring in, the higher you go?" I said. "Kind of like that mountain climber on *The Price Is Right*."

"That's a little simplistic."

"But true," I said. "If I read the materials correctly."

"And that's how you found out about my involvement?"

"Executive board member," I said. "A little bit more than just involved."

"I'll tell you whatever you like, but don't get us involved with the police," she said. "That would be a waste of your time, their time, and Gabby's time. I can assure you whatever happened to her didn't happen on our watch. HELIOS is a sisterhood of professionals. This is a very tough city that supports a very harsh and misogynistic industry. We look out for each other. We guard one another's interest and watch one another's backs."

"Has Gabby had some bad experiences?"

"Of course," she said. "She's young, beautiful, and very ambitious. She might as well have come from Massachusetts with a target on her forehead."

"Maybe with a major head of a studio?"

"Like I said, she didn't share personal stories with me," she said. "She worked for me. We were friendly. But not friends. I'm not privy to her personal details."

"But you did get her into HELIOS?"

We walked for a few moments, Nancy Sharp thinking on the question. She took a deep and very long breath and let it out slowly. "Yes," she said. "I brought her to her first meeting. But HELIOS is like a river with endless branches and tributaries. She started with me but went on her own journey."

"Perhaps she's still on that journey?"

Nancy Sharp stopped cold and stared at me. "If you want to accuse me or the group of some kind of hidden agenda, go ahead. I'd really like to hear it. All we do is help people. Enable people. Gabby was a broken woman when she came back to me, needing my help. Used up and spit out by some horrendous people."

"I thought she didn't discuss personal matters?"

"Goddamn you," she said. "Are you always this insufferable?"

"Always," I said. "I've worked on it for years and years."

She rubbed her neck with her free hand, tired, and cut her eyes at me. She closed them for a moment and then opened them wide, asking me if I'd like to come back to her house and have a cocktail. "Let's slow down," she said. "Okay? Let's talk about things like rational people. HELIOS does great work for so many. Dragging us in the mud isn't what Gabby would want."

"Do you know a woman named Mallory Riese?"

"Of course," she said. "She's the director of communications. Her mother is a great mind. A visionary. She assisted in designing many of our programs."

"I met with Mallory earlier today and she explained the entire HELIOS directive."

"And that didn't set your mind at ease?"

"For a few minutes," I said. "Until a couple of really nasty guys, one who'd doused himself in a quart of Axe body spray, started to follow me back to my car. I'd seen them before when they shot my friend not long after I spoke with you."

"And what does that mean?"

"They didn't follow me," I said. "They came with her."

"That's crazy."

"Mallory Riese was pretty fast to want to meet with some guy who just walked in off the street to a HELIOS center."

"She was being generous with her time."

"I want to meet Joe Haldorn."

Nancy Sharp started to laugh and pressed her hand to her mouth. She made it seem like I'd just asked if Jesus Christ or Buddha might be willing to meet me at the corner bar to answer all life's questions. She laughed some more, the hysteria seeming to bubble up involuntarily.

"Or I can call the police and tell them what I know."

"Do whatever you want," she said. "This is harassment."

"Might make it easier on ol' Joe to talk to me than a bunch of detectives with search warrants."

"Search warrants for what?"

"Gabby Leggett."

"HELIOS saved Gabby," she said. "Why would you blame us?"

"Call me tomorrow," I said. "Let me know where and when."

I walked back to the car and crawled back in with Z. I started the engine and pulled away from the curb.

"How'd it go?" Z said.

"I believe I just got us an audience with the Great and Powerful Oz."

"Is that a good thing?"

"Once you get through all the green smoke."

24

"Y ou caught one of the dudes who ambushed you and Sonny Sixkiller and then let him go?" Samuelson said. "Why the fuck would you do that?"

"He gave me a lead."

"A lead?" Samuelson said. "What is this, fucking *Adam-12*? I was calling you to let you know these people are coming for your head. We jammed up Sarkisov pretty good the other night and he wasn't exactly thrilled about it. In fact, he was downright pissed."

"Arrests?"

"Nope," Samuelson said. "None of the guys on camera were there. Because they were out and about, looking to finish what they started."

"This guy said Sarkisov would eat up my asshole."

"Jesus," Samuelson said. "What the fuck does that even mean?"

"I don't know," I said. "But it sounds unpleasant."

We were seated at a long table on the bottom level of Philippe the day after I spoke with Nancy Sharp. The place was so old it still had a row of wooden telephone booths by the front door, sawdust on the floor, and a candy counter where they offered a check-cashing service. On the walls were pictures and newspaper clippings from old L.A. One close to us offered the headline FATTY AR-BUCKLE CHARGED WITH MURDER.

"Did Sarkisov tell you about his interest in Gabby Leggett?" I said.

"Says he never even heard of her," Samuelson said.

"I'm shocked," I said. "You ask him about Yamashiro?"

"Sure," he said. "He said he didn't know Yamashiro or know anything about blackmail."

"That part actually may be true," I said.

"So did you want to meet with me about something or just shoot the shit for old times' sake?" Samuelson said, tossing his tie over his shoulder so it wouldn't land in his au jus. He dipped his sandwich and jabbed its pointy edge at me. "I took it that you had come across something important. Or did you want to just underscore all the shit that my detectives don't know?"

"Ever hear of a group called HELIOS?"

"Nope," Samuelson said. "Should I?"

"They claim to have thousands of members over several continents," I said. "Empowerment. Sisterhood of strength. The leader claims he's found a way to hack into the human brain to unlock a treasure trove of potential."

"Sounds like a truckload of bull crap to me," he said. "And I know of about a thousand other groups just like them in this city."

"Gabby Leggett was a member," I said. "When I went to one of their centers they shooed me away. And then yesterday morning, out of the clear blue, the director of communications for HELIOS wanted to buy me a nice cup of coffee and chat."

"And?"

I took my first bite of the French dip sandwich. I'd had one before, and ever since I'd looked forward to having one again. Maybe better than Kelly's on Revere Beach.

"Lots of bullshit," I said. "But also two of Sarkisov's guys were loitering outside. They'd been sent to tail me after the meeting."

"Aha."

"Exactly what I was thinking."

"And now you want me and an LAPD SWAT team to bust down the doors of these HELIO fucknuts and demand to know where they put Gabby Leggett?"

"Sure," I said. "For starters."

"Need a little more, pal," Samuelson said. "All I have is your word that some guy you snatched up might be connected to these people. Can you see my position here? A judge might find the situation slightly humorous."

"Gabby Leggett was also working for a high-ranking member of HELIOS," I said. "And when I called on her, she didn't say a word about their organization."

"Maybe she's a private person."

"Maybe she's hiding something."

"Again," Samuelson said. "My detectives would need more."

"Just like Jimmy Yamashiro?"

"Jimmy Yamashiro is a better suspect," he said. "Now we know about the blackmail. He had quite a bit to lose."

"And Eric Collinson. That's where you're going, right?"

"Tell me this, Spenser," he said. "When you were a cop, how many times was it the husband or the boyfriend?"

"Almost always," I said.

"Nearly ninety percent," he said. "This is between me, you, and the pickle on my plate. But the detectives are taking a serious look at Collinson. He had a pretty unhealthy fascination with Miss Leggett for a very long time."

"How so?" I said.

"Nope," he said. "That's all I got for you. But you seem to think they're looking in the wrong direction."

"When a crew of Armenian gangsters ask you to butt out and then shoot your partner, you get a little suspicious."

"Somebody doesn't like you asking questions," he said. "I'll give you that."

"That's all I get?" I said. "I bought you an extra pickle."

"I'm saying keep all options on the table," he said. "And watch your ass with those people. You pissed someone off for sure."

"What can I say?" I said. "It's what I do."

Samuelson bit into his free kosher pickle. He gave me a hard look from behind his tinted glasses. Chewing, he seemed to be deep in thought. "Next time you see that son of a bitch Sarkisov, he's gonna put one right behind your fucking ear," he said. "You got that, Boston Blackie?"

"You do realize I'm not on my own," I said. "I have the best backup in town."

"Really?" Samuelson said. "You got a one-armed Tonto and fucking Pedro Infante trailing along. These guys aren't nice. They don't play fair. And you'll never see them coming."

"Pedro Infante?"

"What can I say?" Samuelson said. "My old man played 'Cielito Lindo' about a thousand times when I was growing up."

"That's okay," I said. "The other night I asked a bartender to play Johnny Hartman."

"Why not Mel Tormé?" Samuelson said. He dug into his potato salad. "Or the fucking Ink Spots. How old are you, Spenser?"

"Age has nothing to do with it," I said. "I am a man of the classics."

"Kind of like the Hollywood Forever Cemetery," he said. "That place is filled with all types of fucking classics."

25

It was a bright blue and cloudless day in Los Angeles. Chollo and I were parked a few blocks away from Haldorn's gated mansion along West Adams. The mansion had been built in an Italian renaissance style, with elegant columns and balconies, and, from what I could see through the gate, offered precisely manicured grounds of bright blooming flowers and more species of palm trees than I knew existed. We'd been watching the property since sunup and had watched many cars come and go. Lots of cargo vans and trucks, workers unloading tables and chairs, setting up for some type of event in the back of the mansion.

"Looks like a wedding," Chollo said.

"Is this mansion to your liking?"

"*Sí.*" Chollo nodded. "It's even larger than Mr. del Rio's. But this neighborhood is not Bel-Air."

The old neighborhood was far from Beverly Hills or

Bel-Air, a hodgepodge of decrepit mansions and rows and rows of aging bungalows in a variety of conditions. Some of the mansions had been split into apartments and many of the old houses looked as if they'd been slathered in stucco and left to rot. Chollo said it had once been the toniest neighborhood in Los Angeles, with movie stars and millionaires. In the last few years, it seemed to be making a slow comeback.

There was a tall stucco fence and black metal gate in front of the HELIOS property. Several guards patrolled the grounds.

"For a man who eschews wealth," I said. "This is quite a place for Joe Haldorn to hang his hat."

"And what do we know about this man?"

"He is a riddle wrapped in an enigma and then deep-fried in an egg roll."

Chollo turned to stare at me from the passenger seat. He was dressed in black jeans, a black T-shirt, and black boots. All he needed was a bandolier strapped over his chest. Without it, he resembled a Mexican Johnny Cash.

"That means we know nada."

"This girl," he said. "Miss Leggett. Might she be inside?"

"It's worth asking," I said. "Since the police seem to think we are on shaky ground."

"The police are only on shaky ground when it comes to money," Chollo said. "Where I grew up, in my neighborhood in East L.A., the police were never shy about kicking in a door. Here, this might as well be a castle on a hill."

"And Haldorn the king and spiritual ruler."

I got out of the car and stretched, crossing the street to the mansion and again walking past its gates. Whatever they were setting up for had culminated in a symphony of drills and hammering. A woman emerged from a black cargo van holding a large and intricate flower arrangement. The air was cool, a nice breeze along the sidewalk as I doubled back to the car.

I texted Z to look into what kind of event the HELIOS people might be hosting over the weekend. I crawled back into the car and thumped at the wheel.

"This woman you met," Chollo said. "What did she say about Miss Leggett?"

"Mallory Riese said she didn't know her," I said. "And couldn't confirm if she was among the rank and file of HELIOS."

"And now?"

"She hasn't returned my calls," I said. "Nor will Nancy Sharp. I think the proverbial gate has been shut on the castle. My meet-and-greet with the king has been denied."

Chollo nodded. "If we are sure Miss Leggett might be alive and inside, Mr. del Rio said he'd be honored to loan you Bobby Horse and some more of our people. But only if you are positive. He doesn't want trouble with the Armenians."

"A rescue mission?" I said.

"If you wish."

I watched as the black metal gate swung back and a white SUV pulled out ahead of us on West Adams. It appeared very different from the workers and delivery vehicles we'd been watching all day, with its tinted windows and bright silver wheels. I pressed start and knocked the car in gear.

"What did you see?"

"Not a thing," I said. "But I've run out of ideas."

"You think it's maybe Haldorn?"

"Maybe," I said. "Or maybe someone of importance."

"Sixkill showed me a picture of this woman, Gabby," he said. "She is very beautiful. The kind of woman who might break a man's heart in many places. Her eyes are so large and green. I have seen few like them. Like emeralds."

"Since I touched down in L.A., it seems I've been following a long list of lovers," I said. "Her former agent. A couple more boyfriends, a movie executive, and now it appears Joseph Haldorn."

"Have you thought perhaps this woman brought on her own demise?" he said. "Playing games with the wrong people?"

"It's one of my working theories."

We followed the white SUV down West Adams, toward the USC campus, and then turned toward downtown on Olive Street. They turned again on Seventh and we followed for a long way through downtown and the urban sprawl of storefronts and office buildings. I had the windows down and played a local station offering up a nice mix of Gerry Mulligan, Chet Baker, and Dave Brubeck. A fitting soundtrack to the scenery.

"These people don't seem to know where they are going."

"Nice day for a drive," I said, tapping at the wheel in time with the music.

"I think they know we are here, *amigo*," he said. "They are leading us somewhere."

They continued slow and steady for a long while before turning south and dipping under the 10. The storefronts and offices were soon replaced with modern steel buildings and old brick warehouses. The streets were cracked and broken and colorful graffiti decorated the old brick walls. Telephone poles, not palms, adorned the sidewalks.

"Maybe they came to do business."

"With us?"

"With the Armenians," Chollo said. "We are going into Furlong."

"Nice town?"

"If you like to be beaten and shot," Chollo said.

"Sounds lovely."

We followed the white SUV in and out of several small streets by welding shops and grocery distribution warehouses. I hung back as far as I could without losing sight of them. But down here, there were few cars, mainly trucks and trailers coming and going. I thought I'd lost them for a moment and took a U-turn on a long stretch of industrial road.

"There," Chollo said. I slowed but kept on moving.

We saw the SUV parked at a crooked angle behind a large chain-link fence topped with concertina wire. I turned down the Jerry Mulligan and parked a few blocks away. I killed the engine and we sat and waited for the car to back out.

"You can run the address," Chollo said. "But one way or another, it's Sarkisov."

"Will Sarkisov speak with Mr. del Rio?"

"Not without a gun stuck up his *culo.*"

"Can that be arranged?"

Chollo gave a gentle shrug. He didn't seem to dismiss the idea. "Is this what you Anglos called a Mexican stand-off?" he said.

"*Sí,*" I said.

26

After I dropped Chollo back on Olvera Street, I returned to my hotel, made some phone calls, and drove a short distance to Runyon Canyon Park. I'd changed into my shorts and Nikes and a navy sweatshirt with the arms cut off at the elbows. I needed to sweat and think. Sitting in a car for more than six hours hadn't done my body any favors.

Along the street, a man under a small canopy sold fruit slices and chilled whole coconuts. I bought a bottle of water for two bucks and walked inside the gates. At the base of the canyon, thirty or forty people practiced outdoor yoga en masse. There were professional dog walkers and shapely young women in micro–workout clothes. I chose one of the most difficult trails and started off on the paved path, getting a fast walk going before transitioning into a run. I stopped at a tight turn in the hills and stretched against a park bench.

I watched a young woman, blond and comely, taking a selfie with Los Angeles stretching out behind her.

Gabby had lived less than a quarter-mile away. Her mother had told me she'd often visited the park to exercise or take Nancy Sharp's dogs for a walk. It was warm, a mugginess covering the hills with a smoldering haze down into the basin. I pushed off the bench and loped into a slow run. My gait wasn't pretty and the run wasn't easy. As my regular path was flat along the Charles, I wasn't used to making a vertical climb. There were evergreens, sage, and what I figured might be tumbleweeds. I spotted warnings for snakes and coyotes but had yet to see either of them. As I ran, I was mindful of my surroundings. As I'd been followed twice since I arrived, I hadn't grown complacent.

Two older women in bright blue tracksuits passed me on the way down. One of the women had had so much plastic surgery, her features seemed to have been formed of clay. Almost no nose and blooming red lips. She looked like a house cat brought to life.

I continued to climb up along the canyon.

Gabby Leggett had disappeared. The credit cards I tracked hadn't been used. Her phone had remained inactive, no longer connected to her Apple account. Her laptop contained some nasty emails to Jimmy Yamashiro but no replies. Eric Collinson had done his best to scrub it clean but had been no match for Jem Yoon. She'd even found the infamous video of Gabby and Yamashiro's tryst. It was dimly lit and poorly acted, a reject from Cinemax After Dark and easily forgotten.

I was sweating now, steadying my breath, my quads aching as I glanced up at the hilltop goal that seemed as far away as Katmandu.

The last time Gabby was spotted was her infamous last brunch with Jade. The last time we knew where she'd been was leaving her apartment building that morning. There was a charge on her credit card at a Starbucks on Sunset. And then nothing. No one had seen or heard from her. No one had found her car.

All I had now was a trail of fibs that seemed to center on an organization that prided itself on its anonymity. HELIOS advertised human and spiritual growth but partnered with someone like Vartan Sarkisov. Gabby Leggett had been a member of HELIOS for many months, but Nancy Sharp had done all she could to keep that detail private.

Those most likely to hold the answers I needed had steeled themselves behind a brick wall. I could press Samuelson to get his detectives to make inquiries into HELIOS, but I'd need more.

As I ran, I started to wonder what Hawk would make of the hiking trail. I think he'd like the challenge. I know he'd like the women. Dozens of them going up and down the Hollywood hills. Old ones. Young ones. Few unattractive ones. Many taking photos. Some walking slow. Others passing me on the way up, their backs shiny with sweat and calves bulging from the climb.

A muscular man carrying a green rucksack jogged down the winding trail. The sleeves had been cut from his sweaty gray T-shirt, showing red arrow tattoos on his delts. I nodded at him and he nodded back, my reflection in his mirrored sunglasses.

I missed mornings in Cambridge with Susan and Pearl. Taking Pearl for a run along Memorial Drive, cooling off at Magazine Beach Park, and walking slow among the reeds and goose droppings down along the Charles. The rowers on the water, steam lifting in the early morning as they'd disappear under bridge to bridge. The coach shouting instructions to pull harder and faster.

I missed afternoons at the Harbor Health Club. Henry Cimoli strutting around in his white satin tracksuit that never seemed to fit the times. I liked the metallic smell of the old weights and the sweat in the boxing room. I liked the feeling of pushing myself to exhaustion on the heavy bag until my arms felt dull and heavy, knowing the only direction was forward.

I missed drinking coffee and eating corn muffins, waiting for the next client who always walked through the door of my office in the Back Bay. I liked the simplicity of working for myself, paying my bills, and not having to answer to anyone. I liked Mattie Sullivan, now a student at Northeastern, dropping by when she could to help with errands and begging me for some real work.

I missed nights with Susan. Waiting for her upstairs while she finished with her final session of the evening, making small talk in her kitchen. Her with a glass of Riesling and me with a beer, deciding on dinner. Sometimes I cooked. Sometimes we went to Harvard Square. There was the Russell House Tavern, Harvest, or Legal at the Charles Hotel. Cambridge our oyster. We were friends with bartenders and waiters. Old-fashions poured over a large cube of ice and no fruit. Vodka gimlets in a perfectly chilled glass.

I thought of Susan waiting for me alone in the bedroom, smelling of good soap and wearing nothing else but her La Perla lingerie and a devilish smile. Her curly black hair worn loose across her bare shoulders.

I missed Boston. I'd never feel at home here. Los Angeles seemed like a sunny, silly void to me. Everything was concrete and palm trees and overpasses and emptiness. It seemed the perfect place to drop off the face of the earth. Or be swallowed whole into nothingness. Samuelson was right. There were no rules here. I had few contacts. No one cared about history or allegiance. It was the snake trying to eat its own tail.

I'd made it to the top. I stood tall on the Hollywood Hills and looked down along Runyon Canyon and into the haziness of Los Angeles. I was breathing very hard. My sweatshirt was nearly soaked through. I checked the time on my phone and noticed I had a text from Jem Yoon.

It simply read: **Received invite to HELIOS fund-raiser. Want to join?**

27

How do I look?" Jem Yoon said.

"I might just break into 'On the Street Where You Live.'"

"I don't know that song," she said. "Is that good?"

"Only for you and Eliza Doolittle," I said. "Mainly for you."

Jem Yoon had on a lacy coral-pink dress that hit her just above the knees and a pair of very tall beige stiletto heels. Her blue hair had been pulled back into a loose little bun with strands of hair hanging down below her elfin ears. The only jewelry she wore was a silver necklace with a mini-padlock as a pendant.

"You don't look half bad yourself," she said. "I thought you didn't have a suit."

"Off the rack from Brooks Brothers," I said. "They had a little trouble finding a forty-eight-long jacket."

"I like the tie," she said. "It fits you."

"I asked for one with a dancing hula girl," I said. "But they were out."

"Shall we?" she said.

I finished the beer I'd been working on before her arrival, paid the tab at the lobby bar, and offered her my arm. We walked out the doors and I handed the valet my ticket. It was a breezy early evening in Hollywood and the sky above the hills was dusky.

"Is Sixkill jealous?" I said.

"I could only get two tickets," she said.

"And what do they call this wealthy Korean socialite?"

"Jem Yoon."

"Creative," I said.

"Yes," she said. "She's exactly like me. Only with much more money."

"And how did she get her money?"

"Her horrible father," Jem Yoon said. "A real Bond villain a-hole. He sells lasers or something. That would explain my date. I have repressed issues and prefer to be with an older man."

"Much older?" I said.

"How about respectably older?"

"Is there any such thing?" I said.

"Of course," she said. "We'll make it so."

Jem Yoon cut her eyes at me, a slight grin on her lips, as my rental glided into the roundabout and wheeled its way to the curb. I opened the door for her and walked around to pay the valet. She slid into the seat, knees locked in the tight dress, and the doorman closed it with a snap.

"What do we do if they recognize you?" she said.

"Once I'm inside?" I said. "Nothing. In fact, the plan is that I hope they do."

"You want to agitate them?"

"Mainly I want to agitate Joseph Haldorn."

"And what if he has us thrown out?"

"Then we know we're on the right track."

We headed out onto Highland and then took La Brea south back to the old mansion where Chollo and I had spent the morning. We drove for almost forty minutes before reaching the West Adams neighborhood. Out front, a car valet service had set up for the event. Instead, we parked a few blocks away, just in case we needed to make a hasty retreat. Jem Yoon was not pleased about the walk in the stilettos.

The entry gate was guarded by two men with thick muscles. One black and one white. Both were bald and wearing black shirts, black pants, and sunglasses. They looked like guys who'd almost made it to the NFL, but didn't make the cut.

"Jem Yoon," she said. "And guest."

"And your guest's name?" the white guy said. Speaking as if I weren't present.

"Busby Berkeley."

"I don't see your name on the list, Mr. Berkeley," he said.

Jem Yoon moved her body between me and the man. I watched as she touched his shoulder and smiled, head tilting, mouth parting, and becoming a new person. She spoke in a high, lilting tone, using a lot of the vocal fry. "That's why it read *and guest*," she said. "Right? Wow. *Oh my God*. You look so strong."

The man smiled and let us through the front gate and onto the lawn peppered with tables overflowing with food and drink. There were two open bars before we even got to the steps of the Italianate mansion that glowed gold from its windows and open doors.

"Fucking idiot," she said.

"I would like to say men are more complicated than that."

"Than reacting to nice tits and a bouncy little ass?"

"Would it be sexist if I said we all have our gifts?"

"Yes," she said. "It would."

We found a long, linen-covered table where champagne had been poured. I grabbed two glasses and followed Jem Yoon up the marble staircase and into a grand house from another age. The room was polished dark wood with tall wooden columns rising into a vaulted ceiling. I craned my neck up to see an intricate fresco of angels frolicking in the clouds, a beam of sunshine shooting down from the heavens. A trio of violinists played Strauss. Or at least I believed it was Strauss. Whatever it was, you could definitely waltz to it.

"See anyone you know?" I said.

"I only met a couple of recruiters," she said. "With the bullshit profiles I created, I'm sure they will be finding me soon. Crazy rich Korean with *mucho dinero*."

"How rich?"

"Did I mention I took a private jet to Napa yesterday to collect a case of my favorite cab?"

"Save any for me?"

"No," she said. "But you're welcome to what's left of a six-pack of Pabst in my fridge."

I'd been to countless fund-raisers in Boston and Cambridge with Susan, but there was something odd and surreal about the energy in this room. Everyone was so upbeat, laughing and smiling as if nitrous oxide had been pumped into the air ducts. I finished the champagne and set it on the tray of a passing waiter. Coming down the staircase, I saw a man in a gold metallic dinner jacket with a black shirt and black pants. He had a longish beard and long hair swept back off his high forehead. Despite the tux, he still appeared dirty.

Jem Yoon elbowed me hard in the rib.

"You know I am a trained detective?"

"Just making sure you are paying attention."

Across the room, through the din of conversation and music, I spotted Nancy Sharp standing with Mallory Riese and a much older woman who looked as if she might be Mallory's mother. They looked to be in deep conversation, whispering into one another's ears, and not-so-furtively glancing in my direction. They did not appear to be members of the always popular Spenser Fan Club.

"How do you say 'the jig is up' in Korean?"

She said something in Korean. "Is it?" Jem Yoon said.

"Two of my biggest admirers over by the staircase."

"Shit," she said. "And I was all ready to play the part of the ditzy socialite. I had to borrow this damn dress from my cousin. Lace. I don't usually do lace. I'm more of a leather girl."

I looked away from Sharp and Riese as they met Joe Haldorn at the landing. I stood back and took stock of the room, looking for anyone else that might seem familiar. Or anyone that I could recall seeing in Gabby Leggett's thousands of photos. Before I could, I felt the short shadow of two of the security guards at the front. They were wise enough not to place a hand on me.

"Sir," the white guy said. He had a thick neck and large arms but was several inches shorter than me. His bald head gleamed under the chandeliers.

"Busby Berkeley," I said. "I was just about to ask that trio to play 'I Only Have Eyes for You,' and there you appeared."

"Please come with us, sir."

"Not yet," I said. "Mr. Haldorn wanted to see me."

"I don't think so."

"Oh, I do," I said. "Let's go ask him. Joe is such a huge fan."

"Sir."

"Ask him," I said. "I'll stand right here and wait until you get back."

Jem Yoon walked up to him and patted his cheek. "So cute," she said. "Like Vin Diesel. Only dumber."

Three more men in black T-shirts and black pants had joined us. I took it they were either security or trying to form a boy band. I glanced across the room and caught the eye of Joseph Haldorn. He saw me but looked away, trying not to acknowledge my presence. As I turned back, the short, thick guy grabbed my right wrist.

I punched him with a hard left in the solar plexus. He stepped back as if he'd swallowed an Everlasting Gobstopper whole. Another man wrapped his arm around my neck and I reared my head back until I heard the crunch of his nose. The classical music stopped; the attention was on me.

I was pretty sure Joseph Haldorn knew I'd joined the party. And to punctuate the point, I took on a third man who tried to karate-kick me in the groin by catching his foot, twisting it hard, and sending him onto a long linen-covered table neatly adorned with a delightful assortment of crudités.

There was a lot of noise. And mess.

And then good ol' Joe walked up, his hand raised in a gesture of peace and calm. The jewelry on one wrist looked like he'd looted the tomb of an Egyptian cat. Everyone watched and listened to him. A spiritual twin to E. F. Hutton.

"Leave him alone," he said. He spoke with a hard intensity but with a low volume. "This man is welcome here."

I looked to Jem Yoon. She was confused. I was confused. The guards were confused. Mostly the one whose black tee was splattered in some kind of white herb sauce.

"This is not a closed group," he said. "There's no reason for deceit and misdirection. You could have simply asked to speak to me about what we offer."

"How much does it cost to drink the Kool-Aid?"

Joe Haldorn's eyes were an icy blue and possessed a weird tranquility. "Why are you causing trouble?"

We were within inches of each other now and he continued to smile his odd, tranquil smile. "I've been hired to find a woman named Gabby Leggett," I said. "She's been missing for more than two weeks. I understand she's one of your faithful followers."

"I know Miss Leggett."

I nodded. Someone told the band to play on and they did, diving into a Mozart concerto.

"If you care about your people so much," I said. "Why don't you tell me the last time your people have seen her? And why she's disappeared without checking with her family and friends?"

"I have no idea," he said.

"When is the last time she checked in to the Mickey Mouse Clubhouse?"

Haldorn's smile faded as he continued to stare at me. "I teach my students to never keep secrets," he said. "Secrets can devour your soul. We want to rid ourselves of anything that binds the intellect."

"So pleased to hear that," I said. "Where's Gabby been for the last two weeks?"

"I'm not exactly sure," he said. He paused to stare at me and then cocked his head and jacked his thumb over his shoulder. "Why don't you ask her yourself?"

I turned to where I'd last spotted Nancy Sharp. She was speaking with another woman, and as Sharp said something to her, the woman turned around and looked in my direction. She was tall, blond, and rail-thin, with large eyes. She wore an oversized black jacket on top of a short cocktail dress. The woman smiled in my direction and offered a short, friendly wave. Her hair was much shorter and seemed much darker and the face scrubbed clean of all the makeup and false eyelashes.

There was no doubt it was Gabby Leggett.

28

"Y ou made a real mess," Gabby said.

"I'll pay for dry cleaning on the guard's T-shirt," I said. "Can't do anything about a broken ego."

"I mean all of this," she said. "This is a private event. An incredibly special night."

"Your mother is more than worried," I said.

"My mother worries too much," she said. "So dramatic."

"She thought you might be dead."

We were sitting on the steps behind the mansion, facing a long rectangular reflecting pool. Blue and red flowers, miniature trees, and climbing plants filled several concrete pots. People walked past us, down the steps, and around the pool. They chatted and laughed. None of them even gave us a sideways glance as we spoke. Jem Yoon stood nearby, speaking with an older woman with white hair. The older woman had on a floor-length white satin dress. Lotus blossoms floated in the pool alongside lit candles.

"So you're okay?" I said.

"Of course I'm okay," she said. "My mom sent you all the way out here from Boston? That's so much like her. So hysterical and wanting to be involved in my every move. Did she tell you that she never wanted me to leave? She wanted me to come work in her little dress store in Harvard Square. That silly little boutique. She can't stand that I'm doing so well."

"But are you?"

Gabby Leggett took in a long breath and touched her temples. Up close, her eyes seemed an even brighter green against the pale skin. Her hands shook as she held a bottle of water in her hands. "God. This is all so crazy. So embarrassing. Did you say the police were looking for me, too?"

"Yes," I said. "And they suspect your ex-boyfriend might've had something to do with your disappearance."

"Who?" she said.

"Eric."

"God," she said. "Oh, God. Eric. Why Eric? We haven't been together for more than a year. He's my goddamn agent. How in the hell will that look to everyone? I'm still out there trying to get jobs."

I noticed her black jacket still had the maker's tag stitched on one of the sleeves. She held the coat over her, shivering and cold. It was nearly eighty degrees. Her white skin looked a little pink, not a trace of makeup, and the blond hair showed dark roots.

"I think this goes without saying," I said, "but perhaps you should call your mother."

She shivered again and drank some more water. "Of course I will," she said. "I have a lot to tell her. She can't keep on trying to control my goddamn life."

"The police will want to speak with you, too," I said. "To make sure you're all right."

"I'm all right," she said. "Why don't you just tell them? Don't I look fucking all right? I went on a retreat. Can't someone go on one goddamn retreat without notifying the world? Leave the world behind. Isn't that the whole damn point? This is so embarrassing."

"To you?" I said. "Or to Joseph Haldorn?"

"Dr. Haldorn is a very important man," she said. "He doesn't need this mess. God. You just flipped out at his birthday party."

"This is Haldorn's birthday party?"

She nodded.

"Damn," I said. "I should've popped out of the cake."

Something in the light caught my eye, the faintest purple bruise against her long neck. I reached out and turned her chin away from me. She jumped to her feet as if she'd been stabbed with a dull stick and pointed down at me. "Don't you touch me," she said. "Don't you fucking touch me."

Jem Yoon looked in my direction. She had a confused, do-you-need-help expression. I shook my head. Across the pool, Nancy Sharp looked my way before lifting a flute of champagne to her lips.

"Where did you go on this retreat?" I said.

"That's none of your concern."

"What did you do on this retreat?"

"Go to hell."

"I'm sensing a pattern," I said.

"You're getting involved in my personal life," she said. "And I don't even know who the hell you are."

"I told you," I said. "Spenser. With an *S*."

"I'm sorry you went to all this trouble, Spenser with an *S*."

"No trouble," I said. "And I found you."

"Don't worry," she said. "You'll be paid for your time. My mom can afford it. She can afford to make as much trouble as she likes. Are we done here?"

"Almost," I said. "How about you sit back down for this one?"

"Don't touch me again."

"Nasty bruise on your neck."

She didn't answer, but sat. She hugged her knees to her chest and gathered up the long coat sleeves in her hands in an effort to pull herself farther inside it.

"Did you send Jimmy Yamashiro a video clip and demand payment?"

"What?" she said. "Are you fucking kidding me? Did Jimmy say that? What a piece of shit. That's a lie. A video clip? What are you even talking about?"

"A little clip of you guys playing house."

"What?"

"It's a euphemism," I said. "From my generation. It means having sex."

"Oh."

"Ring any bells?"

"Of course not."

"So you never had sex with Jimmy Yamashiro?"

"What does that have to do with you or my mother?" she said. "I'm an adult."

"You never taped you and Mr. Yamashiro having sex?"

"God, no," she said. "That was a mistake. A big mistake. Please don't mention it. Please don't tell my mother. God, no. Don't tell Eric, either."

"Eric knows," I said. "When you went missing, he tried to wipe your laptop of any correspondence with Mr. Yamashiro. Including the art film of you and Yamashiro."

"You know this is an invasion of privacy?" she said. "My computer? Where is it? Who has it?"

"I have it."

"I want it back."

I nodded. She stood up for a second time, the black coat hitting her at the knees. Susan would be the first to tell me that I wasn't an expert on women's fashion, but Gabby Leggett looked very hastily dressed. No makeup, hair that looked as if it had been chopped by dull scissors, and someone else's coat thrown over her dress. Even her shoes looked off: dirty suede ballerina slippers at a formal cocktail party.

"Do you know anyone who might want to extort Mr. Yamashiro?"

"No."

"Was your relationship with him consensual?"

She shook her head, swallowing. Gabby Leggett started to cry, but then just as quickly stopped herself, wiping her eyes. She looked hard at me and shook her head as she ground her teeth. "I was used up and humiliated by that man," she said. "I was promised things that didn't and never will happen. There's too much to that story that I don't have time to answer. And never want to answer. But no, it was not consensual. And without HELIOS, I wouldn't have made it out alive."

I nodded. The guests around the pool began a slow trodding walk back inside the brightly lit mansion. Inside, I heard the strings of the violins break into a rousing rendition of "Happy Birthday." There was a lot of clapping and the murmured voice of Joe Haldorn starting to speak.

"He's a very great man."

"So you've said."

"So everyone says."

"And Jimmy Yamashiro?"

"Isn't even human," she said. "He tried to destroy me."

"And again, you are okay?" I said. "Just for the record."

Jem Yoon walked up to us. She looked from me to Gabby Leggett and Gabby didn't seem to even notice. We stood there all together by the dim light of the reflecting pool. A brisk wind crossed the garden and sent more flower petals into the water.

"I am more than okay," Gabby said. "I am whole."

She sauntered up the steps and handed her coat to Nancy Sharp, who stood by the door, waiting. Gabby's bare back in a black cocktail dress looked as if it had been constructed of toothpicks. Her neck as thin as a bird's.

"I guess that's it," Jem Yoon said.

"Did they ask you for money?"

"Funny enough," she said. "They did."

"And what did you say?"

"I said I'd like to know a lot more about HELIOS."

"Me and you both."

We walked up the steps together and into the great and very old room. Brushy-bearded Joe Haldorn stood at the marble staircase, talking about the power of forgiveness and the need to accept trauma as our own personal doing. Gabby Leggett beamed as he spoke, clapping hard, tears streaming down her gaunt face.

29

"As any therapist would ask, can you please tell me what the fuck is going on?" Susan Silverman said.

"Pardon me?" I said.

"Does my direct language offend you?"

"I'm clutching my pearls as you speak."

It was the next morning and I'd ordered room service for breakfast. I hadn't even lifted the silver plate cover from my omelet when my phone started to buzz. Outside my tenth-story window, the sun rose high over the Hollywood hills without a cloud in sight.

"I was about to have breakfast," I said. "After that, tie up some loose ends. Maybe check out the La Brea Tar Pits."

"I just got off the phone with Amanda Leggett," she said. "Gabby finally called her this morning."

"Wonderful."

"Not so wonderful," Susan said. "Amanda is more

scared than ever. She told me she couldn't believe this was her daughter saying these crazy things. Gabby said her relationship with her family has been toxic and stifling. Even abusive, which I don't believe to be true. Gabby was furious that her mother had hired you and said you'd made a big scene and embarrassed some very prominent people."

"Pissing off so-called prominent people is my specialty."

"Who the hell are these HELIOS people?" Susan said. "I looked them up but couldn't get past all the feel-good doublespeak and general bullshit. Tapping deep into unexplored parts of the brain? Every page written with all the emotional depth of a greeting card."

"HELIOS is a multinational executive success program," I said, remembering what I'd read in the pamphlets. "They offer a proven system to maximize your full potential through time-tested psychological techniques."

"Okay," Susan said. "And what the fuck does that exactly mean?"

"I have no idea."

"Neither do I," she said. "And I'm a goddamn shrink."

"I read they know how to hack into the human brain to unbridle the mind and offer untapped resources."

"I'll alert my professors at Harvard," Susan said. "I'm sure they'll be thrilled with the breakthroughs."

Holding the cell between my shoulder and ear, I poured some coffee, added a sugar, and took a seat in a little grouping by the window. I could look down onto Highland at Z's office and beyond into downtown Los Angeles coated in fine morning haze.

"From the little I understand, Gabby was recruited into HELIOS by a woman named Nancy Sharp," I said.

"The woman with the dogs."

"I know," I said. "I thought you could always trust a dog person. Not to mention she came on to me. At least we know she has excellent taste."

"In dogs?" she said. "Or men?"

"Is there a difference?"

"So Nancy recruited her into this HELIOS thingy—"

"She said Gabby had quit working for her but came back after a bad time of it with Jimmy Yamashiro," I said. "Gabby confirmed all this last night when we spoke. She all but said Yamashiro used her for a while and tossed her aside. After she joined the group, Gabby said it transformed her life. And now it seems she has become enamored with a man named Joseph Haldorn."

"I know who he is," Susan said. "The golden boy with the bushy beard and the crazy pale blue eyes. And I also saw he has zero training or experience in psychology. Did he happen to mention to you how he's mastered the understanding of the human brain?"

"My time with the master was brief."

"Is that what they call him?" she said. "The master?"

"No," I said. "I made that part up. Thought it seemed to go with the program."

"And your time with Gabby?"

"Also brief," I said. "To the point, she said her life was in the dumpster before being rescued by the HELIOS method."

"Did she say where she'd been?"

"At a retreat," I said. "But she wouldn't say where."

"With Haldorn?"

"I don't know."

"And why the hell would she not let anyone know?" she said. "And why would some local thugs try to get you to quit looking?"

"I don't know."

"And why would someone trash her apartment?"

"I don't know."

"And why would some sleazy Hollywood mogul say Gabby was blackmailing him if she said she never did?"

"These are all very good questions, Suze," I said. I stood up and walked over to my breakfast, lifting the silver plate cover. A Western omelet with home fries was still warm. "Does Amanda Leggett wish to keep me on the pad until I find the answers?"

"You bet your ass," Susan said. "Amanda told Gabby that she wanted to fly out and see her, but Gabby refuses to see her or talk with her. I think Amanda is coming out anyway."

"Can you talk her out of it?" I said. "At this point, it would only complicate matters."

"I can try," she said. "Where will you go next?"

"We know Gabby is alive, but we don't know she's safe," I said. "Last night, she looked like a nervous wreck. She was also very thin. Not L.A. thin, but thin to the point of looking malnourished."

"Do you think she might have been held against her will?"

"I do."

"Do you think they produced her to get you to leave them alone and shoo you back to Boston?"

"Absolutely."

"To hell with these people," Susan said. "I can make some inquiries on my end with some professors and therapists I know in Southern California."

"And for me, starts the long and very unsexy part of my profession."

"There is an unsexy part of your profession?"

"*Shh,*" I said. "Don't tell anyone."

"The records trail."

"Yep."

"Good luck," Susan said. "Is there anything else I can do?"

I gave her several ideas of what I'd like when I return home. She listened very thoughtfully and patiently and paused after I finished. I was very detailed in the description. "That's a tall order," she said. "Glad I'm both in shape and an experienced yogi."

"I wouldn't have suggested it otherwise."

"And what do I get in return?"

"Answers," I said. "I hope."

"For what you just asked for?" she said. "You better bring Gabby home safe."

I'd stepped out of the Loews lobby to the roundabout when a large black sedan wheeled beside me, a side window sliding down ever so slowly. It was an extra-large Cadillac with very shiny silver wheels that showed my elongated reflection in the rims. I liked it. It made me look svelte.

"Get in," a man said.

I peered in. It was Jimmy Yamashiro's right-hand man. The guy with the leathery skin and the crew cut. He kept his eyes straight ahead on the driveway.

"Sorry," I said. "My mother warned me against getting into cars with strangers."

"Christ," he said. "Would you quit yanking my goddamn chain, Spenser?"

The passenger window slid down and Yamashiro himself appeared. He waved me over and also requested that I get in the extra-large car. He had on a dark suit with a white shirt. Dark sunglasses covered his black eyes.

"I don't see any puppies or candy," I said. "Gee, guys. I don't know if this is such a good idea."

"Money," Yamashiro said. "We need to talk money."

Yamashiro had my attention. I walked around back of the black Cadillac and opened the passenger door. The grizzled driver/bodyguard took off, jostling me back into the plush seats as I turned to Yamashiro. The inside of the car was all black leather and shiny chrome. A small flat-screen television hung from the ceiling, showing the local TV news. Smiling L.A. TV types chattered on about the wonderful weather they'd been having. More expected.

"You found Miss Leggett alive?" Yamashiro said.

I nodded. The car headed up Highland and turned on Franklin, driving fast and running parallel to the 101.

"And no harm had been done to her," he said.

"That's debatable."

"I heard from her as well," he said. "And you need to know any concerns I had earlier have been rectified."

"She's no longer blackmailing you?"

"Like I said, Gabby is a very high-strung, passionate woman," Yamashiro said. "Some statements were made in the heat of the moment. I just want to make sure that you don't leave this situation still concerned with my private affairs."

In the console were six neatly aligned bottles of spring water set in cup holders glowing with blue light. I took one and unscrewed the cap. The water promised to have come from an Alaskan glacier but still tasted like tap to me.

"You know she is involved with HELIOS?"

"What's HELIOS?" he said.

"Really?" I said.

Yamashiro pulled off his sunglasses and tucked them into the inside pocket of his suit jacket. He pinched his nose and closed his tired and bloodshot eyes.

"Again, Mr. Spenser, these are personal matters," he said. "Surely Gabby's quest for self-discovery has no bearing on your work. And finding that she is indeed alive and well should conclude your services to her family."

"You would think so," I said.

"But that's not the case?"

"Nope," I said. "I'm on my own mission of discovery. What do you know about HELIOS?"

"I know Joseph Haldorn is very well respected," he said. "And he's done a great deal of good for many women in the industry. I heard you made a real ass of yourself at his birthday party."

"I was supposed to pop out of a cake but got so damn excited, I ended up knocking a couple of his men into the crudités."

"Yes," he said. "I heard all about it."

"Not to be rude," I said. "But when you enticed me into the backseat of your car, you said something about money."

His face lit up, feeling himself back in comfortable territory discussing finances. "I want you to be paid for your time."

"A payoff," I said. "How old-fashioned, Jimmy."

"Not a payoff," he said. "A compensation for your time

out here. You became entangled in my personal life and I want to make sure you don't leave with a bad taste in your mouth."

"Are you offering me cash," I said. "Or Listerine?"

Yamashiro pinched the bridge of his nose a second time. I could smell booze on his breath. Scotch. He looked like he'd had quite a bit of it the night before. His suit jacket was rumpled and there was the faint trace of lipstick on his collar. I was relieved he had such a modern and mature arrangement with Mrs. Yamashiro.

He reached into a leather pocket by the door and extracted a white envelope. He handed it over to me, the envelope feeling as thick and heavy as a paperback of *War and Peace*.

"Are we good?" he said.

I opened the envelope and flicked through a great deal of hundred-dollar bills. I lifted my eyes to him as we headed like a bat out of hell toward Fairfax.

"You didn't answer my question," I said.

"Which is?"

"Is Gabby Leggett still blackmailing you?" I said. "Or did you come to a financial arrangement with her? Or with her people at HELIOS?"

"That's none of your concern."

"That's the entirety of my concern."

Jimmy Yamashiro gave me a long, hard stare, the kind that would strike fear in the hearts of ambitious producers and coffee-fetchers alike. As I lifted the water to my lips, I tried to make sure my hands remained steady. The water still tasted like tap but was very cold.

"Are we going somewhere?" I said, looking to the driver's eyes in the rearview. "Or are you just taking me for a ride?"

"I want your word," Yamashiro said. "That you're done."

"Nope."

"Is the money not sufficient?"

"If it ever got out that I took payoffs to lay off a case, I'd no longer have any cases."

"This is between you and me," he said. "Harvey can drive you to the airport."

"Harvey?" I said. "Damn, that's funny. He doesn't look like a Harvey."

"And what does a Harvey look like?"

"A six-foot-tall rabbit," I said. "Loves martinis."

I could tell Jimmy Yamashiro, major movie studio CEO, had absolutely no idea what I was talking about. God help us. It was nearly enough to get me to stop believing in the magic of Hollywood.

"So, do we have a deal?"

I tossed the heavy package of money in the space between us. "The answer is no."

"Harvey," he said. "Take Spenser back to his hotel."

"Why do you care if I look into HELIOS?" I said. "Or if I find out if Gabby Leggett was trying to shake you down? Something, for the record, she denies."

"Just walk away, Spenser," he said. "It's best for everyone."

"For Gabby?"

"For everyone."

Harvey made a grand, sweeping U-turn at Fairfax and headed back from where we came on Highland. We drove at a brisk pace under a highway overpass. The interior of the car was thrown in and out of shadow like the flickering of a black-and-white film.

"All is fair in love and career moves in Tinseltown."

"What does that matter?" he said. "Why would you even say something so ridiculous? She was a beautiful girl. I am a rich and powerful man. We had an arrangement. We both had needs. It worked for several months just fine."

"I think it would matter why you'd be willing to let such an indiscretion go."

Yamashiro swallowed. He reached into his suit pocket for his eyeglasses. Traffic gathered at the stoplight, and as we sat there, I could hear his slow and ragged breathing. He wet his lips and nodded ever so slightly. The traffic started to flow and Harvey made a hard left turn back to my hotel.

"Please don't speak to me, Mr. Spenser," he said. "Or contact me ever again."

"And here I was thinking this was the start of a beautiful friendship," I said.

Again, my words didn't resonate with Yamashiro. So much for the classics.

31

Two empty coffee cups and a half-eaten box of donuts sat on Zebulon Sixkill's desk. They nestled in nicely along with various downloaded civil suits against Joseph Haldorn, a few Google maps of his properties, and several printouts of background checks from LexisNexis. After my joyride with Harvey and Jimmy Yamashiro, I'd crossed the street and walked upstairs to Z's office. For more than three hours, we'd perused online records and newspaper stories. The information was voluminous and not surprising.

"So Haldorn is a complete fraud and a phony," Z said.

"Which makes him what in L.A.?" I said.

"Highly respected."

I saluted him with my fresh cup of coffee and debated whether to take on the second half of the old-fashioned donut laying on a napkin. I had been told all Californians embraced a healthy lifestyle. And yet I hadn't so much as tried a kale smoothie.

"Used-car salesman, president of a failed multilevel marketing company," I said. "No college education we can find. No experience in business, philosophy, or psychology. He's really worked his way up the self-help ladder. A man from nowhere now rubbing shoulders with the Hollywood elite."

"Not exactly nowhere," Z said. "I found a registration to a 2000 Dodge Neon and a mortgage back in Chesterfield, Missouri. Not to mention three ex-wives. Trying to track them down now."

"Not exactly a man of mystery," I said. "How about HELIOS? And Haldorn's right-hand woman, Riese?"

"Unlike Haldorn, she actually does have a Ph.D. from Stanford in psychology."

"Good thing shrinks can't resist me."

"Perhaps they see a man in need."

"I thought it was my broad shoulders and quick wit."

Z offered me a dubious glance and leaned back into a large leather office chair. He spun from side to side like the captain of an intergalactic starship. Scattered across his desk were several photos of Gabby Leggett in varying states of undress.

Z shuffled through the photos, choosing one carefully and laying it above Haldorn's many bankruptcies and lawsuits. It was a close shot of Gabby Leggett's face: the wide, catlike eyes, pert nose, and full mouth. Her tongue was touching the top of her upper lip. Her hair was blond, lustrous, and shiny, falling against shapely freckled shoulders.

"Funny," Z said. "I leave L.A. to destroy myself in Boston. And Gabby Leggett leaves Boston to destroy herself in L.A."

"Only you put yourself back together."

"With some help," he said. "And it took some time."

"You think she's redeemable?" I said.

"Isn't everyone?"

"Nope," I said. "Not everyone."

"Some people do things that put them past that point."

"When we first met, you thought you had," I said. "You'd quit believing in yourself."

"Yeah," Z said, standing. His left arm hanging tight in the sling across his broad chest. He moved to a tall bookshelf and pulled a football helmet out from among the books, holding it by the battered face mask. "I guess it depends on the company you keep."

"Joe Haldorn promises mental and spiritual self-improvement," I said.

"Back on the Rez, when I was a kid, there was a man who called himself White Elk. He sold trinkets and potions to tourists. And although an outsider, he promised he was raising money for a community center for the kids. We believed him. I thought there would be a rec center with basketball courts and a gym. But one day, White Elk just disappeared. And all the money."

"White Elk?" I said.

"I know," Z said. "But some of the elders vouched for him. They said his mother was full Cree. But he'd paid them off to say that. No one cared he was phony. We all wanted to believe in what he promised."

Z was a little taller than me and had a lot more muscle. His black hair was pushed back from his wide, flat face. The scars, although obtained in violence, offered him a lot of character, making him seem older than in his mid-thirties. A photo of him barreling through the offensive line for a touchdown hung above his California state license.

"You've done very well," I said.

Z looked around the spare, cluttered office on the second floor of a strip mall and smiled. "Living the dream," he said.

"Accept it," I said. "You've built a new life. Through hard work and talent. That's nothing to scoff at."

"I don't know how you've done it all these years," he said. "I've spent all morning downloading court records and files and not finding a damn thing to help us. The only interesting details come from a blog that attacks the HELIOS philosophy and teaching. I tried to find out more, but there isn't any contact information or details of who runs it."

"Could Jem Yoon find out?"

"Maybe," he said. "The blog hasn't been updated in a few months. The last entry had kind of a rambling message about pressure from attorneys that worked for HELIOS. Whoever runs it wants to keep their name a secret."

"Print out what you've got?"

"They don't get much into the teaching or the philosophy," he said. "Mainly the blog accuses HELIOS of being a multilevel marketing scam."

"Sort of a self-help Amway?"

"Members are called Hyperions," Z said. "Each Hyperion must bring in at least five members to serve and train under them. Those members must bring in five of their own recruits, and so on and so on."

"Like Fabergé shampoo."

"If you say so."

"It's kept my locks bouncy and smelling great for years," I said. "You should try it."

The printer hummed to life and started spitting out pages. Z stood up, grabbed the papers, and handed them to me.

"Call me if you and Team Sixkill find something."

"Where are you going?"

"Working out," I said. "Might grab a bite to eat. That's the joy of having an apprentice."

"You want me to do your work for you?"

"Nope," I said. "I want Jem Yoon to do your work and for you to do my work and so on and so on."

"Like the shampoo."

"Super shine, super body," I said. "And my hair smells as fresh as a meadow."

"Gabby is still in trouble."

"Yep."

"And Haldorn may be worse than Yamashiro?"

"I think they may be equally reprehensible."

"Men like them don't do men like us any favors."

"No," I said. "They don't."

He picked up his phone and pressed the button for Jem Yoon. I spotted her contact photo with the bright pink hair. "Behind every great detective is a smart woman who locates a key clue."

I smiled and shot him with my thumb and forefinger. "Couldn't have said it better myself."

32

Twenty minutes later, Jem Yoon found a name, two addresses, and four phone numbers for a thirty-five-year-old white male named Lee Abrams. My workout and lunch would wait. Both addresses were in Santa Monica. On the fourth phone number, a man picked up.

"Mr. Abrams?"

"Who the hell is this?"

I told him.

"And what the hell do you want?"

"To talk to you about charisma," I said. "You seem to have a lot of natural talent."

"Fuck you, man."

I then told him more about my profession, why I was in the greater Los Angeles area, and what I hoped to learn about HELIOS.

"I have no fucking idea what you're talking about."

I then repeated a bit of the information Jem Yoon had passed on to me about IP addresses, geolocators, and the name and brand of his laptop computer.

"Oh," he said.

"See," I said. "What do you have to lose?"

"How about my life?" he said.

And hung up.

I called back twice. No answer. I called back a third time. He picked up.

"Come on, man," he said. "You're going to get me fucking killed."

"How about you meet with me live and in person and decide for yourself if I'm sincere," I said. "I'm good on the phone. But a real charmer in person."

"Okay, sure," he said. "You drive up in a black van, snatch me up, and my parents get a nice phone call in a few weeks. 'Gee, Mr. and Mrs. Abrams, we found your son in a dumpster. How might you pay for shipping?'"

"We make it public," I said. "Choose a location where I can meet you without a black van in sight. That's how they do it in the movies. It keeps everyone honest."

"I don't know."

"Come on, Lee," I said. "I don't like these HELIOS people any more than you do. Your blog is the best information I've found."

"Really?"

"Absolutely," I said. "You're the Hedda Hopper of California cults."

"You think HELIOS is a cult?" he said.

"Indeed I do, Lee."

He agreed to meet with me later that afternoon at the Santa Monica Pier. I decided I was a big boy and didn't need the assistance of Sixkill or Chollo to shadow me. I figured I could make it safe and sound onto the pier to stand toe-to-toe with a dangerous blogger like Lee Abrams.

At a little before six, I found a parking deck on Second Street and headed for the pier. I had on jeans, boots, and a spiffy navy T-shirt with a convenient pocket to hold my Ray-Bans. I put on the sunglasses, ball cap down in my eyes, and walked with the crowd toward the smell of churros, saltwater, and weed.

The big wooden pier jutted out far into the Pacific, crowded with shops and restaurants on one side, culminating in an amusement park with its iconic Ferris wheel. I made it about halfway through the throngs of tourists and onlookers, past the monks in flowing robes selling meditation books, the James Brown cover band offering a funk gospel to the masses, and down toward the agreed meeting spot: Pier Burger.

I had given Lee Abrams my description. He did not reciprocate.

I waited for nearly twenty minutes past our meeting time, without luck. The sun was getting lower and people gathered at the pier railing to watch the surfers paddle into the oncoming waves. A woman in a pink string bikini roller-skated past me. A man wearing jeans, a Hawaiian shirt, and a costume bear head gazed wistfully into the sunset. *Ah, California.*

Among those gathered to watch the cover band, a skinny, loose-jointed man with matted black hair kept peering over at me. He was medium height and scruffy, wearing a black T-shirt two sizes too big with ragged jeans and black Chuck Taylor high-tops. The shoelaces hung out, dirty and untied.

I leaned against an outdoor table at Pier Burger, watching him behind sunglasses while pretending not to watch him. My furtive abilities often staggered me.

After a while, I watched him hitch a backpack up over his shoulder and walk toward the restaurant. I patiently waited as he ordered something at the window, meandered a bit until his number was called, and then set his tray down two tables over.

"I would've bought you a burger," I said.

"Shit," he said. He stood and reached down for his backpack.

"Sit down," I said. "I didn't mean to spook you. Don't you want fries with that?"

"I ordered so fast I forgot."

"Hold on."

I walked up to the window, ordered a Pier Burger for myself and two orders of fries. I sat back down with Lee Abrams while I waited for my food. Several pigeons had gathered. He shooed them away, and they fluttered up into the air, only to return moments later.

"Persistent," I said.

"Flying rats," he said.

"I would assume if you met me that you checked me out."

He took a larger mouthful of hamburger than necessary and chewed, a thick wad in his right cheek. He was so skinny he appeared to not have eaten in days. His eyes darted up and down the pier as he ate.

"And you realize my questions about HELIOS are legit."

He nodded some more and put down the burger. My number was called, and I quickly returned with a heavy tray. The flock of pigeons had doubled in number.

"They like fries," he said.

"Wish I had my dog with me," I said. "She's a pro at scaring off the competition."

Abrams ate some more, polishing off the burger and wiping his mouth with a napkin. He looked directly at me and said, "Everything I read about you was in Boston," he said. "Why the hell are you out here?"

I told him about Gabby Leggett.

"I don't know her," he said. "Haven't heard the name. But that sounds about right for HELIOS. Haldorn likes them young, blond, and beautiful. If they have money, so much the better. Does Gabby Leggett have money?"

"Some," I said. "But not the kind of money you mean."

"I got onto those people a couple of years ago," he said. "I write sometimes for a free newspaper in Venice. There was a woman who called in to our offices one day and told this wild story about her daughter, a decently known TV actress, being abducted into a cult."

"And you were a bit dubious?"

"At first," he said. "Sure. I met with her and we had coffee and the whole thing sounded like pretty wacky stuff. I'll let her tell you more if you meet her, but at some point, all of this stuff starts making sense."

"What's her name?"

"The daughter is Bailee Scott."

Before taking a bite of the burger, I offered an elegant shrug.

"*The Totally Awesome Cami*?"

"Sorry," I said. "My TV only gets ESPN and Turner Classic Movies."

"You didn't miss much," he said. "It was a show on the Disney Channel a few years ago. Bailee played a teenage girl with secret superpowers. It's mainly about her balancing school, boys, friends, and fighting crime."

"I often have to balance my love life with fighting crime," I said. I pushed the untouched french fries over to him. "It's not an easy task."

He selected one and took a bite.

"And where is Bailee now?"

"Dead," he said.

I looked at Abrams as he chewed. He stared back at me, swallowed, and nodded.

"When?"

"Little over a year ago," he said. "It was ruled an overdose. Her family thinks different. From what I understand, Bailee had gotten pretty high up in HELIOS. Right below the woman who helped him start the whole thing."

"The psychologist?" I said. "Riese?"

"Exactly," he said. "I'm impressed. You know more about these people than you think."

"I've met her daughter," I said. "And I read your blog. All of it. So you believe it's a front to make money?"

"Yep."

"Are these people dangerous?" I said. "I believe they may be working with a crew of local thugs who afford protection for Haldorn."

"I don't know anything about that," he said. "But I do know Haldorn is a certifiable and dangerous nut."

"Is that why you haven't gone public?"

"I published a piece two years ago, and we got sued for ten million dollars," he said. "The legal fees bankrupted the paper. Other people who've tried to do the same get scared off from telling the truth. I don't know how, but Haldorn has unlimited legal resources to shut down anyone who speaks out against HELIOS."

"Can I meet your source?" I said. "Bailee Scott's mother?"

I took another fry and tossed it onto the ground. A dozen or more pigeons fluttered onto it and flew off with it onto the boardwalk. One of the workers from Pier Burger came out with a broom and scattered the rest as I finished the burger.

"She'll talk," he said. "She loves to talk."

"I love to listen."

"The only problem will be shutting her up," Abrams said. "And some of what she says is a little out there. She believes the whole thing is some kind of sex cult. She says she has proof that Haldorn is grooming his own private harem. I think Haldorn is a fake and a phony, and greedy as hell. But I'm not sure about the stranger stories I've heard about HELIOS. They're all so damn private, and their former members flat-out won't speak to me. It's very, very difficult to know what goes on beyond those empowerment seminars."

"What's Bailee's mom's name?"

"Charlotte," he said. "She was an actress, too. Lot of B movies. Stuff you'd see late at night on Skinemax. She was Miss July sometime back in the eighties. Really beautiful and sweet woman. But this thing with Bailee, it's consumed her. Her whole house is like some kind of war room to take down HELIOS."

I nodded. When I looked up, the pigeons had returned, eyeing the remnants of burgers and fries. I admired their persistence.

"War room sounds interesting," I said. "Where do you sign me up?"

"Venice," he said. "I'll give her a call."

"And you'll vouch for me?"

He nodded and picked up his cell.

33

Charlotte Scott lived in a small Craftsman-style house that looked as it had been constructed by Bilbo Baggins himself. It appeared original and very period, with a low-pitched roof, intricate carved brackets, and stone work, paths, and chimneys. She greeted Lee Abrams warmly at the door with a kiss on both cheeks. For me, she stood back and studied me like a stray dog that had just knocked over her trash can.

"I'm not so sure about this, Lee," Charlotte said.

"Have to trust someone," Lee said. He shuffled onto one foot and then another, hands deep in his saggy jeans.

"I don't trust anyone," she said. "Look at him. He looks like one of those goons they send to follow me around."

"They follow you?" I said.

"Don't talk to me, mister," Charlotte said. "Not until I've decided what I'm going to do."

Charlotte Scott had one eye closed and the other trained on me. She was redheaded and intense-looking, as many redheads tended to be. Her hair was long, running down her back and spilling across a very amble bosom. The latter being displayed in a white lace camisole number with acid-washed jeans. It had been a few years since I'd seen acid-washed anything.

"Does he know about Bailee?"

"Yeah," Lee said. "I told him."

"And?"

"I'm very sorry about your daughter," I said. "My client is concerned for her daughter as well."

She didn't speak, only turned and walked through the door, leaving it open. Lee Abrams shrugged and gestured me inside.

The furniture matched the home, with a grouping of Stickley chairs and wrought-iron lamps with Tiffany-glass shades. I imagined the home to be subdued and elegant at some earlier point. But it was hard to tell with the stacks of boxes and dry-erase boards set about her living room. The back doors were open, letting in a cool evening breeze that fluttered long white curtains.

"How do we know you're not one of them?" she said.

"Would you like me to recite Keats while performing a one-armed push-up?"

"I don't know what the hell that would prove," she said.

"Intelligence," I said. "Determination."

"Sure," she said. "Go for it, big-time Boston private eye."

I hit the floor with one arm behind my back while extolling the virtues of a Grecian urn. I cranked out a fast ten and then just for the hell of it went for twenty. I finished and hopped up from my knees.

"That was lovely," she said, walking toward me.

"The push-ups or the poems?"

"All of it," she said. "I like him, Lee. He has pep."

Scott was a little heavy, with tired green eyes and skin so white it seemed to lack any pigment at all.

"And you're really a private eye?" she said. "Or is that a gag to get me talking?"

I looked to Lee Abrams and he raised his shoulders and showed the palms of his hands. I reached for my wallet and showed her my license.

"He's real, Charlotte," Abrams said. "And better than that, he's willing to listen. Cops won't even do that."

"What's in it for you?" she said. "I lost my daughter to that rotten son of a bitch."

"Haldorn?" I said.

"Don't," she said. "Don't you dare say that man's name in my presence."

"If it makes any difference, I put a damper on his birthday party last night," I said. "I tossed one of his guards into a nice table of appetizers."

"It makes a difference."

She invited me into the living room and we all sat. My chair faced the wall and a six-foot-tall oil painting of a much younger and much skinnier Charlotte Scott. In the painting, she sat at the edge of an antique velvet chair and wore nothing but a pendant.

The real-life Charlotte Scott reached for a pack of Virginia Slims and fired one up. I looked from her to the painting and the painting back to her. *You've come a long way, baby.*

"It's okay to stare," she said. "You shouldn't feel bad about it. Or pervy. It's beautiful. It's fucking art."

"That's nice to hear." I worried that staring too hard at the painting was akin to looking into the bright headlights of an oncoming truck.

"Thirty years ago, I had the best set of tits in L.A.," she said. "James Caan told me that at the mansion during the Midsummer Night's Dream party. Before he told the next Playmate that. And all of them that followed. All I got out of it was five thousand bucks and an introduction to every casting couch in town. Of course, that's how I met my first husband, Rick, that unholy prick. He was a producer on a few of my movies."

"And he was Bailee's father?"

"Last month she turned twenty-nine," she said, tapping the long ash of the skinny cigarette. "So beautiful. A truckload of talent. More than anyone, I blame myself. I should've stopped her. I should've marched right into that goddamn compound, grabbed my little girl by the hand, and gotten her the hell out of there."

"I understand," I said.

"Do you?" she said. "How could you? Do you have kids, Mr. Spenser?"

"I don't have biological children," I said. "But I have

two young people I care for like my own. A boy—now a fine man—and a tough, smart young woman."

"Okay," she said. "That's something. And you'd do anything in the world for them?"

"You better believe it."

"I would've done the same for Bailee," she said. "If I'd known everything, I would've shot Haldorn right in his Johnson. Would you like to see a picture of her?"

I nodded. Charlotte Scott stood up and padded off on bare feet to the kitchen and returned with a studio head shot. Bailee Scott had been a doe-eyed girl with a lot of big, bouncy blond hair caught in a glossy frame. The photo said Bailee Scott, *The Totally Awesome Cami.*

"That was the good old days," she said. "Before she accused me of stealing her residuals and ruining her life. All of that junk started as soon as she got in with those HE-LIOS people."

"How did she find HELIOS?" I said. "Or did they find her?"

Lee Abrams leaned forward in his seat and rubbed his hands together. His right knee shot up and down with nervous energy as he looked from me to Charlotte Scott. He'd thrown on a threadbare flannel shirt over his black T-shirt. The material so worn it looked like cheesecloth. His face was gaunt, bony, and hard as he rubbed his unshaven jaw.

"One of the actors on her show recruited her," she said. "I didn't think much of it at first. Why would I? They called themselves an executive training course and this was like three, four years after they canceled her show.

She talked about them helping harness her talent to direct, maybe produce. It all sounded fine and positive up to the point I noticed she was writing checks. A shit-ton of checks to those people."

"How much?"

"Last I knew, it was nearly a hundred grand," she said.

Charlotte stubbed out the cigarette and started a new one. A warm breeze blew through the open doors, which overlooked a curated rock garden. The air smelled salty and warm. She'd lit several candles that had been placed around the room and within the stone fireplace.

"The more questions I asked, the more defiant she got. She finally moved out and in with those creeps. I knew from the moment she talked about Phaethon this and Phaethon that."

"Wait," I said, holding up my palm. "Who or what is a Phaethon?"

"Fucking Haldorn," she said. "Fucking Joseph Haldorn only goes by Phaethon to his HELIOS people. They aren't allowed to call him anything else. He may look like a stumblebum with the brushy beard and the long hair, but behind those walls and among his HELIOS jeepers creepers, he is Phaethon. *Numero Uno*. He wears a goddamn white robe, sandals, the works. Jesus Christ Superstar."

"But can he turn water into wine?"

"No," she said, blowing out some smoke. "But he can turn bullshit into money. A lot of goddamn money."

"I was hoping you could explain a little more how that worked."

"You've got to understand, everything they do there, everything the member is supposed to achieve, is about getting closer to Phaethon," she said. "You work your way up the ladder, paying out the fucking nose, and recruiting anyone who will listen, until you get into the inner circle."

"How far did Bailee get?" I said.

Charlotte took out the cigarette and looked to Lee and back to me. She didn't speak but only held up three fingers. I looked to Lee Abrams and he nodded.

"If you don't mind me asking," I said. "How did she die?"

Charlotte got up again and walked back to the open kitchen and returned with a very large box. She placed it on top of the coffee table and slid it toward me. "There," she said. "There you go. That's all that's left of my little girl. Autopsy results. Coroner's inquest. Letters from medical experts from all over the country. According to L.A. County, Bailee died of a drug overdose. But that's absolute bullshit. My daughter may have been naïve, she may have followed the wrong people, but she didn't take drugs. Somebody shot her up with heroin and left her for dead."

I looked to her. I didn't say a word.

"That's what happens when you try to leave," she said. "I have four different medical examiners that spotted signs of restraint and starvation and dehydration. Haldorn and HELIOS kept her locked up tight for nearly two months before they decided to kill her. My whole life now is about trying to get someone, anyone, to fucking listen to me."

I reached for the box, flipped through the file headers. I noticed one labeled BRANDED. I slipped out the file and flipped through several 8x10 photos of a crude-looking scar that resembled the sun. I looked over at Lee Abrams and then over at Charlotte Scott.

"Haldorn's signature," Scott said.

"Does he brand all of them?" I said.

"Only the special ones," she said. She blew smoke from her nose.

"Why?"

"Why does anyone brand anything?" she said. "To prove ownership."

I held the photo in my hand. "Can I take these?"

"No," she said. "But you can copy what you like."

I reached for my cell phone and began to select a few files.

"It won't matter," she said. "Nothing matters to the prosecutors or the cops. They don't believe you. They'll think you're crazy and not hear a word you're saying."

"I can be very persuasive."

"It's gonna take a lot more than that and one-armed push-ups, stud," she said. "To take down Haldorn and HELIOS, you'll need a goddamn army."

34

Traveling the twelve miles from Venice to Hollywood took me an hour and a half.

At the hotel, I debated whether a beer or a workout would put me in a brighter mood. I opted for both. I did forty-five minutes on the treadmill with a quick circuit on the machines and then headed up to my room to shower. I planned to meet Z later for dinner, to trade information on what we'd learned that day.

I changed into a fresh pair of dark green chinos and a black polo and took the elevator back to the Loews lobby. As I saddled up to the bar, I found out my lodging wasn't a well-kept secret. Nancy Sharp was waiting for me, perched atop a barstool and enjoying an extra-large martini with several olives.

"What are the chances?" I said.

"Pretty good," she said. "I've been waiting for you for

over an hour. I was worried you'd left a back way without your car."

"You have people watching me."

"Or maybe just me."

My eyes darted around the lobby as she took a sip of the martini and grinned. Sharp looked nice. Nicer than I'd ever seen her, in a black silk top with small straps over her shapely shoulders. Her silver hair complemented her tan skin and crinkly hazel eyes. Her legs looked long and strong in a pair of expensive jeans, and her arms reflected a woman who worked out. Or did a lot of yoga.

"You went to a lot of trouble," I said. "All you had to do is call."

"Would you have met with me?"

"Sure," I said. "After speaking with Gabby, I'm more committed than ever to joining HELIOS. I want to be the best investigator that I can possibly be. Use those untapped portions of my brain."

"You don't have to be snippy," she said. "This isn't about HELIOS. I felt bad about the other night. I wanted to offer you an apology."

"From the Phaethon?"

Her eyes remained on mine, not registering a bit of annoyance. "No," she said. "From me. I like you, Spenser. I felt we really connected the first time we met. You're smart, funny, and, let's face it, a pretty handsome specimen."

"That may be the only honest thing you've ever said."

"And we seemed to share the same passions," she said. "Good food. Good cocktails. Traveling. Dogs. I don't know. Life is short, why not take a gamble?"

"Am I on camera?" I said. I looked around. "I feel like I'm in one of those eHarmony ads. What's next, walking hand in hand on the beach? A bicycle built for two?"

"If you want," she said. She took a long sip of the drink. It hadn't been her first. Her cheeks were slightly flushed and there was a hazy, unfocused quality to her eyes. "Before you go home, I'd love to show you around Los Angeles. Perhaps have that nice dinner? There's a lovely little sushi place not far from here. We can eat at the bar and catch up."

"I told you some might take issue with that. My dog. My significant other."

She placed her hand on top of my forearm and cocked her head to stare into my eyes. From this distance, she smelled very nice. Jasmine and citrus, maybe a little like the sea. Sharp pulled the silver hair from her neck and over onto one shoulder.

"You're a long way from Boston," she said. "Who would know?"

"Me," I said. I signaled the bartender and ordered a Woodford Reserve neat with water back.

"Do I make you nervous?"

"Any moment I might start pawing at the ground with my right foot," I said. "And blowing snot from my nose."

"Can one little dinner hurt?"

I nodded. The bartender brought my bourbon. I drank half and then sipped on the water.

Sharp leaned in to me and pressed her lips against my ear. She made a bold statement about doing very bold things well into the night.

"That's incredibly nice of you, Miss Sharp," I said. "You must feel really bad."

"I feel awful." She held on to my biceps and squeezed. She asked the bartender for another martini.

"Can we discuss Gabby Leggett?" I said.

"Absolutely not."

"Phaethon?"

"What is that?" she said. But this time, she giggled and covered her mouth a bit. "I wondered what you and that nutcase Charlotte Scott talked about today."

"Eyes everywhere?"

"Everywhere," she said. "A very important man doing important things has a lot to protect. Surely you understand."

"Gabby looked sick the other night," I said. "Like she hadn't eaten for a long time."

"She'd been part of an outdoors retreat," she said. "Some retreats encourage fasting. Many of the world's best-known religions do the same thing. Christians. Jews. Muslims. Is that suddenly a bad thing?"

"I want to see Gabby again tomorrow."

"I thought you were going back to Boston."

"Nope," I said. "You're stuck with me for a while."

"For how long?"

"Until I'm convinced you are doing right for Gabby."

She shrugged, reached for the martini, and plucked out three olives on a toothpick. She bit one off with very sharp teeth and swallowed. "I could arrange another meeting," she said. "That's up to Gabby. And then only if you have dinner with me."

I began to think that perhaps dinner wasn't such a bad idea. If she got to the bottom of another martini, she might just crawl into my lap and recite "Only God Can Make a Tree" and all the top-secret HELIOS doctrines. At the least, I could understand more about Gabby Leggett's commitment. At the most, I could perhaps become the best Spenser I could be.

"I'm checking on a friend's place in Malibu," she said. "After dinner, you can go out there with me and relax a bit. It's a lovely place to watch the moon on the water. The waves crashing onto the shore. The sand between your toes. Whenever I want to put the world in perspective, I return to the sea."

"You and Captain Ahab."

"What's that?" she said. She was beginning to slur her words.

"Good captain," I said. "Terrible placekicker."

She laughed. She flipped her hair again, showing off her long, delicate neck. She tilted her eyes at me and stared for a really long time. "Don't be nervous," she said. "Tonight, I'm yours. You can do anything you want to me."

"Anything?" I said.

"Whatever you like."

My mouth felt a bit cottony. And for the lack of anything better, I finished the bourbon. Sharp's eyes looked up at someone over my shoulder and suddenly stiffened. She stood up straighter, lips parted, and took two steps back.

"I'd take her up on it," Susan Silverman said. "Anything you want? That's a kind and most generous offer."

I turned and saw Susan standing there, leather travel bag over her shoulder and a mirthful look on her face.

"You caught me just in time," I said. "I was just about to take this woman to Malibu and commit acts illegal in most states."

"But not California?" Susan said.

"Apparently not," I said. "They have very open and modern laws."

"Oh, thank God," Susan said. "Is this the psychologist?"

"No," I said. "This is the HELIOS publicist. Nancy Sharp. And Gabby Leggett's former employer."

Sharp straightened up and tried to stare down Susan Silverman. She would've had a better chance of body-slamming John Cena.

"And who the hell are you?" Sharp said.

"That's for me to know," she said, "and for you to go royally fuck yourself."

Sharp looked like she might be choking on the martini olive.

"Beat it, Grandma," Susan said. "This spot is taken."

Nancy Sharp flipped back her silvery hair and reached down for her purse. She locked eyes with me and laid down several twenties onto the bar. She tossed her purse over her shoulder and sauntered out the pneumatic doors of the hotel.

Susan slipped onto the barstool. I smiled and ordered her a vodka gimlet with Ketel One and fresh lime juice.

"How much of that did you hear?"

"Enough," Susan said. "You must really be getting to

these people. She gave you carte blanche at the ole fun factory."

"Fun factory?" I said

Susan Silverman also had a shapely body, more shapely than Nancy Sharp's, and most women's, for that matter, even those half her age. Her black hair was curly and vibrant, her dark eyes big and intelligent. She had on a thin silver necklace with a roman coin I'd bought her on a recent trip to Italy.

"Long time, Suze."

"Too long," she said. She reached under the bar and squeezed my knee. "Gabby's mother wants me to evaluate how far she's gone off-reservation."

"Understood," I said. "But tonight, there's not much we can do."

"There are a few things we can do."

"Are you also offering me carte blanche at the fun factory?"

"Drinks first," she said. "And then dinner."

"And then?"

"And then I'll think about it, sport," she said. "You have some explaining to do."

35

The next morning, we checked out of the Loews and drove straight toward the Pacific and Santa Monica, where Gabby's mother had rented us an apartment. It was big, airy, and modern, chrome and white tile, with three bedrooms and two slick bathrooms and a pool, all within spitting distance of Shutters on the Beach. An Impressionist-style painting of seagulls gliding along the shore hung over a king-sized bed in the master bedroom.

Since Susan had stayed up late and rewarded me for my recent diligence, we took a long, leisurely breakfast at a nearby restaurant called Gjusta. We sat outside at a small table in a rustic courtyard with potted plants and artfully weathered furniture. Birds chattered on a tall privacy fence and swooped down every few minutes, scouring for crumbs. I felt as if I'd entered an aviary.

I had ordered a plate of *huevos rancheros*, almond-butter toast, a kale smoothie, and black coffee. Susan had a tahini croissant and hot tea.

"Kale smoothie?" she said. She picked at the edge of her croissant, popping small bits into her mouth. "Interesting."

"What did you expect?" I said. "I've gone native."

"If I hadn't found you last night, I might have lost you to a much older woman."

"Nancy Sharp is younger than you think."

"I'll say she looked well preserved," she said. "Maybe HELIOS is even better than advertised. Good for the mind and the body."

"We both know better than that."

"Of course we do," Susan said. She added a bit of honey to her tea and stirred. "Nothing is as good as advertised."

"Nothing?" I said.

I smiled. Susan ignored me.

"So after a hearty breakfast and perhaps another session of lovemaking, I imagine we construct a plan on how to get Gabby away from that lunatic?"

"Construct plan first," she said. "Make love later, Tarzan. This will be a lot harder than you and Z storming the mansion, snatching up Gabby, and tossing her into the back of your rented Toyota."

"Must you spoil all my fun?"

"Only some of it," she said. "And if she won't be going willingly, isn't that technically kidnapping in the state of California?"

"Probably," I said, drinking a little black coffee and

tearing an edge off my toast. "If you have to be so damn technical about everything."

I threw the crumbs onto the patio for the birds. The birds swooped in and the crumbs disappeared within seconds. I was making friends everywhere I went. Pretty soon, a nice chickadee would land on my shoulder and start whistling "A Smile and a Song."

"I'd like you to arrange a meeting with Gabby," she said. "We can theorize, but exactly how deep is she?"

"From what I saw the other night?" I said. "I'm no psychologist, but I'd say she's in deeper than the Mariana Trench."

I cut into the *huevos rancheros* and the yolk spilled out onto the plate. Everything was local and very fresh. Cézanne couldn't have arranged the beans and eggs with any more precision.

"She needs someone to challenge her view of reality," Susan said. "I'd try to talk about things that anchor her back to Cambridge. Back to her mother and relationships before moving to California. This kind of mind-set always begins with detachment. A complete obliteration of the past and reality."

"I've worked similar cases but never understood it," I said. "Joseph Haldorn is neither handsome nor charismatic. He resembles a junior college philosophy instructor. Only with worse hygiene and sense of fashion."

"It's not just about Haldorn," she said. "These people have a method. They always do. They may seem nuts, but they are the absolute best at breaking down people to their most vulnerable. It's all about making their followers doubt themselves, making them reliant on those around them to make decisions."

"Okay," I said. "But what if Gabby won't see you?"

"We'll just have to insist."

"You insulted my number-one go-between at HE-LIOS," I said. "I doubt Nancy Sharp is a fan of Susan Silverman."

"I don't give a damn about that woman," Susan said. "If Gabby is really free, then she's free to make her own decisions. She's free to talk about why she disappeared for so long and how she's been treated by Haldorn and these HELIOS people."

"Any fool can make a rule, and any fool can mind it."

"Gabby's no fool," she said. "She graduated with honors from BU. Played on the volleyball club team. She was once a very tough and very smart young woman."

"California changes people," I said. "Gabby is probably a much different person than the young woman her mother knew."

"Has California changed you?" Susan said.

I picked up my kale smoothie and took a slow, deliberate sip from the straw.

"Ah," Susan said. "It's all starting to make sense."

After breakfast, we found a Whole Foods to buy some supplies for the week. I brought the groceries up to the apartment and put them away as Susan pored over the reports I'd printed at Z's office. She had her laptop cracked open and transferred notes with a quick, precise tapping.

I took my computer outside to a small balcony overlooking the pool and dug in deep with the death of Bailee

Scott. Much of the story had been reported in the *Times* and some smaller papers and blogs. I didn't learn anything new and returned back to the files Charlotte Scott had collected from other coroners offering their opinion. What bothered me most, aside from the sun-shaped brand on her left hip, was that Bailee appeared to have lost thirty pounds before her death and showed signs of dehydration. Not to mention the ligature marks on her wrists and ankles.

The same type of burns that I'd seen on Gabby's wrists at the mansion. I read over each report three times.

That night, we took a break and I removed two large portions of fresh mahi-mahi from the refrigerator. I seasoned both sides with salt and pepper while heating up the skillet on the stove. I cooked each portion for about two minutes and then placed the whole skillet in the oven for about five minutes. When they were done, I removed the fillets, set them aside, and added some premade quinoa to the skillet, topping with the mahi-mahi and some chilled mango salsa I'd made earlier. I placed the hot skillet on the table and opened a bottle of sauvignon blanc.

"Don't burn your fingers," I said.

"He cooks," she said. "He cleans. He does one-armed pushups while whistling 'God Bless America.' And by God, despite some somewhat old-fashioned views, actually likes and respects women."

"*Likes* tends to be the key."

"You don't feel threatened by strong women."

"A few times," I said. "But only when a woman was holding a gun on me."

"Why do you think that is?"

"Why I like women?" I said. I scooped out the quinoa and mahi-mahi, careful to keep the artful dab of mango salsa on top. "I think I learned to appreciate and respect women from my father and uncles. I never heard them talk of women in a disparaging way. Or talk about women as conquests. They genuinely enjoyed being around women as people, not as objects. My father rarely spoke of my mother. But when he did, it was in the most glowing terms."

"So for you it was role models?" she said. "Older men you respected?"

"Yep."

"Men who hate women often have a multitude of problems," she said. "But sometimes it's the most obvious."

"Such as?"

Susan raised her hand and crooked her pinkie finger up at me.

"Ah," I said. "You spent how many years training at Harvard and your hypothesis about toxic masculinity boils down to one little thing?"

"A very little thing."

I attended to my own plate, adding a little bit more quinoa and some salsa onto the fish. I poured the wine, sat down, and waited for Susan to take the first bite. If we had Pearl with us, staring up with big adoring eyes, it would nearly feel like home.

I ate for a bit and then took a long swig of wine. "Just to let you know, I'm healthy and confident in my appreciation of women."

Susan laughed, nearly snorting some wine out her nose.

"Haldorn, on the other hand, isn't going to let Gabby go," I said. "Or come to a sudden epiphany about what he's been doing."

"I know," Susan said.

"At some point, you'll have to let me and Z do our thing so that you might do yours."

"Even if you have to break the law?" she said.

"I've been known to do that once or twice," I said. "For the right cause."

"You believe what happened to Bailee Scott might end up happening to Gabby?"

I nodded. Susan thought about it and nodded, too. After dinner, she washed the dishes and set them on a wooden drying rack. We helped ourselves to the last of the bottle and stood out on the balcony, looking down at the small swimming pool, brightly lit from below. The tall palm trees swayed in the ocean wind.

The wind was warm, pleasant, and alluring, but we were far from home. Susan's bare feet rested on the edge of the railing as she sipped her wine.

"What do you think?" I said.

"Do what you need to do."

36

At about midnight, my phone buzzed. It was from a 301 area code, but a number I did not recognize.

"Is this Spenser?" a man said.

"You've reached the voicemail of Hopalong Cassidy and his wonder horse, Topper."

"Quit dicking around," the man said. "This is Miller."

"And who is Miller?"

"Harvey Miller," he said. "I work for Mr. Yamashiro. You know? Harvey the fucking rabbit? We met at the studio and at his place. You know who this is."

"Ah," I said. "Crew Cut."

"What's that?"

I reached for my watch on the nightstand. I was almost right, seeing it was nearly one a.m. Susan shuffled naked under a thin white sheet, the moonlight shining across her black hair and bare shoulders.

"We have a situation," he said. "And I could use some help."

"It's way past midnight and I'm in deep slumber with my significant other," I said. "Can't the situation wait until morning?"

"Not this," he said. "Mr. Yamashiro is missing and I was hoping you could help me find him."

"Why me?"

"Because I think he went to find that little piece of tail," he said. "Gabby Fucking Leggett."

I got dressed and headed back toward the city.

Traffic wasn't a problem at one a.m. I met Miller back in Hollywood, outside Z's office. I left my rental and crawled in the front seat of the Lincoln. His windows were cracked and he was smoking a cigarette. "Took you long enough," he said. His silver hair was barbered into geometrical precision.

"I would've flown, but I left my cape back in Boston."

"Christ," he said, flicking the nub of a cigarette out the window and starting a new one. "I don't know where the fuck Jimmy went. I heard his car start and watched him drive off outside my window. I called him three times. The third time he picked up and said he had important business and not to bother him. When I asked him if this had something to do with the girl, he just hung up on me."

"Gallant," I said.

"Stupid," Miller said, trying to blow smoke outside the window. The wind cast it back into the car. From where we parked, I watched two men enter the all-night massage parlor for what I assumed were therapeutic reasons. A crick in the neck. Misaligned vertebrae. A big upcoming playoff game. The bright red-and-green neon in the window buzzed in the darkness along Highland.

"Did he mention any of this to you?"

"Nope," he said. "None. What about the chick? I thought she denied she was trying to shake Jimmy down."

"That's what she told me."

"That's bullshit," he said. "I knew her before she joined up with that freak show. She was just another dumb party girl. Cooze and cocktails. Another skirt for Jimmy to chase until he got bored. Did you ever see the tape?"

"I did."

"Tell me this, Spenser," he said. "Man to man. Did that girl look like an unwilling participant?"

"Not at that exact moment," I said. "She looked like a jockey riding the Triple Crown to the winner's circle. All that Yamashiro lacked was a saddle and a bit."

"That's the way Jimmy liked 'em," he said. "Big and strong. Won't date a girl unless she's taller than him and can make him feel weak. What the hell's that about?"

"Let's find him and ask him."

"How the fuck are we supposed to find a man that doesn't want to be found in a city of four million?"

"The old-fashioned way," I said.

"Drive around and look for his red Mercedes coupe?"

"Nope," I said. "You give me his phone number and I'll call a friend who can track down his cell phone within a quarter of a mile."

"Bullshit."

"You would think," I said. "But you'd be wrong. We

may be the same age, but I'm the very model of a modern major PI. The only reason I couldn't use it on Gabby is that she'd turned off the phone. If Yamashiro has his with him and it's on, we'll find him."

Miller gave me his number and I called Jem Yoon. She was less than pleased to hear from me at the witching hour and told me it was going to cost me double. Since I didn't know what the daylight rate was and figured on charging Yamashiro anyway, I happily agreed.

Twenty minutes later, she called back.

"Griffith Park," I said.

He cranked the ignition, made a wide, sweeping U-turn in the strip mall parking lot, and we took Franklin over to Western, up to where it became Los Feliz, and entered the park. It was almost three now, and we wound around the gentle curves, headlights sweeping over the hills as we drove farther up. A few cars were parked around the entrance to the trails to the observatory. None of them were a red Mercedes coupe.

"Yamashiro is one of the toughest businessmen in the city," he said. "But he's pussy blind. Protocol says he shouldn't even go to the john and take a leak without me and J.J. But fuck, man, there he is, heading high into the hills in the pitch-black night for a fucking blowjob."

"Maybe it wasn't Gabby."

"If it wasn't Gabby, ten to one it's another piece of tail."

"Gee," I said. "You seem to hold women in high regard."

"You live in Los Angeles as long as I have, seeing the

way these girls work their assets, tossing it in men like
Jimmy's faces, then talk to me about it."

"I understand Yamashiro made some promises he didn't
deliver."

"Oh, yeah?" Miller said. "Show me a contract. These
girls think he's gonna snap his fingers and make them
goddamn Meryl Streep? Your girl Gabby knew this was a
short-term deal. If she couldn't take it, she shouldn't have
jumped on the carousel."

"How about you be quiet and look for Yamashiro's
car," I said. "We don't share a similar worldview."

In the passing half-light, Miller looked poised to re-
spond with a smart remark but shut his mouth as we both
spotted a red Mercedes coupe, top down, parked across
from the Trails Café. "Christ Almighty."

He parked. We got out.

Griffith Park was very dark and very quiet at night.
Miller walked over and looked into the front seats of the
Mercedes. He checked the glovebox and then met me at
the mouth of the trail.

"Maybe he's out for some fresh air," I said. "Healthy
living."

"Ordering room service is Jimmy's idea of exercise."

We headed onto a well-worn path over a small wooden
bridge and past a playground. There were picnic tables
and porta-potties and an old brick structure that looked
to be in renovation.

"It's about a mile to the top."

I shrugged. "Want to race?"

"Don't kid around," he said. "This ain't good."

Along the curve of the trail, we saw a man walk from a brick building. We stepped back into the shadows. A dull glow shone from the streetlamps along the road.

I heard a car winding its way up the hill and then slowing and idling by the Trails Café. I looked to Miller. In the glow of the security lamps, he looked unshaven and worn out. His black suit was wrinkled and his dress shirt fanned out crooked on the jacket's lapels. I heard the sound of men talking and then feet on the gravel. The closer the men got, I could tell they weren't speaking English. Or Spanish. Or even pig latin.

I reached for the gun on my hip. Miller pulled what looked like a Sig from under his coat and we moved into the shadows behind a rock wall.

"A fucking setup."

"Of whom?"

"Whom?" he said, under his breath. "Christ."

The man from the building joined two figures I immediately recognized. One of whom Chollo had taken at gunpoint outside the meeting with Mallory Riese. We watched them walk, the bald man grunting out some orders, walking stiff-legged toward the porta-potties. He called out someone's name, sounding to me like *Nishan*. He called the man again.

They started opening the doors to the porta-potties. More yelling and pointing. They seemed frantic to find something or someone.

Miller looked over at me, taking careful aim at the figures in the dark. I wondered who had set up whom and what Miller hoped to achieve. I knew I'd be the perfect witness to a justified shooting of some men who'd wanted to shake down his boss. I wasn't sure what was happening, but I figured Gabby Leggett wasn't within twenty miles of Griffith Park.

Miller closed his left eye, raised his gun, and fired off a warning shot. The Armenians turned, asking no questions, fanning out and into the woods and shadows.

"Never shoot unless you mean it," I said. "Now they see us."

I took cover and duck-walked behind the wall, watching two of the figures crouching and moving with stealth in the darkness. They had their guns out, communicating with hand signals, going from tree to tree, seeking what little concealment they could find. I, on the other hand, was behind a rock wall and could stay there all night long. At best and in daylight, the short barrel had a range a little less than a football field. I began to wish I'd packed my Browning. And I began to wish I'd invited Chollo along.

Someone was going to be shot. And I didn't want it to be me.

Miller followed me down the rock wall as the third man came up fast beyond the playground. If Miller could actually shoot, he could drop him cold and hard right by the swing sets.

Miller moved with the steady determination of a man who'd only threatened a gunfight but had never been in one. None of these guys were going to throw up their hands and turn tail back to the road. I felt my adrenaline begin to surge.

The two men were getting closer and closer to the rock wall. If they kept that close, I could come right behind them. I wouldn't need a hundred yards. I might not need five.

Before I heard the shot, I had it all worked out. Two more shots. Quick cracks and a brief light in the darkness.

I glanced over for just a moment to see Miller drop halfway over the rock wall. The two Armenians ran toward where he fell. I aimed at them both, and one spotted me, raising his gun. Before he could fire, I dropped him at about twenty yards.

The other fired toward me and I felt a chunk of rock fly against my face. I fired two more times and dropped him as well.

The third man, the one who'd shot Miller, ran up into the hills. I ran after him but soon stopped. I caught my breath and noticed I was bleeding down the front of my jacket. I wiped it away and headed back to the playground.

One of the men looked dead. The other looked well on his way. I took both of their guns and walked toward Miller. His body was bent over the rock wall like a sock puppet. His eyes and mouth were wide open, a little bubble of blood on his lips.

I set down the guns and reached into his pocket for the keys. As I did so, I noticed the door to the small brick building wide open. I couldn't be too sure there weren't more of them, and headed toward the light, ducking under construction tape. I heard the sound of water running in the bathroom and stepped inside, searching for a light switch that worked. The water continued to run and I felt my Nikes splash through the water as I held up my phone to offer a little light.

In the second stall, I found another man, also very dead. Blood colored the water from the overflowing toilet. His head was cocked in a very unnatural way, with black eyes staring straight ahead and reflecting the light from my cell phone.

The body was dressed in a baby-blue polo shirt and white jeans.

It was Jimmy Yamashiro.

37

"How 'bout I drive you over to Anaheim and you can shoot some more people at Disneyland?" Samuelson said. "I think that Donald Duck and his smart attitude has really been asking for it."

"That's nice of you," I said. "But I think I've done enough shooting for the night."

"I'm so glad you're satisfied, Spenser," he said. "That makes my life easier."

It was early morning, nearly eight, and I sat on one of the picnic tables in the park, the entire recreation area taped off as a crime scene. The techs had finished up doing their work in the old bathrooms and two guys from the coroner's office had unceremoniously loaded Yamashiro's body on a stretcher and into a black van.

"How's the guy I shot?"

"You mean the not-yet-dead one?" he said. "You shot

him in the stomach. Don't you remember the Westerns? Gut shot ain't good."

"Will he live?"

"Don't know," Samuelson said. "I'll let you know where to send roses. Maybe you can visit him and ask him to forgive you."

"I didn't have a choice."

"You had a fucking choice the moment you were offered the job," he said. "You know we have an entire police department who does these kinds of things? Blackmail, missing persons, homicides, we offer it all. By the way, after you found the girl, why didn't you catch a flight back to Beantown?"

"My work wasn't done."

"Is it done now?" Samuelson said. "You got two guys with more ink on them than fucking Rand McNally. Are they the ones who shot Sixkill?"

"Yeah," I said. "The bald one."

"You mean the dead one," Samuelson said. "Are you all even now? You can blow the smoke from that .38 and ride off into the sunset."

"Your officers took my gun."

"Good."

"And my phone."

Samuelson shrugged. "And what's next you won't really like. But I can't do a goddamn thing about it. You will be transported to headquarters and then county lockup, where you'll be spending the next few days. That's unless you know someone who knows a real hot-shit lawyer."

I shrugged. "I just might."

"That's on you," he said, reaching into his jacket pocket and handing me his cell. "Here's my phone. Fucking call them. But you have presented me with a fine shit show in a very popular and well-known part of the city. Did you know the chief takes a hike here with his wife most mornings? Now he's going to have to track through this goddamn mess, wanting to know just how in the fuck I'm acquainted with frigging Wild Bill Hickok."

"Old pals?"

"We were never pals, Spenser," he said. "Let's get that straight."

Several vans from the television stations had parked out on the road. The cameramen taking close shots of Jimmy Yamashiro's cherry-red Mercedes coupe being loaded up onto a flatbed. The man I'd shot and Miller were still out in the playground, covered in sheets. A crime-scene tech walked by them and marked brass casings with numbered tags. It was all very efficient.

I pushed myself up from the picnic table and called Susan.

"Thank God," she said.

"Don't thank him yet," I said. "I'm going to be a while."

I told her about what had happened after I met Miller at Z's office.

"Would it be rotten if I say better him than you?"

"Not at all."

"And Gabby?"

"Nowhere to be seen," I said. "I asked Samuelson about Yamashiro's cell phone, but he was reluctant to pass along details."

"But he'd gone to meet her."

"That's what his man Harvey believed," I said.

"Will the police talk to Gabby?"

"You bet."

"And that will be more time before I can speak to her."

"I need you to call Z and tell him what's going on," I said. "Tell him to reach out to Chollo. I need a top-notch lawyer."

"Sorry," she said. "I heard Johnnie Cochran is dead."

"The kind that Victor del Rio has on speed dial."

"Are you okay?"

"Fine and dandy."

"You don't sound it."

"Call Z," I said. "I'll call you when I'm out."

She told me she loved me. And I told her the same. I handed the cell back to Samuelson. He stood with his back to me, arms crossed over his chest, surveying the scene behind his tinted glasses. What was left of his hair fluttered about in the wind.

"A mess," he said. "A goddamn mess."

38

After a long morning and a longer afternoon of questioning, a sharp-dressed attorney named McLaughlin argued for my release. When he joined me in the interview room, he passed along a thick business card with a font you didn't so much read as feel. I felt for the name, rough and bumpy over my thumb, recognized its legitimacy, and placed it in my jacket.

The lawyer had on a navy pinstripe suit with a white dress shirt and red power tie. His hair was long and slick, combed back into a modern pompadour, and seemed to make the two cops pressing me seem uneasy. I liked him immediately.

By early evening the cops let me go and McLaughlin offered me a ride in his spiffy silver Audi a few miles away to a plaza that bridged the space between Chinatown and Olvera Street. When he stopped the car, the lawyer pointed

out a silver-headed figure in a white linen suit sitting on a
park bench. Nearby, a group of children raced around a
gazebo on scooters.

I shook his hand, left the Audi, and walked toward
Victor del Rio. Del Rio didn't move his eyes from the
children, sitting with his right arm relaxed over the park
bench. "Sit," he said.

I sat.

"You should have brought Chollo," he said.

"Live and learn."

"One would think you would have learned by now," he
said. "You are lucky they missed, my friend."

I touched the wound on my head and decided not to
explain it came from a rock fragment. Being grazed by a
bullet offered more credibility among criminals. I looked
over at del Rio. He'd aged a bit since I'd seen him last, his
mustache and heavy eyebrows showing more silver. His
hands shook, tracing the head of a hand-carved cane.

"Maybe next time bring Bobby Horse, too."

I looked around the plaza. I saw Bobby Horse on the
opposite side of the gazebo. The big man had on a black
leather jacket over a black T-shirt and black jeans. I waved
at him. He nodded slightly in my direction. Bobby Horse
was thick-bodied and thick-necked, with long black hair
starting to turn white. He had on an enormous silver belt
buckle that glinted in the fading sun.

"Thanks for getting me out."

"It's nothing," del Rio said. "Nothing at all. We have a
long past together."

"Back to Jill Joyce," I said.

We sat under the wide sprawling branches of a fig tree. Chinese lanterns had been hung from wires over the plaza, rocking in the fading gold light. Somewhere down Olvera Street, a mariachi band began to play. At that exact location, I was pretty sure I could smell egg rolls and fajitas. Perfect L.A. fusion.

"Tell me more about these guys."

"They are very bad," he said. "Bad people."

"I got that idea when they began to shoot."

"This man they killed," he said. "Was he a friend?"

"I barely knew him," I said. "But he didn't deserve to get shot. He was only looking for his employer."

"The movie executive."

I nodded. Bobby Horse left his post and a made a small tour around the gazebo, looking loose and relaxed, sauntering around in a clockwise motion. But I knew Bobby Horse. He was taking in every person, every movement, every passing car. He most definitely had a pistol the size of a rocket launcher under his coat and would quickly expel anyone who might want to harm Victor del Rio.

"Why'd they kill this man, Yamashiro?"

"I don't know."

"Chollo said he was being blackmailed."

"That's right," I said. "I assume he didn't want to pay up."

"Then why come at all?" he said. "And alone."

"Very good question," I said. "You would've brought Chollo and Bobby Horse with you."

"And maybe my new friend, Mr. Sixkill, too," he said. "And none of those men would've cast a shadow in my direction."

"It was night," I said. "Everything was in shadows."

Del Rio smiled and nodded. He said something in Spanish to the kids racing around on their scooters. I only caught part of it. *Faster, faster.* He chuckled with amusement. The kids looked at me funny, and I remembered my bloody temple and blood across my wrinkle-free blazer.

"I take it you would like to know more about this man Sarkisov and what he has to do with these people who worship the sun?"

"Yes," I said. "I would. Although technically they don't worship the sun as much as a man named Joe Haldorn. Ever heard his name?"

"No," he said. "But five years ago, there was some nasty business with me and Sarkisov. He was new to this country and wasn't aware that we have borders, lines you don't cross."

"And you had to remind him."

"Yes," he said. "Quite firmly. People like Sarkisov are nasty, but they can't compete with my business partners in the south. They don't care to be tested and never ask twice. It's better I don't mention them, but they are quite ruthless and unforgiving. My people and Sarkisov's people are happy to coexist, but only up to a certain point."

"Is that why they got banished down to Furlong?"

Del Rio's face split in a pleasant smile. "Yes," he said. "Exactly. From there, in that tiny little town, they can do as they wish. Mostly it is stolen goods. Hijacked trucks.

Cheap electronic garbage from China. Cell phones. Laptops. As long as they stay away from peddling our product, there isn't any trouble."

"Is it true Chollo is now selling churros?"

"Do you find that odd?"

"Only in its alliteration," I said. "It would look amazing on a T-shirt."

Del Rio didn't seem to be listening. He stood up and met a tall, graceful woman who'd walked into the park. She had on a sleeveless white linen jumpsuit and very tall tan heels. Her cheekbones were high and prominent and her shiny black hair was pulled back into a long ponytail. Her skin was bronze, her eyes enormous and black.

She met del Rio and kissed him on the cheek. She looked at me, but he didn't offer an introduction. After she walked away with two of the children, a young boy and girl who looked as if they might be twins, he turned to me with a smile.

"Very beautiful," I said.

"My daughter," del Rio said. "And a rare visit from my grandchildren from the north. She might not be here if not for Mr. Sixkill. It pained me a great deal to hear that he'd been shot by Sarkisov's people."

"It pained him even more."

"And the man you shot?" he said. "This was one of the men who shot Sixkill?"

"Yes."

"Are you sure?"

I nodded. "I never forget an ugly face."

Del Rio stood and waved for Bobby Horse to join us

under the giant fig tree. A sign had been taped to a lamp-post advertising a lantern festival that week to celebrate Chinese heritage. Bobby Horse and I shook hands. He gave the slightest of smiles. High praise for a man who rarely showed emotion.

"I want to arrange a meeting with Sarkisov," del Rio said. "This thing between Sixkill and the Armenians is finished. Whoever they are protecting and for whatever reason, that is finished, too."

"Maybe I should bake him a cake," I said. "Or buy him a potted plant. It might make him feel better about losing two of his men."

"He won't risk our agreement for whatever business he has with this Haldorn," del Rio said. "If I don't like his answer, my associates to the south and I can make life very difficult for him. Furlong won't be far enough away."

"He might lose his head?"

"Among other parts," del Rio said. "Mailed to wives and girlfriends."

"Ouch," I said.

"Very."

We shook hands and walked toward the street. Bobby Horse offered to give me a ride back to the apartment in Santa Monica. I agreed and thanked him.

Del Rio clasped my shoulder and then wrapped me in an unexpected hug. "The world is round, *amigo*," he said, patting my back. "Perhaps I will need your help again one day."

"Anytime."

39

The next day, Susan and I made several attempts to meet with Gabby Leggett. We were shut down on so many fronts, I started to believe the HELIOS people genuinely didn't like me.

We were told Miss Leggett was busy. We were told she didn't wish to have contact with us or her family. We were told she was on another retreat.

I didn't blame her for not wanting to be found. News on the Yamashiro murder and a possible connection with a recent missing-persons case were strewn about America's TVs, computer screens, and cell phones. I assumed that if I stepped outside of the apartment, I might see Gabby's face plastered across the broadside of the Goodyear Blimp.

Susan and I kept our cell phones handy. I spoke twice to Samuelson. He wouldn't confirm, deny, or venture a guess on whether his people had found Gabby. I offered the idea of a wellness check at the mansion at West Adams. Samuelson offered me a blunt reply on what I might do with my advice.

At the apartment, I made a large batch of chipotle chicken salad with feta and avocado and let it cool in the refrigerator. I went for a long run along the beach, and when I returned, Z was seated at the kitchen bar, catching up with Susan. He was drinking one of those Mexican Cokes in the tall green bottles.

"You've replaced me already," I said.

"Can you blame me?" Susan said. "He's like you, only the newer model."

"With that busted arm," I said, "more like a demo."

"Stronger in the broken places," Z said. "Or don't you read anymore?"

I looked from Z to Susan. "Is it too early to drink?"

"Yes," Susan said. "But not too late for lunch."

I doled out the chicken salad onto toasted sourdough slices and made a platter of small sandwiches. I set the table in the dining room and began to cut up some fruit for a small salad. We turned on the cable news as we ate, Gabby Leggett's photo shown during the story on the Yamashiro killing.

"Why are they calling Gabby a person of interest?" Susan said.

"It doesn't mean she's a suspect," I said. "They know the men who were there. They just want to speak with her."

"And can't find her," Z said.

I asked him about her apartment. He said he'd been sitting on it for the last four hours.

"And Jem Yoon?"

"Still nothing," Z said. "Gabby's off the grid."

I ate a sandwich with some black coffee. It was so good, I helped myself to another one with a side of fruit. I didn't care to go head to head with some Armenian Power thugs on an empty stomach.

"And what's stopping this man Sarkisov from luring you both in and then killing you?" Susan said. "His people already shot Z and murdered another man. It seems like they'd like to shoot you most of all."

"They'll have to get in line," I said. "Lots of people want to shoot me."

"That's not funny," Susan said. "Will Chollo go with you?"

"Probably," I said.

"And Bobby Horse, too," Z said. "It'll be the Three Amigos plus some old white guy."

"Who are you calling white?" I said.

"And you think that will be enough for them to let Gabby go?" Susan said.

"Actually, I don't want them to do anything," I said. "Only to drop whatever agreement they have with Haldorn. By now, they've got to realize whatever it was isn't worth the trouble."

"And this is based on what?" Susan said. "A code of honor? A thick layer of machismo?"

I looked to Z and then back at Susan. I shrugged. "Basically," I said. "Yes."

"But even you know most people don't operate with a code," she said. "Especially not these people."

"Perhaps *code* is too strong a word," I said. "How about *fear*?"

"These people are afraid of Victor del Rio?"

Z lifted his eyebrows and nodded. "Very."

Z reached with his right hand for three small sandwiches and stacked them on a napkin in front of him. Susan walked back through the open kitchen and poured us both a cup of black coffee. I looked up at a small clock above the refrigerator. It was nearly three.

"Do you ever worry that one day you might trust the wrong people?"

"I trust del Rio," I said. "And I believe in the healthy fear that Sarkisov will have if something happens to any of his people."

I had on a sleeveless blue sweatshirt, soaked down the chest, with my running shorts and shoes. A Browning nine-millimeter I'd borrowed from Chollo lay in its holster on top of the coffee table. Just close enough in case we had an unexpected knock on the door.

An hour later, my phone buzzed.

"Meet me in an hour at Union Station," Chollo said. "Z can ride with me. Bobby Horse with you."

"Was Sarkisov excited to receive us?"

"I don't know, *amigo*," he said. "I guess we will soon find out."

40

Furlong was even uglier at night than it was during the day. Endless streets and avenues of tin-roofed industrial buildings behind chain-link fences. The only life came from the occasional barking pit bull and the roar of a tractor-trailer making a sweeping turn out from a loading bay. There were a few late-night bars tucked into the side of little standalone brick buildings and all-night bodegas and sandwich shops advertising with neon signs. But mainly Furlong resembled a scene from an apocalyptic movie, only with less character. Everything was asphalt and concrete. Concertina wire and sheet metal formed the basic aesthetic.

"Why'd Chollo want you to ride with me?" I said.

"You shoot and he shoot pretty good," Bobby Horse said. "Z and I can back you up."

"You shoot pretty damn good, too," I said. "And Z when he's not injured."

"Not like Chollo," he said. "No one shoots like Chollo."

"What about the churros?"

"Okay."

"Just okay?" I said.

Bobby Horse shrugged.

I followed the taillights of Chollo's car down a long stretch of road splitting the heart of Furlong, gliding through the cavernous path of metal buildings and brick warehouses. Bright lamps lit the way on the dry, dusty streets. The windows were down on the Land Cruiser and we listened to the wind and occasional bark of a dog. I waited for a tumbleweed to blow past my headlights.

"Lovely place," I said.

"This is the asshole of Los Angeles," Bobby Horse said. "Only the dead end up here."

"A positive attitude is always the key to success," I said.

"A cautious one is better," Bobby Horse said. "A cautious one keeps you alive."

"Native American wisdom?" I said.

"No," he said. "Common sense."

Chollo's SUV slowed and turned at a closed gate to a towering brick warehouse. He idled for nearly a minute before the large chain-link gate began to slide back, and we both drove inside and parked at crooked angles. The headlights of our cars brightened the broadside of the building. The Virgin Mary had been painted on the warehouse in a fading mural, clutching her sacred heart and looking toward heaven. Two men in white undershirts and low-slung jeans met us in the parking lot.

The men held automatic weapons with shoulder straps

that they used to usher us into the warehouse. Both were medium-sized, with shaved heads and razor-thin black beards. I couldn't tell who was who with an automatic weapon aimed at my chest.

I looked over to Z and Chollo and nodded. All four of us fanned out as we followed them into the brightly lit warehouse. The inside was a maze of industrial metal shelving rising thirty to forty feet high, stacked with boxes for chain saws, cases of champagne, laundry detergent, and new leather sofas and chairs wrapped tight in plastic sheeting. I felt as if we'd infiltrated a Costco.

Under the bright lighting, I saw a man standing in a wide-open space, stacking crates into the back of the truck. He wore dirty denim coveralls and had a lot of thick, curly hair. He wasn't large but moved like a strong man, with an oversized belly and skillet-sized hands.

The skinheads walking us in stopped and hung back as we approached him. They rested their hands on their hips and waited.

I looked above the man in coveralls at a catwalk with a small office. Three more men looked down at us, clutching identical automatic weapons with shoulder straps.

"Wow," I said. "Must be a big sale of AR-15s on aisle five."

The big-headed man stopped his loading and turned to us. He was a little out of breath as he placed his hands on his hips. His eyes were large. His nose was big. Even his jaw was big and unshaven. He looked like the very personification of Fred Flintstone.

"You want to buy gun?" he said. "I sell you gun."

"Must be my lucky day."

"We will see about that, my friend," he said.

"You know why I've come?"

Sarkisov nodded. He unzipped his coveralls and slid out of them, kicking his feet free. He was wearing a skin-tight black designer T-shirt with thin black piping. The T-shirt did little to disguise his pear-shaped body and long, hairy arms. He looked at me with bloodshot eyes and reached onto a folding card table for a cigarette. He lit one with a gold Zippo, took a deep drag, and clicked off the lighter with a quick snick.

"I don't like this," he said. "I don't like trouble. I am an easygoing man. I do my business. I let the fucking Mexicans do their business. Koreans. Chinese. Salvadorans. Everyone makes money. Everyone is happy."

I looked to Z in the sling. I looked back to Sarkisov. "Not everybody."

"Unfortunate accident," he said, shrugging. "I do someone a favor. My people come to tell you to lay off. A little argument go sideways and then the *boom, boom, boom*."

I shifted my weight onto the other foot. The men above us stood a little stiffer, not aiming, but paying closer attention to our hand placement. Chollo waited to my left, still and easy, hands resting at the sides of his legs. Bobby Horse and Z to my right, calm and relaxed. Bobby Horse had his thumbs hooked into his hand-tooled Western belt, his eyes droopy, almost sleepy, as he listened.

If Sarkisov's men so much as sneezed, the violence would be quick and ugly.

"What happened at the park," Sarkisov said. "That is

the end. Like I tell del Rio, this over. For us. For you. I am finished. Okay? We okay? We be friends now?"

"Sure," I said. "How about a hug?"

"You joke," he said. "You a funny man. I like you, funny man."

"Shucks."

"All this with the movie man and this girl," he said. "Too much trouble for me. Too many policemen harassing my people and looking for me. Too much on the TV and the Internets. A headache, man. A real fucking headache, funny man."

I couldn't see the two men who'd greeted us outside. But Z had taken a few steps back. Bobby Horse moved a few feet back, watching the men above and below. He wore a chambray Western shirt with his jeans and rattlesnake boots.

"Why'd you kill Yamashiro?" I said.

Sarkisov shrugged again. I couldn't shake his resemblance to Fred Flintstone. I waited for him to give a thickly accented *yabba-dabba-doo* at any moment. He blew smoke from the side of his mouth and shook his head. "I didn't kill that man," he said. "He dead on the toilet when we got there. Ugly. Very disgusting."

Sarkisov sat on the card table and looked up to his men above. He leveled his eyes back at me and shook his head ever so slightly.

"That's some bad luck," I said. "Your people going for a late-night hike and stumbling on the corpse of one of the most powerful men in Hollywood."

He blew out smoke again, slow and easy. He reached up to scratch his cheek. "Very bad luck," he said. "I don't need this trouble. I don't want this trouble. The cops. The news of the TV. I am just—"

"A simple businessman," I said. "And this warehouse is filled with completely legitimate items ready to be trucked to your local Walmart. I could really use a gigantic tub of cake frosting and some paper towels."

"Sure," Sarkisov said, grinning. "You need something? Guns? Champagne? Nice new lawn-mowing machine? Women? I know you like the women. I get you a whole party. Forget this girl."

"I can't."

"Why not?"

"I was hired to bring her home."

"And you want to know why I protect Haldorn?" he said. "Right?"

I nodded.

He smiled. He smoked. He swayed back and forth on the wobbly card table to music that I couldn't hear. I wondered about Armenian music. Did it sound like Greek music with those big zithers people played in their lap? If Sarkisov started to play music, would his men put down their AR-15s and begin to perform a traditional dance? Maybe break a few plates?

"This man may have done me a favor or two," he said. "I repay the favor. But now I am done. How you say, too much heat?"

"Too much heat," Z said.

I looked over at Z and smiled. I nodded my appreciation. Bobby Horse and Chollo hadn't spoken or barely moved.

"You give him money and he washes it through HE-

LIOS," I said. "It's the only arrangement that makes sense to me."

Sarkisov shrugged. "If you say," he said, cigarette bobbing on his lower lip.

"I do say," I said.

Sarkisov nodded and nodded. "You and Haldorn are not so different. Both of you fascinated by this woman with the cool, green eyes."

"I get her back," I said. "And we'll leave you alone."

"What?" Sarkisov started to laugh. And then cough. Smoke came from his nose as he composed himself. "Leave us alone?" he said. "You think you and your Mexicans can take Sarkisov's men?"

"Only one Mexican, *cabrón*," Chollo said. "And two American Indians."

Sarkisov seemed unimpressed with the clarification of ethnicity. Bobby Horse stood still and relaxed. I knew it would take him less time to grab his gun than the men who'd walked us in. Chollo could take out every man on the catwalk faster than Sarkisov could scratch his privates.

"I want you and your men to stay away from Haldorn," I said. "And his place on West Adams. No interference."

"That is it?"

"That's it," I said. "So simple even a man like you can understand it."

"You a funny man," he said. "But Haldorn? He is crazy man. You know this?"

"I suspected it."

"Haldorn thinks he's not a man," Sarkisov said. "He thinks he is a god. That he and his people came from the sun. They worship him like he's more than a man. They would do anything for this man. Including your woman with the bright green eyes. You may get her back. But she'll never be the same as she was. If it were me, I'd say enough. I let her go. She's no good. She's a ruined woman. Spoiled like old meat."

"I disrespectfully disagree."

Sarkisov's nose flared. He didn't like that answer.

We looked at each other for a long while without breaking eye contact. I wondered, if he looked away, would I win a prize? Maybe half-price at checkout here at the Furlong bootleg Costco.

"Why do you care so much?" he said. "I get you ten women look just like her. Only fresh and clean. No more trouble. No sun people. None of the crazy."

"Her family hired me," I said. "And I do what I say."

"Family?"

"Her mother."

Sarkisov sucked on the last bit of the cigarette. He flicked it onto the concrete and nodded. "I give you tonight," he said. "Maybe I look the other way. Maybe we not interfere. But after that, you make trouble for me? For people I do business with? I won't be so nice."

I nodded in agreement.

"See you at the rock quarry, Sarkisov," I said.

Bobby Horse and Chollo waited until I got toward the big rolling door of the warehouse before they followed. Z and I walked step for step, Z watching my back and me watching his.

It was nice to have friends.

41

parked my car in a paid lot downtown and crawled into the backseat of Chollo's SUV.

"Roomy," I said.

"It has a sunroof, too," Chollo said. "Would you like some fresh air?"

"After dealing with Sarkisov?" I said. "Yes. I would."

Z rode shotgun and Bobby Horse sat behind Chollo. We resembled a fun group of friends headed to the local drive-in. I asked Chollo to play some Dick Dale to lighten the mood. He punched up some buttons on his phone at the stoplight. "Miserlou" rattled the speakers in the car as he navigated the streets back to West Adams.

Bobby Horse checked his gun and counted the bullets in the snap pocket of his Western shirt. Chollo turned up onto the 10. It was late and we rode the highway unencumbered by traffic, racing down to the West Adams mansion where I hoped we'd find Gabby Leggett. And where I hoped, but didn't expect, Haldorn's people to not offer a challenge.

We parked on a nearby street and walked along West Adams. Bobby Horse exchanged places behind the wheel with Chollo. Bobby Horse and Z stayed behind in the SUV as Chollo and I headed toward the mansion.

"Like Proctor?" Chollo said.

"Let's hope not," I said.

"Too bad," Chollo said. "Proctor was fun."

I stepped from the sidewalk and streetlight into some bushes by the far-right corner of the mansion. We followed the tall wrought-iron fence for about a hundred yards until I found a good, dark place to jump it. I was glad I wore a pair of loose-fitting jeans that night. It would've been embarrassing to try and take Gabby Leggett back with a hole in my crotch.

I reached for the top of a brick pillar and lifted myself up to where I could slide my shoes between pointy metal spikes. Knowing my foot wasn't caught, I hopped over the fence and found myself in some dense shrubbery and plants. Chollo was beside me before I realized he'd even jumped.

I knew there had to be guards and security cameras. If they called the police, I had several half-reasonable excuses for the social call on Gabby. Susan and I had agreed, she didn't need to spend another night with Haldorn. The maiden needed rescuing. And then the maiden needed some deep and intense psychotherapy.

The pool stretched out bright and cool in the back of the

mansion. I didn't see a single person moving behind the windows or walking the grounds. Everything was still and calm, almost like the house was completely unattended.

I checked the corners for cameras. I stopped as we walked and listened for voices. Absolutely, positively nothing.

"Too easy," Chollo said. He had his gun out by his side.

"Are you complaining?"

"I like a challenge, *amigo*."

"Trigger finger itching?"

"*Sí*."

We waited along the hedgerows until one of the guards from Haldorn's birthday party walked outside and took a seat on a lounge chair. He had a soda can in his hands and absently took a sip. I touched Chollo's shoulder as we made our way around the hedge to where the man couldn't see us. Chollo snuck past me and pointed his gun right behind the man's ear. He was caught in mid-sip.

"Knock, knock," Chollo said.

The man said nothing. He set the can down on the ground. He slowly raised his hands.

"Gabby Leggett," I said.

"She's not here."

"Wrong answer."

"Shit, man," he said. "Don't kill me. Don't fucking kill me."

"Don't worry," Chollo said. "Don't be afraid. You will feel nothing. Just a flash of light. It will be full of peace and love."

"Christ," the man said. "Jesus Christ. She's upstairs. Sleeping. No one is to see her. No one. Her door is locked.

I don't even have a fucking key. Only Haldorn. Who are you? Cops? You can't do this. You can't just break in here. You need a warrant or somethin'."

"Warrants?" Chollo said. "We don't need no stinking warrants."

"Really?" I said to Chollo.

Chollo smiled and shrugged.

"Stand up slow," I said. "Who else is here?"

"Me and Eddie," he said. "Okay. Just me and fucking Eddie."

"Get him."

The man picked up the phone. I snatched it from him. I scrolled down to Eddie and texted for him to meet us by the pool. I walked up toward the French doors and waited. Eddie, my friend who I tossed into the crudités, walked outside holding half a sub sandwich. I tripped him and pushed his face into the concrete, searching his jacket for a gun. I found one and snatched him up to his feet. He didn't speak, only bled a little.

I took Eddie to Chollo and the other guard. I asked the men which room was Gabby's. One of the men tried to explain we were trespassing.

"Which room?" I said.

The first man we'd grabbed told me it was the third door on the right. He again repeated that the door was locked and only Haldorn had a key.

"Now shut your mouths," Chollo said. "You speak and you get shot. It's a nice and simple little game. Who would like to go first?"

Neither of the men said a word. I headed up the marble

steps and let myself into the grand house, walking under the fresco of angels looking down from clouds. I climbed the grand mahogany staircase, taking the steps two at a time to the landing. The house smelled musty and ancient, something of another time. I waited and listened. I heard nothing and followed the hall to the third door on the right.

I tried the knob. It was locked with a deadbolt above.

I stood back and kicked it open. It splintered and cracked open on my second attempt. Haldorn bought locks like he bought security guards.

With my gun, I checked every corner. The light was dim in the room and I saw a hump in the center of a large four-poster bed. I holstered the Browning and pulled the covers back from the bed. Gabby Leggett's eyes were closed and she snored softly. I pushed at her shoulder gently and then harder. I shook her so hard, I waited for the teeth to rattle from her mouth. No soap.

She was out and flying high on some chemical help.

I walked over to the window and looked down upon the glimmering pool. Chollo stood over the two men, seated on the lounge chair. His head swiveled from left to right, making sure we were clear.

I walked back to the bed, lifted Gabby into my arms, and lifted her unceremoniously like Boris Karloff in *Frankenstein*. I carried her through the broken door, down the hall, and onto the landing. I waited and listened. There was nothing. If the sound of shattering wood didn't bring the HELIOS people running, they were either too scared or told to sit this one out.

Downstairs, I set Gabby on a long red velvet couch and opened the door to motion for Chollo. He offered a bit of parting wisdom to the two guards and met me in the grand living room. It seemed dull and empty without the chamber music. I carried Gabby as Chollo took us through the house and to the front door, down the wide marble steps, and into the yard.

He hit the switch on the stately iron gate and lifted his phone to dial Bobby Horse.

The SUV turned the corner and slid to a hard, fast stop along West Adams. The wind was dry and hot out on the street. I could taste dust on my tongue as Z opened the back door and set Gabby inside. She had shuffled awake, briefly, as I moved in beside her, bookended with Bobby Horse. It wasn't going to be the most pleasant ride back to Santa Monica, but she was more doped up than a Kentucky Thoroughbred.

"Trouble?" Bobby Horse said, making a sweeping U-turn along West Adams.

"None."

"Shoot anyone?" Z said.

Chollo shook his head.

"We saw only a couple of trained dogs," I said. "And they rolled over and showed their bellies."

"Haldorn?" Z said.

"Wasn't there," I said.

"Damn," he said.

No one said much more on the slow and uneventful ride toward the ocean. As we turned onto Ocean Boulevard, the big Ferris wheel at the end of the pier flashed and strobed in neon patterns. Bobby Horse let down the window as we cruised along the beach. The palm trees rocked in a warm breeze, people sipped cocktails in outdoor cafés, and couples stood along the concrete railing to look at the Pacific under the moonlight. A lovely Saturday night in California.

Gabby again shuffled against me and then dropped her head onto my shoulder. In the passing light, I noticed the welts on her wrists, chapped and bloody.

She'd been tied up for a long time.

Chollo noticed them, too.

"Should we kill him?" he said.

"Too easy."

"You will never change, *amigo*," he said. "When will you learn? Some people live without rules. And sometimes killing a bad man is the only way."

"I have other ideas for Haldorn."

Chollo nodded. "And I am listening."

42

It was early the next morning.

Z and I sat at the kitchen table and looked up as Susan returned from a back room of the condo. We were drinking coffee and eating warm blueberry muffins fresh from Gjusta.

"Gabby needs to see a doctor," she said.

"You are a doctor," I said.

"A medical doctor," Susan said. "Not just a shrink. Her arms look god-awful."

"She sees a doctor and she'll get free," I said. "She gets free and she'll run right back to Haldorn. Then we'll have to repeat the whole process."

"She'd been given two pills to sleep," Susan said. "God knows what they were."

"You can always trust old Dr. Haldorn," I said. "Top

of his medical class. Musical prodigy. Spiritual leader. Alpine skier. He can both heal the sick and raise the dead."

"She's at least awake now," Susan said. "And coherent. She's patient and listening. No more pacing. No more yelling."

"Is she fighting you?" I said.

"No," Susan said. "But she's very groggy. She definitely wants to leave. She believes you are the main agitator and troublemaker and says Haldorn has called you poisonous. A true pain in his ass."

Z looked across the table at me. "That sounds right."

I looked to Z and raised my coffee mug. "Years of practice."

"I asked her about being restrained," Susan said, taking a seat at the table. "She said the marks on her wrists were from rope burns from climbing during the so-called spiritual retreat."

The patio door was slightly ajar, letting in a soft breeze and sounds of children splashing in the pool. I reached to the center of the table and selected a muffin from the box. I split it in half with a butter knife and set the other half back in the box. Restraint.

"What about her weight loss?" I said.

"She could use an IV to help with the dehydration," Susan said. "She won't eat. I did get her to drink some bottled water. She was very thirsty but wouldn't admit it."

"If you've gone Looney Tunes, can't a family member legally take over?" Z said.

I looked to Z and said, "Medically speaking."

"Medically speaking," Susan said. "Guardianship can be granted. Especially to a family member. But proof of going Looney Tunes can be a long and arduous journey. That's a matter for the courts."

"I'll call Rita Fiore for any West Coast specialists for this sort of thing," I said.

Susan settled in to the table and rested her head in her hand. She'd been sitting by Gabby's bedside all night and was still dressed in light gray pajamas, her curly black hair pulled back into a tight bun at the top of her head. She thought she looked tired. To me, she looked tough, resourceful, smart, and cute as a button.

"Get some rest," I said. "She's not going anywhere."

Z stood up and walked toward the door, snatching up a stray wooden chair and sitting in the hallway by Gabby's bedroom.

"See."

"This isn't something you can rush," Susan said. "She refuses to see her mother. There's a mountain of animosity there. Apparently, that's been going on a long time."

"After Haldorn?"

"Some before," Susan said. "Haldorn only deepened the divide."

"Might she listen to me?" I said.

"God, no."

"Would she listen to someone who lost their kid to Haldorn?"

"Charlotte Scott?" Susan said.

I nodded. Susan looked at me, lifting her chin and narrowing her eyes.

"I think the more information Gabby has, the better," Susan said. "A woman who lost her daughter has a powerful story to tell. Facts very damning to Gabby's ideal of Haldorn."

"I'll see what I can do."

"In the meantime, I'll rest."

I turned to Z. He had the front legs of the wooden chair off the floor, back leaning into the wall. He looked as if he was asleep, although I knew he wasn't.

"Don't worry," Z said with eyes closed. "The Indian will watch the fort."

"Isn't that culturally insensitive?" I said.

"For you, yes," Z said. "For me, no."

"Get with the times?" I said.

Susan smiled. "Finally."

43

"You've got to be fucking kidding me," Charlotte Scott said. "I'm not exactly the kind of woman who leads motivational talks."

"It's less motivational," I said. "More truthful."

Charlotte nodded. She was dressed in blue jeans and a low-cut black top that displayed her most famous assets. She wore a shawl that looked like a Mexican blanket and a gigantic turquoise necklace. Her eyes were lined in kohl and her lips ruby red. If you had a look, even after a few decades, better stick to it.

We sat together outside my rented condo, talking poolside at an iron table topped by a big green umbrella. It was late afternoon and sunny. Few clouds. Blue skies and palm trees and the kind of weather that might make a couple from Boston relocate for the winter. The children had left the pool area, leaving their inflatables and snorkels behind, damp towels hung on a wooden fence.

"How long has she been out?" Charlotte said.

"About twelve hours."

"Any change?"

"Has she rebuked all things Joe Haldorn and HELIOS?" I said.

Charlotte nodded and toyed with some fringe on the shawl.

"Nope," I said. "She's intent on getting back to the party."

"Shit on a stick."

"That's about the tall and short of it."

"Oh, God," she said. "I don't know if I can do this. This is a hell of a bad place to go back to. Thinking about Bailee. I don't want to cry. But I will. Especially when I'm mad. And if she sticks up for that son of a bitch—"

"Which she will."

"Goddamn waterworks."

I tugged at the brim of my ball cap. I smiled. I waited. Finally, I reached out and offered my hand and stood. I pulled Charlotte Scott, star of *Star Chasers 2* and *3*, to her feet. She followed me upstairs and into the condo. Susan was waiting for us.

I closed the door with a soft click and introduced them. Susan leaned against the couch. The door to the room that held Gabby was closed. Z was not there, but I knew he was around, walking the edge of the apartment and keeping a close eye. No one besides Chollo and Bobby Horse knew where to find us.

"It won't work," Charlotte said. "I tried and tried. I know you're a pro. And I respect that. But I hired two professional deprogrammers that didn't help a damn bit. They only ended up leaving me broke. The cult business is a shady fucking racket."

"She promised to at least listen," Susan said. "She knows I can't keep her here any longer. I told her that we'd let her go as soon as you both talk."

I hadn't heard this part of the plan. I looked over at Susan. Susan stared back at me and nodded, ever so slightly.

"It's got to be their decision," Charlotte said. "If not, it's not worth a damn. They'd rather bite though their tongues than to dismiss the great and glorious shithead, Phaethon."

"Are you ready?" Susan said.

"Why the hell not?" Charlotte said.

Susan stayed and I walked with Charlotte back to Gabby's room. We knocked, didn't hear anything, and I turned the knob. Gabby was in bed, under the covers, with her back turned to us. She had on one of my old T-shirts. Karl's Sausage Kitchen in Peabody. After decades of patronage, they'd given me a freebie.

"Gabby?" I said.

She turned her head from the pillow and opened her eyes. She looked like the teenager she'd been not that long ago. Charlotte found a big plush blue chair next to the bed and took a seat. She leaned forward, resting her elbows on her thighs, and looked up at me for some kind of sign.

I introduced them. I called Charlotte a friend. It wasn't

much, but I figured Charlotte would be best to ease into the particulars.

"It's all bullshit, you know," she said.

Or not.

Gabby didn't speak, only turned onto her back and placed her hands under her head to stare at the ceiling.

"Ever hear of a girl named Bailee Scott?" Charlotte said. "She was mine. My little girl. She got a little lost, turned around, and ended up at some strip mall in the Valley. God knows why or how. But they did it. They fucking did it. They gave her some just-add-water purpose and meaning to her life. Her show hadn't been off the air for three years and they told her they could help her reboot her life as a pop star. They knew all the best producers, industry players, and all that crap. She was told the only barriers she had were within herself. Does that crap sound familiar?"

Gabby didn't answer. But she blinked.

"And shockingly, one of her biggest life barriers was her own mother," Charlotte said. "She hadn't been in with Joe Haldorn three months when she met with me for lunch in Venice. We sat, we ate, we talked about the weather and some hard times when she first started out. She gripped my hand, looked me in the eye, and said I was a negative force and that she hoped I understood why she never wanted to see me again."

Gabby threw off the covers and sat up in bed, her feet dangling from the floor. Her long, wiry legs oddly pale and skinny. She cut her eyes to me and back over to Charlotte Scott in the giant blue chair. "Suppressive," she said.

It sounded like a hiss.

"No," Charlotte said. "Like Spenser said, I'm a friend. You remember those? Friends tell you the truth. Friends don't lie to you and keep you from your goddamn family. You see?"

Charlotte's voice had grown in intensity. I held up the flat of my hand.

"What did he give you?" I said. "To make you sleep?"

"Nothing," she said. "I just took a couple of pills. It wasn't a big deal. Thanks for checking up on me. But can I please have my clothes back?"

"What about your arms?" I said. "Why'd he tie you up?"

"You're not leaving here," Charlotte said. "No way you're going back to them. If I'd done the same for Bailee, she'd still be alive."

Gabby looked to me with an open mouth. She shook her head over and over.

"We can't keep you here," I said. "But you're not leaving until you understand exactly who you've thrown in with."

"'Thrown in with'?" Gabby said, laughing. "I didn't throw in with anybody. I am a grown woman who made some major lifestyle changes. And I'm sorry, lady, but sometimes family is poisonous. Sometimes you need to get out from under them to reach your full potential. It's hard. It's ugly. But sometimes it's the goddamn truth."

"It's bullshit," Charlotte said. She leaned back into the thick cushion of the chair. "Everything about that man is bullshit."

"You wouldn't know," Gabby said. "You couldn't know."

"Have you slept with him yet?" Charlotte said.

Gabby stared at her. She shook her head. Her breathing had intensified out of her nose. I noticed a small vein in her temple started to pulse.

"That's none of your goddamn business."

"Well," Charlotte Scott said, pushing herself up from the chair and staring down at Gabby. "I hate to break it to you, kid. But the path to enlightenment isn't at the end of Joe Haldorn's pecker."

Gabby ran to the door. I blocked her as she reached for the knob. She tried and tried but couldn't open it. I was a much larger person who took no pleasure in blocking her path. When Susan and I agreed, we'd let her go. Not a minute before.

"Assholes," Gabby said. She was crying and pacing. "You fucking assholes. You're all going to be sued for this. All of you."

I stayed at the door. As Gabby walked across the wooden floor, she turned her head to Charlotte Scott and spat in her face. Charlotte moved fast, backhanding Gabby and pushing her onto the bed. Before I could make it over, Charlotte had her pressed down on the mattress, pulling down the girl's underwear from her hip bone. When she found when she was looking for, she let her go.

Charlotte Scott looked at me and nodded. "Son of a bitch branded his sun mark on my Bailee, too," she said. "Is that about love and trust? A brand right near your privates? You let that man burn your skin to mark you. Like goddamn cattle."

"You wouldn't understand."

"And you won't understand until Haldorn uses you all up," Charlotte said, crying now. "And is done with you. When he finished with Bailee, all that was left was her body, shot full of drugs and branded like you. How much longer do you figure you have left?"

I touched Charlotte Scott's arm. We weren't making any progress.

"I want my things," Gabby said. "I want to go now. You hear me?"

Charlotte followed me and I shut the door behind us. Z was back in the chair in the hallway. He pressed his lips together in a silent whistle as we walked past.

Susan was in the kitchen, standing at the counter and drinking hot tea. "How'd it go?" she said.

"Terrific," I said.

"It's gone too far," Charlotte said. "Gabby is deep within his circle. She's got the sun brand on her hip and everything. Just like Bailee. I'm sorry, Susan. But you'd have to cage her to keep her."

44

The next morning, I met Samuelson downtown at The Pantry.

He was seated at the counter this time and looked up from a short stack of pancakes, motioning me to join him.

"Your sweetheart Gabby Leggett is missing again," he said. "You wouldn't know anything about that?"

"No, sir, Captain."

"Bullshit," he said. "You do know we'd like to speak with her, too. If it's not too much trouble."

I studied the menu, scanning through several items I had yet to sample. I scratched a place I'd missed shaving along my jaw. "How's the hash?"

"Some woman named Nancy Sharp reported her missing," he said. "Know her?"

"I just might," I said. "She told me she had a thing for men who liked dogs and good beer."

"Watch yourself," he said, stabbing a good bite of pancakes. "She also works with those whackjobs on West Adams. They claim the girl was taken against her will by a large, imposing white dude with a busted nose and a tall, skinny Mexican with a shiny pistol."

"Have any leads?"

"For Christ's sake."

I looked up to the waiter. I ordered the hash and eggs, rye toast, and black coffee. I'd been trying to cut down on the sugar lately.

"How's it coming along on Jimmy Yamashiro?" I said. "I saw some of your press conference. You identified Yamashiro's bodyguard and the Armenian shooter. But no arrests have been made."

"Why would I lie?"

"Want me to draw you a map to Furlong?"

"I've been down there," Samuelson said. "Twice. That son of a bitch has a nice little import/export business going."

"Among other things."

"No shit," Samuelson said. The waiter moved down the counter, refilling coffee. When he got to us, he spilled a little bit on Samuelson's hands. Without a word, Samuelson reached over, snatched a napkin, and wiped off the droplets.

"We had plenty to get his tit in a ringer," he said. "Never would admit a damn thing about Yamashiro. Says you were the one who was harassing his people in Hollywood and again at Griffith Park."

"Ah."

"Sarkisov's lawyer claims the whole fucking thing was a setup," Samuelson said. He took a sip of coffee and pushed away half the stack of pancakes. "Sarkisov said Yamashiro and him did a little business but wouldn't qualify what kind. He said when his people couldn't find him, they searched the shitter and the son of bitch was already dead."

"A claim of which you were dubious."

"You're goddamn right I was dubious," Samuelson said.

He drummed his fingers on the counter as if mulling something over. He looked to me, about to speak, just as my hash and eggs arrived. The platter was so hot steam rose from the eggs and butter melted down the triangles of toast. Perfection.

"What do you know about Leggett and these HE-LIOS people?"

I explained half of what I knew. When Samuelson looked satisfied, I cut into the eggs. The yolk spilled out into the hash and I took a bite. With my mouth full, I couldn't say any more without fear of being rude.

"They brand their what?" he said.

I wiped my mouth and whispered the answer to him.

"Christ," he said. "Fucking Los Angeles."

"It's pretty much an all-girls club," I said. "Your appendage would be safe."

"Then how the fuck did you break into that big mansion with that tall spiked fence?"

"Would you believe I hopped it?"

"At your size?" he said, snorting. "No."

"Gabby is safe," I said. "And she's free to come and go as she pleases. I'll tell her that you want to speak with her."

"It ain't a request, Spenser," he said. "Will she say what she knows about Haldorn?"

"Apparently, he's a really swell guy," I said. "Wants to teach the world to sing and buy everyone a Coke."

"I got a fucking Coke bottle for him," he said. "To ram up his ass. Did you know he did a five-year stretch at Folsom for armed robbery?"

"No, sir. I did not."

"Maybe because he's worked under a half-dozen aliases," he said. "Haldorn isn't even his real name."

"What's his real name?"

"Ernie Sadowski Junior," he said. "From Belle Isle, Illinois."

"He should stick to Joseph Haldorn," I said. "Sounds more cultish."

I ate a little more, lifting up my thick china mug of coffee. The early-afternoon light filtered through the blinds and covered half the tabletops and the old, broken linoleum floors.

"You know how to break him?" Samuelson said.

"Working on it," I said. "What's it to LAPD?"

Samuelson broke off a piece of bacon and popped it in his mouth. He chewed as he thought a bit on the question. He cut his eyes over at me. "Sarkisov wasn't lying," he said. "They didn't show until an hour after Yamashiro got beamed up to that big casting couch in the sky."

"That's hard-boiled," I said.

"Yes," he said. "I know. I can't take credit for it. One of my young detectives broke us all up during the morning meet. Really hit at the right time."

"Good for morale."

"You were a cop," he said. "You know what happens to the ones who can't laugh at this fucking circus."

I nodded.

"Coroner has a time of death," he said. "We got GPS coordinates for the cell phones we took off his people. They were fifteen miles away. Traffic camera verified them coming on scene after the time of death, not before."

"Then why were they there at all?"

"Sarkisov told us it was Big Swingin' Dick Haldorn who told him and his boys to go to the park," Samuelson said. "They expected a payday from Yamashiro. Not his fucking corpse."

"And what does Haldorn say?"

"We've been looking for him for the last twenty-four hours," Samuelson said. "And I have a feeling you might know just where we might find him."

"I don't," I said. "But I do know someone who just might."

45

I met Nancy Sharp at Echo Lake Park.

She'd been hesitant at first. But then I assured her that Susan Silverman wouldn't be joining us. I had the feeling she harbored few good sentiments for Susan after the grandma comment.

"Thank God," Nancy said. "You're alone."

She walked up to where I stood by the boathouse. Nancy Sharp was dressed for working out, in yoga pants and a jogging bra, overlain with a threadbare flannel shirt. She had on leather sandals and wore her silver hair up in a bun.

"Good to my word."

"I shouldn't be here," Nancy said. "You kidnapped one of our members."

"*Kidnapping* is a strong word," I said. "And hard to define. Shall we walk and talk?"

"After everything you've done?" she said. "You really expect me to take a leisurely stroll around the lake?"

"Yes," I said. "I do. You want to know what I know."

We began to walk away from the boathouse and toward the bridge that spanned the lagoon. Out on the water, people pedaled small boats, the light turning a hazy purple orange through the palm trees planted around the edge of the park. To the south, downtown Los Angeles shimmered in the late-afternoon light.

"How is she?" Nancy said.

"Better," I said. "After she woke up. She was a little groggy after you guys drugged her. And sore from where you tied her up."

"That's a lie."

"No," I said. "She had rope burns on her wrists and ankles. Mallory Riese had also given her some kind of sedative that would've made a grizzly bear comatose. I'm no doctor, but I don't think any of this was in my client's best interest."

"Gabby isn't your client."

"No, but her mother is," I said. "And you drugging, tying up, and brainwashing her daughter isn't exactly something she had in mind for her little girl."

I had my hands in the pockets of my windbreaker. I'd chosen a good place to meet. Few places to hide, although plenty of places to park and watch from cars. I had no doubt Nancy had been followed by some friends from HELIOS. There was too much at stake.

"You have absolutely no fucking idea what you're talking about," she said. "You make these broad accusations without any proof."

"I have proof," I said. "And I'm happy to share everything I know about you and your work for HELIOS. Especially what happened with your empowerment group and Bailee Scott."

"What happened to Bailee was unfortunate."

"You bet it was," I said. "Was she trying to leave?"

"Bailee was mentally ill," she said. "And so is her mother."

I shook my head. "Did you know LAPD is looking at your boss for the murder of Jimmy Yamashiro?"

"That's the most ridiculous thing I've ever heard."

Before I could answer, we passed two young women walking a dozen dogs. They moved at a clipped pace, waving to us with broad smiles as they held leashes of dogs hungry for exercise, nails digging into the concrete. The dogs were all kinds. Mutts. A Pekingese, two pugs, and a couple big-boned Labs.

"You can't be that shocked," I said. "LAPD has been searching for him for days."

Nancy didn't answer. She kept moving, pumping her arms now, as if we'd chosen to meet to exercise together. Perhaps she was multitasking for the cult. Discuss shakedown details while burning off calories. Smart.

"Do you plan on kidnapping any more of our members before you finally leave town?" she said.

"I don't know," I said. "How many more are being held against their will like Gabby and Bailee Scott?"

"Your accusations against Mr. Haldorn are slander."

"Truth isn't slander," I said. "I know exactly what Gabby and Joe had planned for that Yamashiro tape. And why Haldorn killed him."

"From whom?"

I didn't answer. I didn't look at her. I just kept on moving, circling Echo Lake, keeping step for step with Nancy Sharp. The water was dark and smooth. Lily pads and lotus flowers choked the small inlets and giant red flowers bloomed along our path. The air smelled of flowers and freshly cut grass. People laughed out on the water as they raced their pedalboats.

"Whatever Gabby told you is a fabrication," she said. "A lie. She's sick in the head."

I didn't answer. I had always found it best to keep quiet when others were willing to fill in the empty spaces. *Spenser's Investigative Tip #13*. It had yet to fail me.

"I've asked before and I'll ask again," I said. "I want to speak with Haldorn."

"He'll never talk to you."

"Try," I said. "We had a real moment at his birthday party. I could tell he liked me."

"He despises you," Nancy said. "You've done nothing but make trouble since you came out here for that goddamn little tramp."

I wasn't fond of hearing her talk about my client's daughter in such derogatory terms. But I sensed she wasn't crazy about Haldorn's obsession with Gabby. Or his extracurricular activities with young pupils. I kept walking. I followed the path in step with my BFF, Nancy.

"What Gabby knows about Joe Haldorn and Yamashiro will destroy HELIOS," I said. "If I knew anything to help the cops, I'd start talking now. Being arrested seldom looks good on a job résumé. Even in Los Angeles."

"You really are a bastard," she said through clenched teeth. "Did you want to see me to get to Haldorn? Or pressure me to cut a deal?"

"I can't cut a deal," I said. "But I know someone who could."

"HELIOS is a wonderful organization," she said. "We do amazing and wonderful work. We groom hundreds of tough-minded, modern women ready and equipped to deal with men like you."

"Sure."

"Your characterizations of it as a fraud aren't accurate."

"Uh-huh."

"If something happened that was wrong," she said. "It should be addressed. The core members won't stand for this. We have enriched the lives of many."

"Pyramid schemes often do."

"You don't understand," she said, shaking her head. "You don't get it. You never will."

"Why's that?"

"Because you're a man," she said. "What was designed and executed here by some brilliant minds is something you'll never be able to tear apart or take down."

"But LAPD can," I said. "Unless someone wants to step forward and separate the wheat from the chaff."

"I can't help them," Nancy said. "I don't have anything at all to offer. What exactly is your damn point here?"

"Haldorn should've never gone after Jimmy Yamashiro," I said. "If he hadn't set that con in motion, I would never have been summoned out to the West Coast and you might've continued on with your sunset retreats, avocado toast, and herbal enemas."

Nancy shook her head. I reached into my pocket and pulled out Samuelson's card. I stopped walking and handed it to her. We stood on the little arched bridge over the island in the lagoon. We were alone as she glanced down at the card and then back up at me.

Nancy didn't take the card, but she didn't exactly tear it up into tiny pieces, either.

"Someone should punch you right in the goddamn nose."

"They have," I said. "Several times. Would you like to examine my profile?"

"Joseph Haldorn is a great man," she said. "Who has done great things."

"Besides running a pyramid scheme and robbing a few banks?"

Nancy Sharp's mouth hung open. She stared at me with wide, unblinking eyes.

"And now his time has come," I said.

"You want me to sell him out?"

"For murder?" I said. "It depends on how much you believe in HELIOS, Nancy."

She clenched her jaw and turned back the way we'd just come, breaking into a jog along the path and heading back toward the boathouse.

I watched as she pulled out and drove off. Two more cars followed, women behind both of the wheels. Sisters to the end.

46

It was nightfall and I drove back to Santa Monica, fighting traffic, jockeying for a position along Pico. I decided not to attempt taking the 10, feeling good on a familiar route to where I once stayed in Westwood, thinking that I might stop by The Apple Pan and bring back burgers, fries, and some pie for Team Gabby. I called Susan from the car to catch her up on the latest fun with her close-and-personal friend Nancy Sharp.

"She's getting worse," Susan said. "Z had to restrain her. I don't like this. This is not why I came out here."

"How bad?"

"The neighbors can hear her pounding on the walls," she said. "She needs more help than I can give her."

"And now?"

"Z calmed her down."

"For a big guy, Z has a soothing effect on people," I said.

"I don't think the soothing part is why she settled down," Susan said. "She tried to throw a chair out a second-story window."

"Yikes."

"Thank God she's weak," Susan said. "That would've brought on the police and more questions than either one of us want right now. I want to help. But I'd rather not lose my goddamn license."

"Would burgers and pie from The Apple Pan help?"

"I don't eat burgers," Susan said. "And rarely pie."

"I'll take that as a maybe."

I passed billboards for new TV shows and big summer blockbusters, breast enlargement and liposuction. Accident lawyers smiled down on me, promising to fight for me at all costs. Everything was pancake flat and spread out into an ever-expanding void of nothingness. More 7-Elevens, 76 gas stations, and endless chain drugstores along the sunbaked streets. I fought the radio dial to find something that I recognized, lucking upon some Art Pepper. Rain began to hit the windshield and I snapped on the wipers. I passed a strip club lit in purple neon. Another billboard advertised a big Cinderella musical coming to town.

I was halfway back to Santa Monica when my phone buzzed. It was Eric Collinson.

"Holy shit, Spenser," he said. "I've called you a thousand times."

"And yet I only received five hundred messages."

"Why didn't you call me back?"

"I've been a little busy."

"Jimmy Yamashiro," he said. "Holy shit. The police kept me almost all yesterday. They knew I knew Gabby and I'd worked with Mr. Yamashiro. This is big. So big. I don't know what to do. I haven't slept or eaten in two days."

"Get something to eat," I said. "Sleep."

"I need to talk," he said. "It's very important. The police say Gabby is missing again. Missing. She's fucking missing, man. I thought you were supposed to find her."

Collinson's enunciation was slightly less than I expected from a Princeton man. I heard a lot of noise and laughter in the background, loud music blaring.

"Yeah, I've been drinking," he said. "And if you'd been through what I've been through, you'd be drinking, too."

"I cast no stones."

"I need to talk with you."

"I need a burger," I said. "And hot apple pie with a slice of cheese. We all need something, Eric."

"This is about Gabby," he said. "I love her, man. I really love her. I'm going out of my damn mind."

"She's fine."

"How do you know?"

I didn't answer. I drove west listening to Art's alto sax, thinking of burgers and pie.

"Do you have her?" Eric said. "If you have her, man, you need to let me know, like now."

"She's safe," I said.

"Thank God," he said. "Oh, thank God. I really need to see you, man. I have something that you need to see."

"A hot script?" I said.

"Something better," he said. "I should have showed you this shit a long time ago."

47

I found Eric at a dive called Mandrake on La Cienega.

The bar was dark, cool, and barely lit by neon bar signs. It was too hip and clean to be a true dive bar, but that wouldn't stop the kids from believing it. Several Millennials flitted about a jukebox, clutching tall pints of the most local of microbrews. A disco ball twirled in the back room by a NO DANCING sign. Steely Dan played from the speakers. Ironic. The cocktails and draft were listed on a fancy font on a thick menu. I chose a local IPA without paying attention to the description.

"What took you so long?" Collinson said.

"You called fifteen minutes ago."

"Took your time," Collinson said. "Just saying."

"Does anyone like you, Eric?"

"Sure," Collinson said, staring straight ahead. Looking a bit wobbly on the barstool. "Everyone fucking loves me."

"Of course they do," I said.

"Where is she?"

"Who?"

"Son of a bitch," Collinson said. He looked up from his empty glass and snapped his fingers at the bartender. I never liked people who snapped their fingers at bartenders. It was also a sure way to get rat poison shaken and stirred into your martini. Although whatever he was drinking looked red, probably the Mandrake's version of the negroni.

"She's safe," I said.

"So you say."

"Yep."

"God," he said. "What is going on? What the hell is going on? I did everything I could for her. I am. I still fucking am."

"Sure you want another drink?"

"What are you, my dad?" he said. "My damn dad. What a flaming asshole."

I was probably about the same age as his dad. But I didn't appreciate the comparison. And I bet Eric's dad was a wonderful guy. Just look how he turned out.

"You got her away from those people, didn't you?" he said. "You and that big Indian guy? You rescued the goddamn maiden from the tower while I sat around with nothing but my dick in hand."

"Looks more like a negroni."

"What?"

"In your hand."

"Smartass," he said. "Damn smartass."

"What do you want?" I said. "Or did you just want someone to knock you off that barstool?"

I lifted my beer and took a long pull. The beer was very cold and tasted as if it had been handcrafted by angels. I would need a replacement in a very short time.

"I love her," Collinson said.

"I know."

"But she's crazy," he said. "She's definitely crazy."

"I detected a little of that, too."

"No," Collinson said. "No. No. No. Not just with HELIOS and Haldorn and all that crapola. I'm talking about off-balance. Psycho. She's obsessed. Obsessive. She was a little like that with me."

"Before or after she dumped you?"

He muttered something under his breath. He lolled his head around at me and squinted somewhere in my direction. "Whatever. Whatever."

I drank more of my beer. I looked at my watch. Fleetwood Mac had replaced Steely Dan. I eagerly anticipated The Eagles. I knew somewhere that "Hotel California" waited for us all. I set down the beer at the same moment as Collinson landed a thick brown accordion folder on the bar.

I looked at the folder. And then over at Collinson. He looked very pleased with himself, stroking his thin hipster beard.

"I left my cheaters in my car," I said. "Want to tell me what's in the file?"

"You were right," Collinson said. "I did clean out Gabby's apartment. I tried to get rid of a ton of emails that would've made her look bad. And I took a lot of letters that would've made her look even worse. These are letters she wrote to Jimmy Yamashiro that for some reason she never sent. She just squirreled them away. Dozens of them in a nightstand. The whole thing was really weird."

"And how does that help her?"

"It helps you protect her," he said. "I didn't know what I was dealing with. Not until much later. You have to be careful. Watch your back. She looks like an angel. A true and authentic angel."

"But she's the devil in disguise?"

"She's not evil," Collinson said. He turned up his drink and drained most of it. He set it down and wiped his mouth with a napkin. "She's just messed up in the head. Very messed up. All this was fun and games until they killed Jimmy Yamashiro. He may have been an ass-hole. But he didn't deserve to get shot on the toilet."

"Only the lucky ones."

"Gabby wanted him dead," he said. "Read the letters, you'll see it."

"You think she killed Yamashiro?"

"Take the files," Collinson said. He stood, reached into his pocket, and handed the bartender his credit card. He nodded toward me. "His, too."

"Thanks."

"Can I see her?" Collinson said.

"Nope."

"When?"

"When all this is over," I said.

"And when the hell will that be?"

I took a sip of beer and leaned against the bar. On a far wall, there was a pinkish neon sign that said UNHAPPY HOUR. I looked over to Collinson as he stood in the middle of the bar, waiting for me to say something profound. The far wall by the door was made of glass brick, and every few moments car lights would shine through as they turned onto the street.

I just stared at him until he shook his head and left.

48

I drove back to the Santa Monica condo and started to boil a large pot of water.

"What are you doing?" Susan said.

"Thinking," I said.

"Looks like you're cooking," she said. "Did you abandon The Apple Pan?"

"I figured you and Z deserved a nice home-cooked meal."

"We can't really go out," Susan said. "With Gabby chained to the bed."

"She's not chained," I said.

"She might as well be," Susan said. "We can't keep her."

"And we can't let her go," I said. "She'll run straight back to Haldorn."

"That's her decision to make."

I pulled a box of soba noodles from the cabinet and

three pounds of fresh shrimp from the refrigerator. I had already started to roast a cookie sheet full of sliced rounds of sweet potatoes sprinkled with sea salt. I checked in the oven and they appeared about done. I closed the oven door, feeling the heat, and turned back to Susan.

"Her mother can't get here until tomorrow afternoon," Susan said. "She tried talking to Gabby again today. It didn't go well."

"What's her mother want to do?"

"She said to let her go," Susan said. "I almost did this afternoon during one of her rages. This isn't doing anyone any good."

"Chollo and I took her because we believed she was being held against her will."

"She denies it," Susan said. "And she is an adult. What we're doing now isn't right."

"What if I told you her ex-boyfriend believes Gabby might've killed Jimmy Yamashiro?"

"I would say consider the source."

"What if I said I've returned with a large stack of incriminating letters?"

"I'd say she's been under the influence of a sociopath," Susan said. "I don't care what she's said or what she's written over these last few months."

"She's safer with us."

"Of course she is," Susan said. "But what are we going to do? Tie her up, stick her in the trunk, and drive her back to Boston kicking and screaming?"

I looked up from where I was peeling the shrimp in the sink. "That's an idea."

"A terrible idea," Susan said. "So terrible that I could never work again and get my pants sued off as a bonus."

"Can I comment about getting your pants off?"

"Now?" she said. "No. You may not."

I removed the roasting pan from the oven and moved the rounds of sweet potatoes off to one side. I added in some more olive oil, dropped in the three pounds of shrimp, and returned the pan to the oven. "I'm not going to just let her go."

"Staying or leaving is Gabby's call."

"I appreciate you being open-minded on her condition," I said. "But getting Gabby out of that mansion wasn't exactly a cakewalk."

"Actually, you said you and Chollo waltzed in and waltzed out," Susan said. "Sounded like a cakewalk to me."

"A waltz requires practice and talent," I said. "And a meeting with the Armenian Power glee club to make that happen."

Susan tilted her head, started to say something, and then changed her mind. She moved closer to me and put her hand on my upper arm, whispering in my ear, "Just because you let her go doesn't mean you and Z can't keep watching out for her."

I nodded, adding the noodles to the boiling water, and set the timer for six minutes. I walked to the sink, washed my hands, and dried them with a dish towel.

"LAPD can't find Haldorn," I said.

"And that scares you?"

"It scares me for Gabby," I said. "Then again, he may never be found."

"We've done all we can," Susan said. "We even brought in a woman who lost her daughter to those people. But now, like it or not, we have to allow her to act on her own. Whether you do it or I do it, she needs to understand she is free to walk out of that door."

I nodded. "Okay."

"Okay?"

"You expected more pushback?"

"Frankly, yes," Susan said. "A lot more."

"How often do you change your mind after making a decision?"

Susan smiled. The smile could've lit up most of the San Fernando Valley.

"You sent me out here to find Gabby," I said. "I found Gabby. What to do with Gabby and what is best for Gabby is not my department."

Susan walked up on me, toe-to-toe, and kissed me hard on the lips, offering something much more powerful than mind control. I wrapped my arm around her waist and pulled her in even closer. She smelled like lavender and good soap and sunshine. Her dark skin radiated heat.

"Do we have wine?" I said.

"That's a ridiculous question."

"Pour some wine."

She poured while I rinsed snap peas in a colander. When the noodles were ready, I dumped them over the peas, careful to keep a little water back in the pot. I poured the noodles and the peas back into the pot and set them on a rear eye to simmer.

"More healthy than burgers and apple pie," she said.

"With great sadness, I agree."

"Z said you two are customers of the month at In-N-Out Burger."

"Traitor," I said.

"Will he be back for dinner?" Susan said.

"I'll set aside a plate for him."

"And then?" Susan said.

I started to hum the first bit of "Born Free." Susan scowled at me as I checked on the shrimp and sweet potatoes and set about to make the sauce. I gathered the forces of tahini, lemon juice, chopped garlic, and red pepper flakes. I whisked like there was no tomorrow.

"How bad was it?" I said.

Susan lifted up her arm and showed me the bottom of her elbow.

"That little bitch bit me."

"I would ask if that's a first," I said. "But I think I know the answer."

"Patients seldom bite their shrinks," she said. "At least not in Cambridge. We're too damn expensive."

I dumped the noodles and peas into a large bowl and then added in the shrimp and sweet potatoes, mixing it all with the tahini sauce. Susan made a small plate for Gabby and started to walk it back to the bedroom.

"How about I take it from here?" I said.

"Maybe she'll like the food so much, she'll decide to stay."

"What are the chances?"

"Slim to none," Susan said. "It's time."

49

"Lovely night," I said.

Gabby, riding in the passenger seat, didn't reply.

"Slight chance of rain tomorrow," I said. "A high in the mid-seventies."

Still no answer.

"Sometimes I feel we are all trapped in a kind of living death that suppresses everything natural and wonderful about being human."

Not even a sideways glance. If Thoreau didn't shake up the kids, I didn't know what else would. I wondered what ol' Joe Haldorn did to motivate the faithful. Joe probably had an entire TED Talk about existential plight. Lucky bastard. Heading back on the 10, streetlamps skimming across the shiny red hood of my rental, Chet Baker crooned "The Thrill Is Gone" on the radio.

"A man like Haldorn won't stop until he uses up all

you have," I said. "I've known guys like him. He can't feel things for other people. He wants your youth and energy until it's gone. Just ask Nancy Sharp. She was with him, wasn't she? Now she's in a more ancillary role."

In the passing, flickering light Gabby looked healthier than she had when I'd found her. There was color back in her cheeks and she'd showered and pulled her hair back into a neat blond ponytail. She wore no makeup and a simple scoop-neck black T-shirt and yoga pants that Susan had purchased for her. As we drove, her hands were folded neatly in her lap. Her immense green eyes stared straight ahead at the highway, showing not a drop of emotion.

She was a striking young woman. Her bone structure, long limbs, and feline eyes were the kind of stuff that people paid ten bucks to see on the big screen. I could see why her agent in Boston had told her to go west, young woman.

"Can I ask what makes Haldorn and HELIOS important to you?"

The exit onto Fairfax was coming up in a mile. I veered into the right lane, passing by flickering lights atop construction barrels. Gabby wet her lips and took in a deep breath but didn't speak. I had the windows down and the warm air circulated in the space between us.

"What was it that moved you?"

"You'll only make fun of it," she said. "Someone like you only sees what they want. You have preconceived judgments based on your Western worldview."

"Actually, more Eastern," I said. "I have a Boston-centric outlook."

She glanced over at me, but didn't speak until I slid off the interstate and turned onto Fairfax, driving as slow as possible, making the most of our quiet bonding time until I dropped her off at her apartment. The roads were almost white and sunbaked, tar shot into the cracked grooves.

"How could I even try to explain a sisterhood to a man?"

"Try," I said. "We have time."

"Would you agree we live in a selfish, male-driven society?"

"Sure."

"What if you could give up the ego and be a part of something larger?"

"My ego is often the thing that keeps me alive."

"How so?"

"I have belief in myself and my skills," I said. "And I often prefer being alone."

"So you have a fear of being part of a group?" she said.

"No," I said. "But I don't believe joining a group adds strength."

"Typical male bullshit."

"Being self-contained and independent?"

"You just can't understand how freeing it is to be part of something larger than yourself, to just let go and realize that you're not the one in control. It's like a pile of bricks get lifted from your shoulders. You feel support. You feel love and strength."

"I've heard many people describe that relationship with God."

"I'm not implying that Dr. Haldorn is God," she said. "But he is a prophet."

"When exactly did he become a doctor?" I said. "Before, after, or during prison?"

"He has degrees in a lot of subjects," she said. "A normal mind can't even comprehend how he views this world. He could dedicate his energy and talents only to making money, serving himself. But he wants to actually make the world a better place. I guess something like that sounds pretty corny to you."

"Nope," I said. "It sounds wonderful. If it were true. What does HELIOS do to make the world a better place? I didn't see him volunteering at the local leper colony."

"Dr. Haldorn helped me become the woman I've always wanted to be," she said. "He's broken down a rotten and broken belief system. Cultural norms and expectations limit our abilities. Being afraid stops our potential. We can fly if we break off pride, ego, and unnatural inhibitions. We can fly together as people."

"I can't fly," I said. "But I can leap tall buildings in a single bound."

She didn't answer. She either thought I was making fun of her or had never heard of George Reeves. We were coming into Hollywood, the land of eternal dreams. It was late, but the streets were crowded, and the lights of million-dollar homes twinkled across the hills.

"What if I told you Haldorn was a fake?"

"He warned us of people like you," she said. "People who would dismiss his accomplishments."

"Oops," I said. "What if I told you he was only interested in money? And most likely sex?"

"Are you a puritan?" she said. "What's wrong with sex? Do you think it's only for men to enjoy?"

"Not in the least," I said. "I'm definitely pro-sex."

"Then why should men be the only ones with multiple partners?" she said. "Shouldn't women be powerful creatures? We can use sex for pleasure or for power. I don't feel guilt about it. Not in the least. I'm free of all those hang-ups that were beaten into me as a little girl."

"Do you have sex with Haldorn?"

"That's none of your goddamn business."

"Maybe not," I said. "But it strikes a blow at his pro-women movement."

"Dr. Haldorn has many partners and many relationships," she said. "Many great men do."

"That must mean I'm not a great man."

"One woman?"

"Yep," I said. "For a very long time."

"That must be very limiting," she said. "In many ways."

"Actually," I said. "It's not limiting at all."

"Don't you want to be with other women?" she said. "You don't find other women attractive?"

"Sure," I said. "I like women."

"They why don't you act on it?"

"To quote Paul Newman, why go out for hamburger when you have steak at home?"

"Who's Paul Newman?" she said.

I had no answer to that question. I felt there was quite a gap between me and Gabby Leggett as we turned onto

Hollywood Boulevard and headed back toward her apartment. It seemed an ice age since I'd arrived in Hollywood, finding her apartment a wreck and the laptop Eric Collinson had clumsily tried to erase. We turned onto Yorba Linda, lined with back-to-back midcentury-modern apartment buildings.

"What's the difference between Jimmy Yamashiro and Joe Haldorn?" I said. "If any."

She started to laugh, covering her mouth. She was shoeless, clutching a grocery bag filled with the clothes she'd had on when I'd found her at the HELIOS complex. I slowed to a stop in front of her apartment and parked in front of a black van on jacked-up tires. The side of the van advertised something called Vagina guitars. I looked at it twice to make sure I'd read it correctly. The shape and design of the logo made it so.

"If you get scared," I said.

"I won't."

"If you want out," I said.

"Why would I?"

"They tied you up," I said. "They held you against your will."

Gabby nodded, pulling a few loose strands of hair away from her eyes. She looked at me with those sleepy eyes, breathing in and out from her cute upturned nose. "So did you," she said. "Lots of irony in that, Spenser. Don't you think?"

I watched her leave the car and march across the small lawn of the apartment complex, shoeless, key in her entry code, and disappear. I drove off, parked a block away, and returned on foot, finding a concrete bench across the street, quiet in shadow.

I texted Susan. And then Sixkill.

He would relieve me in a few hours.

I waited for what seemed like a very long time, although only an hour and a half. I got up and returned to my car, circled the block, and found a slot about five hundred feet from Gabby's apartment. I turned on the radio and scrolled around. Not finding what I wanted, I played a little Dave Brubeck from my phone. I never saw Brubeck in person. I'm sure Ron Della Chiesa saw Brubeck. Probably sat five feet away from him as he launched into "Take Five" on the piano. Ron was lucky that way.

It was nearly two a.m. when a car pulled in behind me and flashed its high beams in my rearview. I reached for my gun and grabbed the door handle. I watched as a man crawled out and stretched, moving into the swath of light from the streetlamps.

It was Samuelson. And he didn't look happy.

50

How'd you know I was here?" I said.

"I didn't," Samuelson said. "I came for Gabby Leggett."

"How did you know she was back?"

"We have people," Samuelson said. "Some private eye. You didn't see them?"

"I noticed a suspicious car down the block," I said. "I thought it might be Haldorn's people."

"Haldorn's gone," he said. "We think he left the state. That whole Norma Desmond mansion on West Adams is empty as a church on Monday. I spent the whole night combing through it. What a weird goddamn place."

"What'd you find?"

"Oh, just the usual L.A. setup, eighteen bedrooms, ten baths, a swimming pool, and a tricked-out basement. A fucking sex room down there that would make Marquis de Sade blush."

"Yikes."

"You said it," Samuelson said. "I've been around the block, seen a thing or two. He had devices, contraptions, fucking swings, and tables with straps and locks. *Christ.* Looked like he was setting up to be a damn gynecologist."

We stood between my rental and his unmarked cop car. A hard, warm wind blew down from the hills and into the basin, ruffling the back of my shirt.

"Any witnesses?"

"One of the guards you subdued," he said.

"I have no idea what you're talking about."

"Sure you don't," Samuelson said. "Fucking guy wouldn't shut up. He'd seen it all. Girls come and go. Some real *Eyes Wide Shut* kind of crap with the masks and naked as jaybirds, flitting around, swapping partners while they guzzled champagne. Jesus. This damn town."

"Gabby called it female empowerment."

"So did your pal Nancy Sharp."

"You spoke with her?"

"At length," Samuelson said. "The woman had a lot to say. To the point, she believes in the system but not so much in the founder."

"I had heard there was a rift."

"She claims she didn't authorize or condone the freaky-deaky sex shit," he said. "She says he's perverted the whole damn operation."

"Can't charge him with that."

"Nope," Samuelson said. "But we can charge him with murder. Nancy Sharp says Haldorn killed Yamashiro. We got some other stuff, that I can't divulge at this time, that puts him right at Griffith Park."

"What about Sarkisov?"

I kept what I'd learned about Gabby from Collinson to myself. LAPD didn't need to know what a jealous boyfriend suspected.

"As much as it pains me," he said, "the son of a bitch was telling the truth. The Armenians were set up and Haldorn is the guy who left them holding a big flaming pile of shit. Haldorn sent them to the park to find Jimmy on the john."

"Wow."

"Yep," he said. "And they're not pleased. I understand that Sarkisov wants Haldorn's schlong served up like a Coney Island special. Has most of his guys out there searching for him."

"Armenian Power."

"Haldorn better pray to God or the planets that we find him first," he said. "I can't imagine that we will find him alive. Or intact."

"Why would he kill Yamashiro?" I said. "That doesn't make any sense. Seems like Yamashiro would've been the gift that kept on giving."

"We intend to ask him," he said. "If we can find him."

"And why do you now need Gabby?"

"We understand she's the current golden girl," he said. "Haldorn believes she offers him some kind of special powers. Like some kind of fucked-up muse. He told

Nancy Sharp that Gabby was someone really special to HELIOS and that he'd been waiting for her arrival."

"Preordained."

"These fucking people," he said. "You have flakes like this in Boston?"

"Mainly in Cambridge," I said. "But yes."

"Come with me to get Gabby?" he said. "She might go more quietly with you around."

"Don't bet on it."

We walked up the concrete walkway to Gabby's apartment and buzzed her apartment. There was no answer after several tries. Two units showed up soon and four more officers. We all stood outside the gate, waiting for the apartment manager to let us in. The air had the acrid tinge of eucalyptus.

The manager was a funny-looking guy in saggy jeans and a dirty yellow T-shirt, short, with more hair in his ears than on his head. He griped about the hour but let us in and took us up to the second floor and Gabby's apartment. We knocked several times without an answer, and the guy, still griping, reached for a large set of keys on his belt and let us in.

Samuelson called out Gabby's name.

I turned on the light. We checked the bedroom and bathrooms. Under the bed and in the closets. Gabby was gone. "Is there another way out of here?" Samuelson said.

"There's a wall out back," the manager said, sticking a pinkie into his ear and itching. "Pretty damn tall. I could've hopped it twenty years ago. Not anymore."

Samuelson looked to me and shook his head. "Some detective."

I felt my phone buzz in my pocket. I recognized the number.

"Eric?"

"I have her, Spenser," he said. "She's with me. She's safe."

"Where are you?"

"She's safe," he said. "That's all you need to know."

"And Joe Haldorn?"

He didn't answer. The line silent between us.

"A lot of people want him dead," I said. "I can't protect you if I don't know where you are. You're being used, kid."

"She told me she loved me," Collinson said. "I'm doing what is best for Gabby. And that's all you need to know."

Before I could answer, the connection clicked off. It was nearly three in the morning, and dark behind Gabby's apartment. In the slanting artificial light, I could just make out the six-foot concrete block fence she'd hopped. I'd made a mistake, a long time ago, with another client in L.A. I had a sickening feeling we were headed to a similar spot. I recalled a time of a lot of wind and rain.

Such a long time ago.

51

I met Sixkill at Eric Collinson's apartment atop a tall hill in Silver Lake.

We knocked several times. We both broke and entered. Collinson wasn't there.

"This woman is confusing," Z said. "Why Collinson and not Haldorn?"

"She needed his help," I said. "She wanted someone who'd do what she said and ask few questions."

"And Haldorn is hiding because of the Armenians," he said. "Who want to seize his parts."

"Samuelson says Sarkisov has a bounty on one specific part."

"I'd leave the country."

"I think that's the plan."

Z shrugged as we walked back to his car, parked on the slope of the hill, the nose of the Mustang edging upward. It was pitch black except for the odd streetlight. The air had grown warmer, palm trees dancing at the edge of the road. The winds scattered the black hair across his face, a strong gust nearly slamming the door from his hands. "Santa Ana winds," he said. "In August, they blow so hard and hot, they make people crazy."

"Out here," I said, "how can you tell?"

"Even crazier than normal," he said. "Back in the day, the Spaniards would forgive those who'd committed crimes during the winds."

As Z opened the driver's door, his cell phone rang. He spoke for a few quick seconds and pocketed the phone.

"Jem Yoon," I said.

He nodded. "Says her guy got a ping on Collinson's phone. Close to LAX. Somewhere on Manchester. She says her guy is usually accurate within a block or two. Remember what Collinson was driving?"

"BMW M240i in alpine white."

"You're good," Sixkill said.

"Some might say the best."

"Some might," Sixkill said. "With a new guy closing in second."

"Pride went before," I said. "Ambition follows him."

Z got in behind the wheel and I climbed into the passenger seat. We didn't talk as he hit the interstate at speeds only possible before dawn. In Boston, we called interstates by number, here it seemed all big roads have *the* in front of them. It wouldn't do to hop on 110, we had to hop on *the* 110 on over to *the* 405. Didn't call them routes here, either. Only seemed to have routes back home. I liked routes. Gave a road character.

"Did you tell Samuelson about Collinson?" Sixkill said.

"Nope."

"Figure we can reason with him better."

"You and I might offer more expediency."

Z found the rough slice along Airlines that Jem Yoon had pinpointed. We drove slow, searching for Collinson's alpine white car. We passed several gas stations, long-term parking lots, McDonald's, El Pollo Loco. The road was lined with telephone poles, wires dancing in the high wind. All-night convenience stores brightly lit and lonely. The winds blew so hard, they buffeted the Mustang.

We traveled up and down Airlines four times without spotting a thing. Z called Jem Yoon to check again. Her people had narrowed the search to the western edge of Airlines, beyond the road and into a construction site, blocked off with concrete barriers. Small construction trailers had been set up with what looked like a parking deck taking shape beyond the cleared land. Z dodged in and out of the barrier maze, headlights shining far into the distance onto a bright white BMW parked at a haphazard angle by a battered CAT earth compactor.

Z hit the high beams and we both got out at the same time.

The driver's door to the BMW was open and the interior light glowed. The motor was still running, giving a soft, even hum in the buffeting winds. Trash bags and paper coffee cups skittered past the reach of the headlights. I could taste the sand and the grit swirling about us.

We walked toward the car together, silent and slow. A huge plane passed close overhead, drowning out everything, red lights blinking on its wings.

I took a deep breath and pushed the door open wider.

Inside, Eric Collinson lay slumped over the center console, his face down in the plush leather seat. There was a lot of blood across the dash and down onto the floorboards. His cell phone lay on the floor, display lit showing five of my missed calls.

Another plane, this time smaller and more quiet, flew overhead. There was silence and then the winds blew even stronger, pushing at the dirt and the grit, twisting the cleared land into a brown swirl.

"What did I say about the winds?" Z said.

In the headlights, I could make out several different footprints in the soft, powdery dirt. They were grouped in tight patterns, seeming to walk in spirals before moving in a straight line toward a halting tire print that then veered out back toward the road.

"Isn't tracking a job for an Indian?" Z said.

"I didn't want to go for the stereotype."

"A blind man could feel his way through that scuffle," he said. "Looks like a big truck or SUV."

"Sarkisov."

"Why would he kill Collinson?"

"He must've gotten in the way," I said. "I think Eric was taking Gabby to Haldorn. Sarkisov found them all."

"Stupid."

"Love is blind," I said.

Z looked back at the BMW, the sloping figure of Collinson over the console. "Damn sure is."

52

At nearly four a.m., we wound our way up into the leafy green hills of Bel-Air and into the open wrought-iron gates of Victor del Rio's mansion.

Chollo stood at the top of the drive as we entered and walked us through the house and into a study. The room was dark and wood-paneled, with plenty of leather-bound volumes that interior decorators collect but their clients seldom read. Del Rio was seated in a big brown leather chair, half lit by a spindly brass lamp. He had on a white terry-cloth robe and blue silk slippers.

Del Rio didn't seem happy to see us. Chollo took a seat beside a giant marble desk. Bobby Horse came in after us, closing the sliding doors of the study.

"Your girl and Haldorn were going to fly out to Mexico," he said. "But they were followed."

"Did you hear anything about a young man named Collinson?"

"No," he said. "Why?"

"They killed him."

"Would he be the kind to put up a fight?" he said. "For the woman?"

"Probably."

Del Rio shook his head. He rubbed his tired eyes and stood up, pacing before the big desk. Chollo didn't move at all, his eyes lingering on far wall, hands loose and relaxed by his sides. At one point, he seemed to stifle a yawn.

"I think he was taking Gabby to Haldorn," I said. "One of them was followed."

Del Rio continued to pace. He walked over to the desk and reached for a thick crystal glass full of a brown liquid. He took a sip, set the glass back on the leather blotter, and wiped his salt-and-pepper mustache.

"Sarkisov can't be trusted," he said. "He told you he'd let you take the girl."

"Yes."

"And now he has her."

"Probably a package deal," I said. "It sounds like he only wanted Haldorn."

"How would you feel if someone set you up for killing one of the most powerful people in Los Angeles?"

"I'd be a little hurt."

"Sarkisov doesn't hurt," del Rio said. "He bleeds with anger. If he hasn't killed this man already, he will soon.

And the girl. How again did the girl get free of you? I thought this matter was all handled."

I looked across to Sixkill. The big man raised his eyebrows and tilted his head.

"Easy come, easy go."

"Not a good answer, my friend," he said. "This woman. She is probably dead, too. I would leave it. I would pack my things and let Mr. Sixkill take you to the airport. I would fly home and let this be behind you."

"A loss on the road?" I said.

"If you say so."

"I can't let that happen again," I said.

"You?" he said. "I didn't think you ever lost. Or at least admitted it."

"Long time ago," I said. "I don't want it to happen again."

Del Rio crossed over to the great desk again and reached for the crystal glass. He drained it quickly and set it down empty. He stood, hands in the pockets of his robe, beside Chollo, and then looked to me and Sixkill. Bobby Horse had left us alone in the room. A trapezoidal pattern of artificial light filtered through the leaded glass window and across a big Oriental rug.

"I don't owe you anything," del Rio said to me. "Nothing."

"Nope."

"And it would be foolish for a man in my position to make trouble with Sarkisov," he said. "In such changing and tempestuous times."

"Tempestuous," I said. "Agreed."

"But him," he said, lifting his hand from his robe and pointing to Sixkill. "Him, I owe. Him I owe many favors for what he did. So perhaps we leave it up to our friend, Zebulon. Do you want to find this woman?"

Z looked to me with his hooded eyes and then back to del Rio. He nodded. "Sure," he said. "Why not?"

"Okay," del Rio said, circling the desk and finding a place in a large rolling chair upholstered with thick leather and brass studs. He turned on a desk lamp, lifted the top on a humidor, and selected a fat cigar. "I would offer you a cigar. But I know none of you smoke."

We waited as del Rio clipped off the end of the cigar with a pen knife and reached for a giant lighter on his desk. Once he got the cigar going, he leaned back in the padded chair, his face half shadowed and half in the desk light.

"Sarkisov keeps a house outside of Furlong at the edge of Hollywood," he said. "It's an old motel where many of his people live and sometimes work. They keep it like a clubhouse, full of drugs and booze. Sarkisov has new women from the old country brought in. This is where he breaks them in to do his work."

"Nice," Sixkill said.

"These people," he said, "are not like the people who watched the false messiah on West Adams. The old motel has a big surrounding wall and a chained gate. If, and I don't know if I am correct, this is where he is keeping this man Haldorn and your girl, they will make a lot of trouble. They are mean people with short tempers and many guns."

I nodded. "Wonderful."

"But if it's as I suspect and they are dead, what does it matter now, anyway?"

"It matters," I said.

"Leave it for the police."

"We do that and she's absolutely dead."

"And this Haldorn?" del Rio said.

"He's on his own," I said. "All his parts."

Del Rio leaned back into his chair, letting the smoke drift up from his cigar. His eyes lingering on me and then Chollo. He looked to Chollo and simply lifted his chin.

"Chollo knows where," he said. "He's watched this place many times for me. I never trusted that son of a bitch."

I offered my hand. Del Rio reached out and shook mine.

53

The Motel Hollywood was a motel only Norman Bates's mother could love. The place had probably offered clean rooms, color TVs, and AC long before Neil Armstrong had visited the moon. Now the entrance to the motor court was secured with a rolling and padlocked chain-link fence and blocked from Sunset Boulevard with a tall decorative concrete block wall. I looked for a historic marker for famous people who might've died there.

Z and I had strolled past separately twenty minutes ago, peering inside the gate and spotting a decrepit two-story house that had probably served as an office/lobby at one time, and six, maybe eight cabin-style buildings that had been built around it.

"If it's all the same," I said, "I prefer the Beverly Wilshire."

"I'm getting bedbugs just looking at it."

We exited the Mustang at the same time, Z circling

behind to pop his trunk and pass me a pair of wire snippers. He grabbed his twelve-gauge, holding the stock under his jacket and letting the short barrel hang down by his thigh. I had the Browning 9 I'd borrowed.

We didn't see Chollo, but we both knew he was there.

As we crossed the street, the wind pushed the grit and trash down the sidewalks, the tall palms shaking back and forth in the dark. One or two cars passed on Sunset. No one seemed to pay us any mind. I hoped Sarkisov's people wouldn't, either. Maybe it was past their bedtime and they were exhausted from a long, hard day of cutting drugs and dealing in stolen TVs and mattresses.

I snipped the lock from the rolling gate and slid it back far enough for us to pass.

I moved first, holding the Browning. Z followed.

I heard music inside, a melodic sitar and electronic keyboard coming from behind a tiny English Tudor with a slanting metal awning instead of a shingled roof. An ancient neon sign in a dirty window flashed NO VACANCY.

"No shit," Z said, walking beside me, skirting the edges and keeping in shadow.

"Maybe they'll make an exception," I said. "I'll tell them I used to date Dorothy Lamour."

The asphalt had been broken up and hauled off long ago. The parking lot was now fine, packed dirt. The grit shifting back and forth in the high winds, glowing a pale red in the neon from the motel sign. Our feet made distinctive crunching sounds in the dirt as we walked over to a black Chevy Tahoe and crouched behind it.

Two men walked around the old motel office carrying

automatic weapons on shoulder straps. They were both wearing black denim jackets and smoking cigarettes. One of them stopped cold and looked around, nodding to the other, and headed back to the front gate where I'd cut the lock. The wind pushed down off the mountains and into the basin, kicking up the dirt into whirls of brown dust. The men turned their heads and covered their eyes as they made their way back to the main house. Coughing. One of them had a shaved head and clipped beard. The other was shorter and fat, with small eyes and longish black hair. He had on an untucked black silk shirt and loose and sloppy black pants.

Z was on them first, raising his shotgun and asking them to stand still with some artful expletives.

They didn't listen. And raised their guns.

I shot one. And Z blasted his friend. We knocked them both off their feet and onto their backs. It was quick and dirty work.

We continued to move forward. Two cabin doors flew open. A kid ran out holding a handgun while trying to pull on his pants. His hands were shaking.

A fat man rushed outside in black bikini briefs with an AR-15 rifle. He had black hair everywhere but the top of his head. Before he could get off a shot, we heard a crack from behind the fence and he tumbled onto his back like a flipped turtle.

I looked behind me. I didn't see Chollo, but he had made his presence felt.

The kid dropped to the ground and tried to crawl back into the cabin. The wind was strong against us, pushing at our backs, as we moved forward in the dark, pointing our guns at the kid before he could get back inside. Z kept watch from behind a pillar, scanning the empty dirt courtyard. The loud rap music from the third cabin hadn't stopped the entire time, the inside lit up like a dollhouse.

Shadows passed in front of the windows. I reached down and grabbed the boy's hair and lifted his head. "Sarkisov?"

He nodded. I dropped his head and picked up his pistol. I reached down again and snatched the collar of his shirt and pulled him to his feet. "Call him."

The boy shook his head. Chin quivering. I knocked him hard across the back of the head with my Browning. I didn't like doing it. I would've rather drop-kicked a kitten.

He stumbled, grasping the back of his head, but moved forward, finally getting off his knees, and approached the motel cabin with all the lights and music.

The boy just stood there.

I pushed him forward.

He shook his head again. I raised my gun.

The boy moved ahead, squinting through the wind and the dirt. He knocked on the door.

The door flew open and a man behind it blasted the kid with a quick sputter from his automatic rifle. He didn't stop, spraying the weapon at us as we both shot at him. Z with three rapid blasts from the shotgun and me with four shots from the Browning.

The man fell hard and fast. A woman screamed.

There was a lot of shuffling. And yelling in what I figured to be Armenian.

On the front steps of the cabin, the boy stared up at me with wide eyes and an open mouth, trying to speak some words that didn't seem to come. I called for Sarkisov. The lights went out in the little cabin. It grew very dark and hollow. The wind quieted down, leaving everything in an electric stillness.

My ears rang from the gunshots, the wind smelling burnt and acrid.

Sarkisov had lost four of his people. If he were in there, he wouldn't come out easily. Sixkill and I headed back behind the Tahoe, waiting. The wind scattered paper and leaves, bright flowers fluttering down from a vine along the wall on Sunset. Z reached into his pocket and jacked in more shells. I reloaded my Browning.

The cabin was dark and quiet. Behind us, the two men we'd shot lay sprawled out in the dirt parking lot.

"What now?" Z said.

"In the Old West they'd smoke him out."

"And the New West?"

"We wait."

"Not as much fun," Z said.

"Tom Mix would've gone in with both guns blasting."

"And he'd be dead."

"Already is," I said. "Killed by a stray piece of luggage."

We waited all but two minutes before Gabby Leggett appeared in the wide doorway, wearing gray sweatpants and a man's white undershirt splattered with blood. She was shoeless and wide-eyed, appearing to be wandering as a man screamed her name over and over inside.

Sarkisov followed, with a shiny new AR-15 at her back. He had blue track pants and what appeared to be a Members Only jacket. His head was even larger than I remembered, and he wore a big grin on his face as he walked toward us. He held the gun expertly in his hands, aimed right at the small of her back.

"Where's Haldorn?" I said.

"Some is here," Sarkisov said. "Some of him elsewhere."

"And her?" I said.

"Too much, my friend," he said. "She's seen too much."

"She's not a part of this," I said.

"Oh, yes?" he said. "You think? Joe Haldorn told us she killed the movie man, this Yamashiro. Haldorn wanted the movie man's money, but she shot him instead. She is crazy in the head. Set things off for all of us. *No. No, no, no.* You can't have her. She's broken. No use to anyone."

I was about to argue the point when I heard the crack of a rifle and Sarkisov's left eye disappeared into a black hole. He fell hard to the ground, the wind picking up, scattering brownish dirt over his body. His mouth moved and made shapes but offered no words.

Sixkill got to Gabby first, wrapping his leather jacket around her shoulders, as we moved fast for Sunset Boulevard. Chollo was out there somewhere, in the dark, watching our backs.

Miles away from Hollywood, I dialed Samuelson's cell.

54

Susan and I sat at the bar at Musso & Frank five days later.

The last few days hadn't been pleasant. Lots of discussions with LAPD. Lots of yelling from Samuelson. They'd taken the gun I'd borrowed from Chollo in addition to the .38 they'd gotten after the shoot-out at Griffith Park. We were finally headed back to Boston in the morning and Gabby Leggett had been checked into a posh rehab facility in Malibu by her mother. I wasn't so sure the herbal teas and yoga sessions Susan had told me about would make up for her killing Yamashiro or erase Haldorn's bloody end from her mind. However, I remained an optimist.

I knew she'd killed Yamashiro. Susan knew. And so did Samuelson. But making a case and removing the blame from the late Joe Haldorn was something else entirely. The press was all over Haldorn's shady past, and who was

I to correct them? Besides, Haldorn and Riese had mentally manipulated Gabby for financial gain. Yamashiro had manipulated Gabby for pleasure. You didn't need a Ph.D. from Stanford or Harvard to understand who was the gun, who made it, and who fired it.

I held a cold martini in my hand while Susan squeezed my knee under the bar.

"Careful or I might spill a drop."

Susan reached for her gimlet with vodka and fresh lime juice. She offered a devilish smile that would've been the ruin of a weaker man.

"Did you go?" she said.

I nodded.

"And does it get any easier?"

I shook my head. I took a drink and recalled slow dancing on a balcony long ago. Earlier I'd left red roses on Candy Sloan's grave. Susan called it penance.

"You don't have to anymore," she said.

"It's more for me."

Susan nodded. She understood. There were few things that Susan Silverman didn't understand, watching me with her enormous black eyes. Without saying a word, she seemed to take everything in, evaluating me and contemplating all that had swirled around us.

We drank together in the cavernous dining room, surrounded by the ghosts of Billy Wilder, Ernest Hemingway, and Tom Mix. The bartenders were old men with starched white shirts and black ties overlaid with red jackets with black lapels. They knew things. They spoke little and always offered an extra vial of your cocktail on the side.

"I miss Pearl," Susan said.

"She's up to five hundred followers on Instagram."

"God," she said. "Next thing you know, she'll get an agent."

I nodded. I selected a lovely green olive from a small bowl and popped it into my mouth.

"I don't know if Gabby even remembers the shooting."

"What did she say?" I said. "If it isn't patient–doctor privilege."

"I would tell you," Susan said, cutting her eyes over at me. "If it weren't."

"Will she ever be the same?"

"We're always the same," Susan said. "Just with more wear."

"Twenty-four is pretty young to screw up your life."

Susan looked around at the rich, paneled wood and soft glowing yellow lights. "Youth is wasted on the young."

The air seemed to hold space and time like a vacuum inside the doors, as if at any moment Bill Holden might saddle up to the bar for a double Jack Daniel's, startling no one at all. I looked across the bar to our reflection in the mirror, very glad to see it.

"It's an awful thought," Susan said. "But maybe Jimmy Yamashiro got what was coming to him."

"That is an awful thought," I said. "And very un-shrink-like."

"Maybe I hear about too many like him," she said. "In his world, women are disposable objects. Too many are dismissed or discarded too easily."

"I am not like Jimmy Yamashiro."

"Or Joe Haldorn."

"I'm glad," I said. "Because they're both dead."

"Let's drink to that," Susan said.

I looked down to see Susan had completely drained her gimlet.

"Yikes," I said. "Who are you and what have you done with Susan Silverman?"

"I'm right here," she said. Her black eyes grew sexy and sleepy. "And so are you."

"Anywhere else you'd like to be?"

"Nope," she said. "But if you see that Nancy Sharp again, I just might punch her right in the nose."

"I wouldn't worry too much about Nancy Sharp," I said.

"Do you know something I don't?" she said. "I thought she'd sold out the high priest to become the high priestess."

"At a small cost."

Susan widened her eyes and tilted her head toward me. I whispered what Samuelson told me about an ongoing federal investigation into HELIOS's ties with organized crime. He called the case the legal equivalent of shooting fish in a barrel.

"As long as she keeps her hands off you."

"Are you calling me a kept man?"

Susan squeezed my knee again. "Absolutely, sweet cheeks. Now order me another round."

"With pleasure."

ACKNOWLEDGMENTS

Special thanks to pals Alison Quinn, Robert Crais, Steph Cha, and Jeremiah Chechik for their hospitality and guidance in Los Angeles.

Ten years ago, Spenser helped a teenage girl
named Mattie Sullivan find her mother's killer
and take down an infamous Southie crime boss.
Now Mattie—a college student with a side job
working for the iconic private eye—dreams
of being an investigator herself. When Mattie's
childhood friend from the South Boston housing
projects is found dead, she decides to take
on the case for the family.

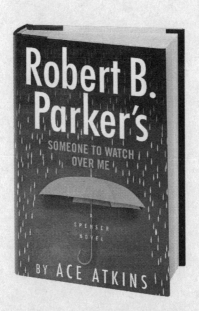

It was early evening and early summer and my bay window was cracked open above Berkeley Street. I had a half-eaten turkey sub on my desk and the sports page from the *Globe* splayed out underneath. Dan Shaughnessy proclaimed Mookie Betts to be overrated. I'm sure many said the same thing about me. But I was pretty sure being overrated was better than being underrated. A mistake few made twice.

I contemplated Mookie's situation as I heard a knock on the anteroom door.

"Second door on your left," I said.

Mattie Sullivan entered my office.

"Still having trouble with the advertising firm?"

"Bad advertising to list their own address wrong."

"Freakin' morons," Mattie said.

Like me, Mattie suffered few fools. And as my occasional secretary, part-time assistant, and sleuthing apprentice, she didn't take kindly to the two-person agency that had rooms down the hall. Mattie leaned into the door frame. She'd grown into a tall girl with long limbs, long red hair, and a heart-shaped Irish face full of freckles. When she smiled, she could light up a room. But Mattie rarely smiled and wasn't smiling now.

"You need anything else today?" she said.

"Nope."

"I paid the rent, deposited the checks, and talked to the painters about next week."

"What happens next week?"

"They paint," Mattie said. "This place hadn't had a touch-up since 1976."

"What do you know about 1976?"

"That's the year my mother was born."

"Ouch."

"Yeah," Mattie said. "Truth hurts, big guy."

Mattie hung in the doorway, green eyes lingering on me as I turned the page of the newspaper. I still bought a physical copy at the newsstand around the corner. I was old fashioned that way. In fact, Susan reminded me I was old fashioned in most ways, from my music to movie choices. But who doesn't enjoy a little Django Reinhardt before their *Thin Man* triple feature?

"Something on your mind?" I said.

"I don't know."

I looked up from where I'd spread out the newspaper

and reached for my coffee mug. Taking a sip, I realized it had grown cold. Mattie, having noted my expression, walked forward, plucked the mug from my hand and dumped out the cold contents into the sink. She refilled the mug from the Mr. Coffee atop my file cabinet, slid it before me, and took a seat in one of my clients' chairs.

"Sugar?"

"Nope."

"So there's this girl I know."

"OK."

"She's a friend, but not a great friend," she said. "Just the younger sister of a girl that I know. She was a Gatey girl, too."

"Gatey girl?"

"Gates of Heaven church in Southie," Mattie said. "Christ. Keep up, Spenser."

I nodded and took a sip of coffee. Mattie demanded a keen mind and reflexes firing on all cylinders.

"So this girl, her name is Chloe Turner by the way, not that it matters to the story, but there you are," Mattie said, leaning forward from the chair. "Chloe comes to me because of the stuff I used to do in the neighborhood. You know, running favors for friends. Asking questions to the right people. Finding shit."

"Sleuthing."

"I call it finding shit out," Mattie said. "But sure. *Sleuthing*. Chloe wanted me to sleuth for her."

"And what does she wish you to sleuth?"

"Chloe lost her backpack and her laptop at some fancy

schmancy club off the Common," she said. "And she wants it back."

"Sounds simple," I said. "Why does she need to enlist your services?"

"Because they wouldn't let her back in," Mattie said. "They threatened to call the cops if she didn't leave. And Chloe had everything on that laptop, not to mention some personal shit in the bag."

"Personal shit is hard to come by."

"And so I went to the club and got the whole 'fuck off' thing from some guy working the door," Mattie said. "Not only did they say they'd never heard of Chloe Turner. They told me that if I, or anyone connected to her came back, they'd call the cops. How do you like that?"

"Not at all," I said. "What club?"

"Place called the Blackstone Club," Mattie said. "Down toward Chinatown in some crummy brick building. No sign. Just a big door and a buzzer. What kind of freakin' club doesn't have a sign?"

"One that wishes to be elite and confidential," I said, starting to stand. "Shall we?"

"Sit down, Spenser," Mattie said. "You know the rules. When you need help, you ask. When I need help, I ask."

"So what do you need?"

"Advice."

"I am an open book of knowledge."

Mattie nodded. I nodded. I took a sip of coffee. It tasted much better hot but I still missed the cream and sugar. Small steps.

"Here's what happened," Mattie said. "Chloe doesn't want to cause any trouble, and more than anything doesn't want to go to the cops. Her mother would go bullshit if she knew what she'd been up to."

I leaned back in the desk. Outside, down on the street, I could hear the whine of an industrial drill and planks of wood tossed against the pavement. A car without a muffler passed and headed out of earshot. A symphony of the Back Bay.

"Chloe knows a girl who knows a girl who promised her an easy five hundred bucks."

"To meet a man at the club?"

"And give him a massage," Mattie said. "Chloe says she was promised that was all there was to it."

"Had she ever met him?"

"Nope."

"Did she have any expertise as a massage therapist?"

"Christ no," Mattie said. "She's just a kid."

"How old?"

Mattie tossed her head to the side and leveled her eyes at me. "Fifteen."

I felt the hair raise up my neck. My stomach turned a bit.

"I know," Mattie said. "But part of what I promise is confidentiality."

"This sounds like a felony."

"Hold on," Mattie said. "Only gets worse."

I listened.

"Chloe says when she first got there, a woman met her

at the club and gave her an envelope stuffed with cash," Mattie said. "The woman told her the guy was some big-time executive hotshot. She didn't need to speak unless spoken to, had to wear this special outfit, pay attention to his feet."

"His feet."

"All creeps are into feet," Mattie said. "Anyway, she goes in there, the room all dim with scented candles and all that. And there's the man, laying on his back with a sheet covering the lower half his body. Chloe says she was so nervous her hands were shaking and starts to rub the man's feet like she'd been told. The man makes some small talk with her. *What's your name? What music do you like? Do you have a boyfriend?* All that kind of stuff. She said he was nice. And not bad looking for an old dude. She said he was polite until things got weird."

"Massaging a grown man's feet is the definition of weird."

"Chloe said she thought the whole thing was legit until at one point the man raised up, threw off the sheet, and started going to town on himself."

I felt my face flush. I wasn't comfortable talking about such matters with Mattie. I remembered when she was fourteen, coming to see me with a collection of crumpled bills in the hope of finding her mother's killer. She was tough as old boots but would always be a lost little girl to me.

"Chloe said she just froze up," Mattie said. "She couldn't scream. She couldn't talk. She couldn't move. She just stood there as the man got finished with his business."

"Ick," I said.

"Yep," Mattie said. "That's when she bolted from the room and the club and left her clothes, her laptop inside that backpack. She doesn't want any trouble. She doesn't want to see that man again. All she wants is her stuff."

"OK," I said. "Let me help."

"Advice," Mattie said. "I only want advice."

"I'd much rather assist."

"Maybe I shouldn't have told you."

"You made the right move."

"You want to beat the hell out this guy," she said. "Don't you?"

"Chloe should file a complaint with the police."

"She can't."

"Why?"

"Because she took the money," Mattie said. "Don't you see?"

"That doesn't make what happened right."

"What would you do?"

I leaned back in my office chair and kicked my Nikes up onto the side of the desk. I began to mentally run through the collection of creeps I've known over the years. My go-to action would have been physical or public humiliation. Perhaps tacking his manhood to the tallest tree in the Common.

"Does Chloe know this man's name?"

"No."

"Does she know anything about him?"

"Nothing," she said. "I already asked."

"If it were me, I'd go back to this club and tell them

they can either turn over the backpack or else you'll tell your story on Channel 7. Say you have Hank Phillippi Ryan on speed dial."

"But I don't."

"But I do," I said.

"And she'd show up with cameras?"

"In a heartbeat."

"OK," Mattie said.

"I want you to have Chloe talk to someone in sex crimes," I said. "I'll call Quirk and arrange it."

"She won't," Mattie said. "But I'll try."

Mattie let herself out, the anteroom door closing with a light click. I reached for my coffee and turned to stare out the window. I spent a lot of time staring out windows. Perhaps if I stared long enough, a sign would appear somewhere in the clouds. I peered into the sky but there were no clouds today. So many creeps. So little time.

I turned back to my desk. Besides the sub and the newspaper, it was bare. I hadn't had a decent case since returning from Los Angeles earlier that year. Maybe it might be time for me to dig into my 401k, if only I had a 401k.

I picked up the phone and dialed Quirk.

"That sounds like one sick fuck," Quirk said.

"Kid's fifteen."

"Jesus Christ," Quirk said. "I got two granddaughters that age. What's the vic's name again?"

"I'll need to clear it with Mattie."

"Mattie Sullivan?" Quirk said. "She's a kid, too."

"Not anymore," I said. "She's twenty-two."

"She still wants to be like you?"

"Yep."

"God help her."

The Dean of American
Crime Fiction

Robert B. Parker